KAIJU

RISING

AGE OF MONSTERS

EDITED BY **N.X. SHARPS & TIM MARQUITZ**

KAIJU RISING: Age of Monsters
Outland Entertainment | www.outlandentertainment.com
Founder/Creative Director: Jeremy D. Mohler
Editor-in-Chief: Alana Joli Abbott
Publisher: Melanie R. Meadors
Senior Editor: Gwendolyn Nix

Published by Outland Entertainment
3119 Gillham Road
Kansas City MO, 64109

Paperback: 978-1-947659-79-7
Worldwide Rights
Created in the United States of America / Printed in China

Editor: N.X. Sharps & Tim Marquitz
Editorial Assistant: D.L. Seymour
Cover Illustration: Tan Ho Sim
Interior Illustrations: Robert Elrod, Chuck Lukacs, and Matt Frank
Cover Design & Interior Layout: STK•Kreations

MONSTERS ARE TRAGIC BEINGS.

They are born too tall, too strong, too heavy. They are not evil by choice. That is their tragedy. They do not attack people because they want to, but because of their size and strength, mankind has no other choice but to defend himself. After several stories such as this, people end up having a kind of affection for the monsters. They end up caring about them.

—Ishirô Honda, Japanese film director (1911-1993)

CONTENTS

FOREWORD

JEREMY ROBINSON

A JOLT ROLLS THROUGH THE boy's bedroom floor. A truck going by? *No,* he thinks, *too powerful.* Eyes wide, he stands slowly and turns toward an east-facing window. A streak of blue ocean cuts across the view, a mile off and two hundred feet below. The water of Beverly Harbor is hard to see through the maples lining the backyard, but his imagination fills in the blanks. He's spent enough time on the coast of his home town to mentally render the craggy shoreline.

The window grinds open. Early summer heat, thick with recent rain flows into the room. The wet metal screen, warming in the sun, smells so strong he can taste it. Staring out at the ocean view, the boy mindlessly picks at the chipping paint covering the wood between window and screen.

He watches, patiently waiting, until...

Thrum.

The room shakes again.

He's coming, the boy thinks.

The distant ocean swells. A massive form pushes up, the film of water falling away in great sheets of hissing foam. The monster is huge. Massive. Larger than the boy remembered. Fully exposed, rising high above the ocean and higher above the boy's home, the gargantuan roars.

Smiling, the boy watches the creature's approach.

Buildings implode under foot.

Others explode.

Smoke rises. People flee. Chaos reigns.

And yet, the boy smiles.

A flash of blue light flickers along the spines lining the green behemoth's back. The light bursts from the giant's mouth, carving an arc of destruction through familiar neighborhoods, through the cemetery, through Shane Dillon's house.

Yes...

The monster, a Kaiju of epic proportions, stands at the bottom of Prospect Hill, atop which the boy's house is located. And yet, it towers over the boy, turning its head down and roaring again.

Blue light flickers.

The monster turns it eyes downward, connecting with the boy's for a moment.

The boy smiles and speaks for the first time. "Godzilla."

THE STORY I JUST TOLD you isn't fiction (so calm down, Toho), it's a memory. The boy is me, circa 1983. I'm nine years old. It's Saturday afternoon, and I've just returned home from a victorious soccer match. I've shed my shin guards, but I'm still wearing my orange jersey, number 37, and cleats. However, I'm not thinking about the game, I'm thinking about how I spent my morning before the game. *Creature Double Feature*, which aired in the Boston area from 1977–1983, was my Saturday morning routine. The show introduced me to Godzilla, Gamera, King Kong and the slew of Kaiju they battled. I was also exposed to other monsters like zombies, gargoyles, vampires and a variety of aliens, but none got so thoroughly lodged in my imagination as the city destroying giants.

In my room, I imagined Godzilla rising from the ocean, which I could barely see, and laying waste to my hometown of Beverly, Massachusetts. In the winter, I became Godzilla, stomping up and down the snow-plowed roads, using chunks of snow for buildings, roaring, as I laid waste to the neighborhood.

Flash forward thirty years, I'm an author. I've written 40+ novels and novellas, and nearly all of them feature monsters—aliens, ancient Nephilim, Greek myths reborn and modern legends, but no Kaiju. While I personally consider all my monsters Kaiju, which means 'strange beast' in Japanese, I had yet to conjure a beast capable of flattening a city. Then, two and a half years ago, I decided to fulfill some childhood fantasies, and Nemesis was born.

Nemesis is a Godzilla-sized Kaiju that stomps down the New England coast, all the way to Boston. On the way, she (yes, she) makes a stop in Beverly Harbor, rises from the ocean and wipes out a good portion of my hometown. The child in me had been waiting a long time to tell that story. Even more than that, the home base for the government agency tasked with handling the Kaiju threat in the story, is located at the top of the hill I grew up on.

A short time later, the movies *Pacific Rim* and the new *Godzilla* were announced, and Kaiju started getting attention. I released *Project Nemesis* in November of 2012, eight months before the release of *Pacific Rim*, which helped Kaiju become a household term. Project Nemesis quickly became the bestselling original Kaiju novel—ever. A bold claim, sure, but let's dissect it.

The word 'original' means a non-Godzilla novel, because if we look at the history of novels, the only other Kaiju novels of note, up to this point, were the Godzilla novels published in the 1990s. The fourth novel in the series, *Godzilla vs the Robot Monsters* was published in 1999. The fifth novel in the series, *Godzilla and the Lost Continent* was written, but never published...meaning the series failed. I suspect this would be different now, but the result was that between 1999 and 2012, there wasn't a single noteworthy Kaiju novel published.

Which means that my claiming *Project Nemesis* is the bestselling original Kaiju novel is 1.) Accurate, and 2.) Not especially impressive. Kaiju, as a genre, has been largely ignored by the publishing world. But thanks to technological advances in publishing, small presses and self-publishers now have the ability to tackle subgenres considered too risky by large publishers. Unfortunately, the genre (as of writing this foreword) is still largely represented in popular fiction by *Project Nemesis* and its sequel, *Project Maigo*.

But not for long.

Enter *Kaiju Rising: Age of Monsters*. This collection of Kaiju shorts continues the traditions begun by Kaiju pioneers, bringing tales of destruction, hope and morality in the form of giant, city destroying monsters. Even better, the project was funded by Kickstarter, which means *you*, Dear Reader, made this book possible. And that is a beautiful thing. It means Kaiju, in pop-fiction, are not only alive and well, they're stomping their way back into the spotlight, where they belong. Featuring amazing artwork, stories from some of the best monster writers around and a publishing team that has impressed me from the beginning, *Kaiju Rising: Age of Monsters* is a welcome addition to the Kaiju genre and an anthology of epic proportions. My inner nine-year-old is shouting at me to shut-up and let you get to the Kaiju. So, without further delay, let's all enjoy us some Kaiju Rising.

—Jeremy Robinson, bestselling author of *Project Nemesis* and *Island 731*

BIG BEN AND THE END OF THE PIER SHOW

JAMES LOVEGROVE

THE FOREVER FUN PIER HAD stood for more than a century, surviving everything the world could throw at it: two wars, three recessions, innumerable storms, and the endless corrosive lick of salt water. But it was no match for a two-hundred-foot-tall sea monster and an almost as gigantic robot.

IRONICALLY, ON THE DAY THE pier was destroyed, owner Keith Brown was trying to decide its fate.

He was on the horns of a dilemma which were, to him, no smaller than the horns of the Kaiju currently wending its way up the English Channel towards his hometown.

On the one hand, he had a firm offer from an entertainment consortium to buy the pier. They would take it off his hands, lock, stock, and barrel, no questions asked, for a cash lump sum.

The money was not retiring money, not head-off-to-the-Bahamas-and-drink-margaritas-for-the-rest-of-your-days money. Once tax was deducted and business debts paid off, there wouldn't be much left. Barely a few thousand. But the pier would not be his headache anymore; it would be someone else's, someone with deeper pockets and friendlier creditors.

*Illustration by **ROBERT ELROD***

On the other hand, Keith had been contemplating an insurance job. A fire would do the trick. A jerry can of petrol left in the fuse box room. A burning rag. It would look like an electrical accident, a stray spark from a circuit breaker igniting a terminal conflagration. The pier's ancient, weathered boards would go up like tinder. Its wooden superstructure would be a raging inferno in no time. The fire brigade would have no chance of saving it.

The benefit of this option was that the insurance company would cough up the pier's full market value, giving him twice the amount the entertainment consortium was tendering.

The drawback? Well, if he was caught and convicted of arson, there'd be no payout. Instead, there'd be a hefty fine and a stretch in jail. Besides, how *could* he burn the pier down? It had been in his family for four generations. His great-grandfather built it. His grandfather paid off the last of the initial bank loan. His father presided over the pier's long, slow decline as a going concern. Keith inherited a sizeable overdraft and a crumbling, barely profitable business that incurred eye-watering overheads in maintenance and upkeep and was dependent on the vagaries of tourist crowds and the British summer.

But it was still the Brown family pier, their livelihood since 1885. Keith's attachment to it went beyond the merely financial; was rooted in his psyche. The pier was in his DNA, in his soul. Its rusty cast-iron stilts were his legs. Its white-and-blue finials and cupolas were his brain, his dreams. Its rickety helter-skelter was his heart.

THE KAIJU, NICKNAMED RED DEVIL, toiled eastward up the Channel, inbound from the Atlantic. Sometimes he swam, thrashing himself along with great sweeps of his tail. Other times, when his feet could reach the seabed, he waded, neck deep. Puffs of smoke curled from his cavernous nostrils with every exhalation. His horns rose proud like two galleons.

Already he had downed a Portuguese Puma attack helicopter just off Madeira, incinerating it with a single fiery exhalation, and had crippled a French naval frigate.

A Royal Navy Astute-class hunter-killer submarine was now shadowing his progress, awaiting word from the top brass. If Red Devil strayed too close to the British coastline or looked as though he was attempting landfall, the sub's captain could be ordered to unleash Spearfish heavy torpedoes and try to blow the beast's legs out from under him.

This was a precaution, though, a last-resort measure. Subaquatic Kaiju kills were hard to pull off and, more often than not, simply resulted in an even more irate monster.

Meanwhile, the United Kingdom's very own special defence measure was being prepped for action in its hangar at the Deepcut Barracks in Camberley, Surrey.

Big Ben.

The alert level at Deepcut was high amber, meaning that, if necessary, in under half an hour the engine could be cycling, the weapons primed, and the three-man pilot team installed in the cockpit, ready to go.

Should Red Devil decide not to circumnavigate the British Isles but instead strode out of the sea onto the nation's sovereign territory, Big Ben would be deployed to intervene.

KEITH, LIKE EVERYONE ELSE, WAS keeping half an eye on Red Devil's approach. BBC News 24 was tracking the monster step by step, with maps and satellite surveillance, like meteorologists monitoring the course of a hurricane. Talking heads—defense officials, Kaiju experts, naturalists—debated the likelihood of the creature actually attacking the country. The consensus of opinion was that Red Devil would bypass the south coast and carry on up the North Sea, making for the Arctic Circle. Possibly, he might stop off at Denmark or Norway en route, to snack on Scandinavians. This view, however, was offered more in hope than expectation, as was the similar notion the creature might prefer France to the UK. Once Red Devil reached the Straits of Dover he would be as close to either nation as could be, more or less equidistant from both. Who was to say he might not turn right instead of left and go in search of Gallic cuisine?

Kaiju were hopelessly unpredictable. Those who anointed themselves experts on the beasts were more like educated guessers than anything. Gypsy Rose Petulengro, who told fortunes in a booth on the Forever Fun Pier, would have been a better predictor of a Kaiju's movements than any of them. Her tarot cards and crystal ball were at least as reliable and credible as the prognostications of these amateur know-alls. The only thing they were interested in was a TV channel inviting them into the studio and crossing their palms with silver.

THE TOWN WAS QUIET AS Keith bicycled down to the pier that afternoon. Traffic was thin to nonexistent, pedestrians few and far between. The hotels had the hollow look of the dead—their guests having gotten into their cars and headed back home. The fish and chip shops lacked paying customers, and several had closed up, with hand-scrawled signs in the windows saying they would reopen once the all clear was given.

Along the south coast there had been an exodus inland. Anyone who had somewhere else they could go to, had gone there.

The seafront was somewhat busier than the center of town. There were a few determined dog walkers, a handful of elderly local residents who were damned if they were going to let some sea monster interfere with their daily constitutional, and the inevitable gaggles of Kaiju chasers who were camped out along the promenade, cameras at the ready, waiting on tenterhooks for Red Devil to lumber by.

Keith pedalled past a coachload of Japanese tourists who, from what he could gather, had forgone a trip to Brontë country in favor of coming down south to snap shots of the latest behemoth to emerge from the Romanche Furrow breeding grounds. There were news crews from as far afield as Italy and Spain, along with casual opportunists who lived in the vicinity and knew pictures and footage of Kaiju could earn them a few quid when sold to the papers or the right online outlets.

A drizzle was falling but the mood was oddly festive. Nobody seemed to think Red Devil would get it into his head to besiege the town. Why would he be interested in a faded, if still architecturally lovely, seaside resort? Kaiju were drawn to bright lights, big cities. They loved to topple a skyscraper or knock down some cultural landmark in the course of their ravenous rampages.

There was nothing *here* for Red Devil. There weren't even that many people for him to pluck up in his taloned clutches and cram into his hungry maw. Portsmouth, Southampton, Brighton, the major conurbations to the west—any of them would be attractive to him, a human smorgasbord spread out for him to gorge on. Or he might round the rump of Kent and travel up the Thames Estuary to slake his hunger on London itself, a capital feast.

But not this humble little gathering of Victorian villas and Edwardian terraces perched on the end of a railway spur. This shingle-beached nowhere which in long-ago, simpler times had been the holiday destination of choice for large swathes of the British working class and, before that, a Mecca for genteel urbanites seeking the restorative powers of sea water and salt breezes as an antidote to smog, stench, and tuberculosis.

Cocooned in kagoules and cheeriness, believing they were safe, the Kaiju chasers chattered and speculated. Keith left them to it. He leaned his bike against the railings outside the Forever Fun Pier, his pier, and passed under the entrance arch.

Sally, the kid manning the turnstile, barely glanced up as Keith went through. She was concentrating on her iPhone, alternating between catching Red Devil updates and texting friends. She was eighteen, a responsible girl with a disabled mother to support.

That morning Keith had sent a round-robin email to all his employees in which he insisted that the pier would remain open unless, or until, Red Devil came within twenty miles of the town. He left it up to them whether to turn up for work or not. It was their choice, but he wanted those who were keen on earning a day's pay to have that opportunity.

He was, he thought, a fair boss. He had a light-touch, lenient attitude, reckoning you got more out of people the less you swaggered and shouted, and he paid generously, well above minimum wage, even though he could not realistically afford to. He suspected that if he had been harder-nosed, more bullying and miserly by nature, more of a Scrooge, the pier might not be in such a parlous state.

But a pier should be fun, that was the thing. A pier should be a bright, happy place, a palace of dreams. If the workforce were relaxed and content and glad to be there, it would show. It would communicate itself to the punters, and they would be happy too— and spend more money.

Gypsy Rose's booth was shut. She had stayed home today. Perhaps she knew something no one else did. But Wheezy Bob was in his kiosk in the amusement arcade, where the shelves of the penny falls machines went back and forth in a ceaseless silvery tide and the one-armed bandits whistled and flashed their come-ons. Not that anyone was playing them. Wheezy Bob was alone, with nobody queuing to have their banknotes changed into change.

"Busy today, Mr Brown," he said. He had been with the pier longer than Keith. He had been young when Keith's father took over. "Rushed off my feet."

"Want to take a fag break? I bet you're dying to."

"And abandon my post when there's work to be done?" Bob let out one of his raspy, phlegmy chuckles. A lifelong smoker, every one of his laughs sounded like a last gasp.

"I think we can manage without you for five minutes."

Wheezy Bob fired off a yellow grin and shambled outdoors, fishing his roll-up tin from his pocket.

Keith moved on. The rock and candyfloss stalls hawked their brightly colored wares, but no one was buying. The tables in the café were empty save for salt shakers and sugar dispensers. The souvenir shop, with its snow globes and brim-slogan bowler hats, waited for customers who weren't coming. Jaunty Muzak—currently "I Do Like To be Beside the Seaside"—drifted ghostlike through the air. Everything glistened under a breath-light sheen of rain.

Keith strolled right to the end of the pier. Here, next to the helter-skelter, stood a three-hundred-seat theater. In times gone by, its auditorium had resounded to hilarity and applause as comedians, novelty acts, singers, and dancers had followed one another onstage in riotous variety bills. Now it was a venue for performers at the tail end of their careers: once-notorious rock 'n' rollers, aged crooners with suspiciously black hair, overweight gag merchants who had toned down the racism in their material but kept the mother-in-law jokes, conjurors who had never heard of street magic and still considered the old rabbit-out-of-a-hat trick an essential part of their repertoire. A full house was a rarity these days. Sometimes the box office was lucky to sell a dozen tickets.

The entertainment consortium had plans to turn the theater into a nightclub. Rip out the seating, install a bar and a DJ podium, maybe some go-go cages. Call it something hip and happening but vaguely nautical such as Trident or Polaris. Why not give a sea-straddling hotspot the same name as a submarine-launched nuclear warhead? *It made as much sense as anything,* Keith thought.

He leaned on the railing at the very tip of the pier. He was 150 meters out from the shoreline, his whole world behind him. Jade waves churned below, curls of ivory surf washing around the stilts.

The impacts of the breakers thrummed through the huge hollow iron tubes and their lattice of cross-braces, as though the pier were some massive, intricate vibraphone. It was a deep and mournful sound, beat after low beat, the throb of nostalgia and loss.

To sell? To burn?

Either way, Keith would be left with nothing. Some cash in the bank, yes, but that wouldn't truly compensate for what he had got rid of. It would never assuage his guilt. The pier was a family heirloom, something he was meant to preserve and pass on to his son, were he ever to father one. But he was unmarried—hadn't found the right woman yet—and he was well into his thirties and all manner of clocks were ticking.

Whatever he did, he had to look on it as a fresh start, a chance to begin again. The single hard fact was that he could not afford to keep the pier running, no matter how he tried. He was up to his neck in debt. The loans were piling up, interest aggregating on interest. Within the next twenty-four hours he would have to go for one or the other of the options available to him.

Although…

There was a third way.

The sea was coldly inviting. How about…?

No. That would never do. No way. Keith Brown was many things but he was not a coward.

A herring gull alighted on the railing beside him, fixing him with a jaundiced eye. Irritably he waved the bird away.

"Flock off," he said, and the gull, in response, squawked and shat on the boards near his feet.

AT DEEPCUT BARRACKS, INITIATION WAS complete.

Big Ben stood to attention, ready.

He was 150 feet tall, one thousand tons of metal and armament, a towering man-shaped hulk, with fists as large as Range Rovers and a head the size of a double-decker bus.

He was high-tech ordnance galore—heat-seeking missile, 120mm cannon, million-volt neuromuscular incapacitator. He was a hexacomb-reinforced armored shell built around cathedral-column servomotors and actuators, powered by a 250,000-horsepower engine salvaged from a decommissioned aircraft carrier. He was ingenuity and resourcefulness and make-do.

He was not the world's tallest Kaiju Response Vehicle. That honor went to America's colossal Major Mayhem, who could go eye to eye with Lady Liberty on her pedestal. Nor was he the mightiest. Russia's fission-powered Spirit of Chernobyl claimed that title. He wasn't even the most recent. Japan was pumping out new marques of KRV at the rate of a dozen a year, in order to counteract the vast numbers of Kaiju that spawned from the nests in the icy deeps of the Mariana Trench.

Truth be told, Big Ben was one of the scrawnier, cruder models. He was over ten years old and bore the scars and dents from nearly a score of Kaiju defence actions. Famously, his left leg was stiff after his bruising fracas with Charlie Two Heads off Lundy Island in the mouth of the Bristol Channel, and the paintwork on his shoulder was still charred and blackened after it had been scorched by Dragon Breath's flames during the Battle of Coventry.

Of course these injuries could have been repaired. "But," said the Department of Kaiju Affairs, "budget cutbacks, economic slowdown, austerity, time to tighten our belts, we're all in this together, blah blah blah."

In any case, people didn't mind. They liked Big Ben just the way he was, flaws and all. He was cranky, dogged, temperamental, a little bit battered, but still game. He was, in a word, British.

WHEEZY BOB TAPPED KEITH ON the shoulder, breaking him out of his glum reverie.

"Sally's just told me. Red Devil's about an hour away. Last place you want to be is on this old pier, stuck out like bait on a pole. Those nutters on the promenade, they might think it's a good idea serving themselves up to him, but anyone with any sense'll get to cover."

They powered down the pier. Lights winked out. The machines in the amusement arcade fell still. The Muzak was silenced.

At the turnstile the three of them went their separate ways, Sally to her mum's house, Wheezy Bob to his bungalow and his parrot and his photos of his late wife, and Keith to the nearest pub that was still serving.

WHY RED DEVIL TURNED INLAND at the precise point he did could never be fully explained. Even the so-called Kaiju experts couldn't fathom the beast's motivations and mindset. Kaiju were impulsive creatures. They were driven by hunger and a love of wanton destruction. Maybe Red Devil just felt peckish and decided it was time for a snack. Maybe the Kaiju chasers on the seafront caught his fancy and lured him in, like a display of food in a deli window. They were in the wrong place at the wrong time, for them; the right place at the right time, for him.

He strode through the threshing shallows, making small tsunamis with his shins. His scaly crimson hide glowed like an atomic sunset. His yellow eyes gazed down from a height of two hundred feet with sulphurous pitilessness. His footfalls were temblors, miniature earthquakes.

The Kaiju chasers became the Kaiju chased. Panicking, they dropped their cameras and ran. All at once, their monster spotting hobby was no longer fun. They had gone from spectators to unwilling participants. Thrillseekers, sanctuary seekers now, fled this way and that along the promenade, making for doorways and hiding between parked cars or in bus shelters or behind the benches where, on normal days, weary old people sat and stared at the horizon, contemplating distances and ends.

Red Devil thundered up the shingle beach, water pouring off him in cataracts. He scooped up a handful of petrified Japanese tourists and gobbled them down like sushi. He snatched a news cameraman off the ground, tossed him in the air, and caught him in his mouth like a teenager with a peanut. The cameraman, to his eternal credit, kept filming even as he vanished inside the monster's gullet.

Screams and wails of despair echoed up and down the seafront. Red Devil bellowed in return, a bomb blast of noise that rattled window frames and shattered panes. He roved to and fro along the roadway like some gargantuan terrier, sniffing out cowering humans, skewering them on an index finger talon and devouring them. Some he popped into his mouth whole like canapés, others he savored, chomping them down in two or three bites as though they were gingerbread men or Jelly Babies.

A fat purple tongue rolled around his lizardy lips in satisfaction. Something akin to a smile creased his serpentine features. The eating was sparse but good, and his prey tasted all the better for the terror-triggered adrenaline that spiced their blood.

IN THE PUB, THE SAILOR'S Rest, Keith and the other patrons supped their pints and prayed Red Devil would leave them alone.

"Feed first, smash property afterwards," said one of the regulars into the timorous silence that filled the room. "That's the pattern. I just hope the bastard doesn't head this way."

"You and me both, mate," said the landlord, with feeling. "My bloody insurance doesn't cover acts of Kaiju. The premiums are too buggering high. He wrecks this place, I'm bankrupt. Orders, anyone?"

"What I don't understand," said a man to Keith's left, "is why we don't try nuking the nests again."

"Because last time it only made them more bloody pissed-off," said the pub's resident smartarse, who organised and compèred the monthly quiz night. "And bigger. Some of them were vaporised.

The rest seemed to absorb the radiation and grow fat on it. Sucked it up like mother's milk. Classic case of whatever doesn't kill you makes you stronger."

"Still reckon we should do it again. More bombs this time. Saturate the seabed with them."

"And poison half the world's oceans into the bargain? Just not worth it. We're better off taking our chances with the occasional rogue Kaiju that goes walkabout."

A tremendous roar from outside made everyone jump and grip their glasses all the more tightly.

"Was that closer? Or further away?"

"Don't know. Can't tell."

"If we can hear him, he's too near."

"Sod this. I'm going home. The wife'll be wondering where I am."

"Are you crazy? Stay put. At least if you're indoors, he can't see you."

"Phone her. She'll understand."

"You've obviously not met my wife."

"Big Ben," said someone. "They'll have launched him by now. Where is he? He's got to be coming. Got to be."

Keith nodded. Everyone nodded.

The landlord switched on the TV. People consulted their phone screens.

Big Ben.

Where was Big Ben?

SPRINTING SOUTH-EAST THROUGH THE leafy woods of Surrey and the grassy wealds of Sussex. Pounding over the ridge of the North Downs. Past Guildford. Past Crawley. Past Haywards Heath. Heading for the South Downs. His giant thumping strides shaking the earth, startling cattle. Seventy miles an hour cross-country, eighty, ninety-five. Gathering speed. Legs pumping, arms swinging. The urgency of his mission prompting him to hurdle busy motorways, take a shortcut right through the middle of Gatwick airport, leap over lakes, bound across farmland as though fields were chessboard squares, until at last the coast was within sight, the sea a strip of murky green beneath a gray, gray sky.

RED DEVIL HAD PROGRESSED TO the demolition phase of his rampage. His belly was full enough. After the slaughter came the wanton property damage.

He took out a couple of seafront hotels with a single, crushing blow.

He picked up the little motorised tourist train that shuttled back and forth along the promenade and whipcracked it like a bushman killing a snake. Its carriages separated and flew.

He lashed out with his saurian tail and flattened the convention center, which had been built in the 1970s in the Brutalist style, all concrete and angles, despite considerable local opposition and protest. Few tears would be shed over its passing.

He stomped on the old cinema, which had lately been repurposed as a bingo hall.

Then his attention was drawn to the Forever Fun Pier.

It seemed to be asking to be destroyed. Poking out into the sea like that. Presenting itself. A provocative finger of manmade structure.

Red Devil gravitated towards it. Fire was mounting in the back of his throat. He had energy again after his arduous transatlantic trek. The human meat slowly digesting in his belly was stoking his inner furnace. It was time to unleash hell.

Then he heard it: *thud, thud, thud.* From far off. Coming closer. Getting louder.

Red Devil swung round in time to see Big Ben come pounding across the swells of chalk cliff to the west of town.

Full steam ahead.

Britain's one and only Kaiju Response Vehicle homed in on the monster, and battle was joined.

THEY CLOSED AND CLINCHED. THEY battered and brawled.

Red Devil had a good fifty feet of height on Big Ben. He outweighed the KRV by many tons. He had thousand-degree fire—organic alcohol sparked by a bioluminescent gland located in his soft posterior palate.

But Big Ben had weaponry, and grit, and a crew who were dedicated to defending their homeland and fellow countrymen, even if it cost them their lives.

Their names, for the record, were Captain Alistair Hargreaves, Co-Pilot Melissa Jackson, and Bombardier Desmond Somersby.

Though the underdog, Big Ben acquitted himself well and with honor. He hit Red Devil with everything he had. The Kaiju's cries of pain and distress could be heard thirty miles away.

Big Ben did his best to divert the fight away from the main part of town. He grappled Red Devil down the beach and into the sea. The two of them wrestled ankle-deep in the water, dredging up enough muddy sand to make the water as thick and turbid as a chocolate milkshake.

Gradually they wore each other down. It became a war of attrition. Red Devil bled a kind of satanic green ichor from his wounds. Big Ben bled oil.

A kick to Big Ben's already damaged leg left him limping, barely able to stand upright.

The crew fought with the controls to compensate and adjust. They unleashed a volley of armor-piercing anti-tank shells that tore gouges out of Red Devil's hide.

The combatants were within just a few yards of the pier.

Big Ben was failing now, internally. His systems were crashing, his servos juddering. The cockpit was ablaze with warning lights. A cacophony of alarm signals whinnied and hooted. He planted his good leg, putting all of his weight on it, and beleaguered Red Devil with punches that would have flattened a mountain.

The Kaiju retaliated with a sweep of his tail that nearly toppled the KRV. Big Ben grabbed hold of the monster, mostly for support.

Then he reared back and headbutted him.

Red Devil staggered backwards, and with that, half of the Forever Fun Pier was gone. Trampled. Timbers became splinters and flinders. Iron stilts snapped like wheat stalks. The theater was knocked clean off into the sea. The helter-skelter fell pell-mell.

Big Ben pressed home the advantage. He jolted Red Devil with his neuromuscular incapacitator—essentially a jumbo-sized Taser. As frying Kaiju flesh sizzled, Big Ben hammered the beast's skull repeatedly. He could reach now, because Red Devil had collapsed onto his haunches amid the debris of half the pier.

Beneath Big Ben's fist, something broke. Bone. Bone broke like a slab of marble. A crack in the Kaiju's cranium.

Red Devil's yellow eyes registered surprise and fear. Not to mention agony.

He flailed. A gout of fire jetted from his mouth, but it was feeble compared with previous bursts, more cigarette lighter than flamethrower.

Big Ben hammered again, and again, and one more time, right between Red Devil's horns.

Then it was over.

The beast let out a tumultuous, gasping sigh and his eyes rolled and acid-green blood spurted from his slitty nostrils, and all at once he slumped sideways, straight into the intact half of the pier, which immediately became no longer intact.

Big Ben fell, too. He sank onto one knee. His arms went limp. His head bowed. Smoke began pouring from vents and crevices in his back. It was black and noxious, evidence of catastrophic mechanism breakdown.

The crew, very sensibly, performed an emergency evacuation.

They swam ashore, leaving their inert KRV smouldering beside the body of the defunct Kaiju and the few sparse, shattered remnants of the Forever Fun Pier.

CLEANUP UNITS ARRIVED, AND FOR the next fortnight the entire seafront was cordoned off as they carved up Red Devil's corpse into manageable chunks, which were then trucked off in container lorries to be incinerated before the rotten meat became a health hazard.

The same courtesy was not extended to Big Ben. He stayed where he was, half-kneeling, head bent, as though genuflecting before some power far greater than even himself.

Officially, there was no money to deal with him. The military performed a thorough examination and evaluation, after the fires inside him had burned themselves out. The conclusion was that Big Ben was beyond repair. This battle had been his last. The damage was too extensive. There were no funds available to keep him going. Nor were there any available to transport him elsewhere, to a breaker's yard, say.

An online petition to have Big Ben retrieved and refitted— revived—gained well over a million signatures, but the government steadfastly refused to listen. Big Ben had been expensive to run. He was uneconomic. He had done exemplary service in the name of his country, and his crew were to be awarded the Military Cross in recognition of their gallantry and bravery, but now, to all intents and purposes, this particular KRV was RIP. Just so much scrap metal.

The good news? The government said it was prepared to invest in a joint European Union project to build a new set of KRVs that would defend the whole of the continent against the ongoing Kaiju threat. The existing fleet of European Kaiju Response Vehicles was starting to show its age, so it seemed logical that the EU countries collaborate to replace it with a generation of brand new super-KRVs. Germany would be doing the majority of the design and manufacturing, since Germany was the only Western nation with a still thriving industrial base. So it was there that the super-KRVs would be headquartered, and it was the German chancellor who would have final say over their command and deployment.

The time for a solely British KRV had passed. "The future," said the prime minister to parliament, "lies in this pan-European initiative, which I believe will bring us and our neighbors much closer, and presents a much more financially sound means of protecting ourselves against the most pressing danger of the modern era."

BIG BEN REMAINED JUST OFFSHORE, immobile, a husk, a relic. The sun shone on him. The rain rained on him. On stormy days, the waves crashed against him and burst into spray. Seagulls perched on his head and shoulders and streaked his metal hull white with their guano.

KEITH, LIKE THE LANDLORD OF The Sailor's Rest, had not taken out act of Kaiju indemnity on his business premises. It was ruinously costly. Basically, no one but the ultra-rich could afford it. Insurers were obliged by law to offer the product but priced it so that hardly anyone would buy.

After some wrangling with his insurance company, however, Keith did receive a token compensation payout amounting to just shy of £10,000.

Nowhere near enough to rebuild the Forever Fun Pier.

But Keith had an idea.

NOW YOU COULD VISIT BIG Ben. You could reach him via a catwalk which extended from the last vestiges of the seaward end of the pier. You could clamber inside him through a specially cut portal in his leg. You could travel up stepladders and traverse suspended walkways through his workings.

You could inspect for yourself his burned-out engine and his emptied weapons pods. You could sit in his cockpit at the inactive controls and gaze out through the windscreens that were his eyes. You could imagine yourself piloting him into the fray, meeting a Kaiju head-on and giving that marauding leviathan what-for.

You could purchase tea and cakes in the horizontal cylindrical chamber of his right thigh, looking out at the view through newly installed portholes. You could spiral down a helical slide built inside his arm, to land safely on an airbag cupped inside his hand. You could venture into a tunnel maze of cleaned-out fuel pipes and coolant ducts.

The hero who had defeated eighteen Kaiju, Red Devil being the last of those, was now one of the south coast's most popular attractions. Customers flocked. Some days, weekends, and bank holidays in particular, the queue stretched from the pier entrance halfway down the promenade.

KEITH HAD OFFERED THE GOVERNMENT a thousand pounds for Big Ben.

Eager to be shot of him, and of the responsibility for him, the government had come back with a counteroffer of fifty. Not fifty thousand. *Fifty* pounds.

Keith spent the rest of the insurance payout on tidying up, refurbishment, the relevant permits, and promotion.

The Forever Fun Pier was no more, and good riddance. It had never been anything except a millstone around Keith's neck.

The Big Ben Experience, though, was his, and his alone. Not a legacy. Something he had developed himself. His inspiration. His brainchild.

Keith had faced an enemy older, heavier and more implacable than a Kaiju, an opponent who had sentiment and the weight of time on his side.

And he had overcome.

THE CONVERSION

DAVID ANNANDALE

And did those feet in ancient time,
Walk upon England's mountains green?
And was the Holy Lamb of God
On England's pleasant pastures seen?

TENS OF THOUSANDS STRONG, THE CHOIR SANG "JERUSALEM."
IT WAS THE SEVENTH YEAR OF THE RAGE.

THE BEAST HAD COME AT last, and was there, in truth, any point in pretending that there was somewhere to run or hide?

Chadwick Ginther didn't think so. Neither did Matthew Carpenter. So they had driven from Manchester to the coast at Carmel Head. They would meet the inevitable upon its arrival.

"I saw Bickford yesterday," Ginther said.

"Oh? Has he tempered his views at all?"

"Hardly. Proceeding full steam ahead."

Carpenter shrugged. "Well, maybe he's right."

"We'll know soon enough, I expect." Ginther surprised and pleased himself with his calm. He wondered if he would be able to keep it when the moment came.

Sitting in the passenger seat of Carpenter's car, eating a ham and chutney sandwich, he found it hard to believe in that approaching moment. It was too abstract. Carpenter had parked by the side of the road. To their right, a field and hills were between them and the coast. They couldn't see the military operations from here, beyond the occasional helicopter or fighter passing overhead. The sound of the deployment was white noise. It could pass for the crash of surf.

Carpenter glanced up from his notes as a squadron streaked toward the sea, engines scraping the early afternoon raw. "Give them credit," he said. "They're still trying."

"Their way of coping," Ginther answered. "Same as we're doing. Same as Bickford, though he won't admit it."

"I suppose so." Carpenter turned to Ginther, and the fear beneath his brittle detachment was visible. He rubbed absently at his chin. "Do you think Bickford could be correct?"

Ginther paused before answering. Thirty years of collegial disagreement urged him to say no. The knowledge that he would die today made him hesitate. "Maybe he's half-right," he said. "I don't believe he has a more direct line to the truth than we do. Anyway, whether he's right or wrong, what does that change about today?"

Carpenter did not look reassured. "What comes after."

Ginther shook his head. "About that, Bickford's wrong." He was more emphatic this time. He could feel his own anxiety growing with Carpenter's. He didn't want that.

"But in the footage of the thing, I see elements that—"

Ginther interrupted. "Footage taken by missile cams and fleeing journalists. Hard to see anything conclusive."

"And its name?"

"That is troubling," Ginther admitted.

There were quiet for a bit, then. They finished eating. There was farmland to the left, and Ginther heard sheep bleating. Fifteen years of living in England, and the sound was still a novelty for him. It was a verdant isle echo that made his heart lurch with an Arcadian nostalgia that was no less acute for being false.

"Plenty of time for reading, the last few days," Carpenter said. The universities, along with so much else, had shut down when confirmation of the approach had been received. "Been going back over a lot of Blake. Yeats, too." He was staring at the hills. Clouds were starting to roll in. Their shadows crawled down the slopes. "You?"

"The Eddur, mostly." A return to the familiar. He had found no comfort there. Only a discomfiting relevance.

The thunder of guns began, joined moments later by the shrieks and deeper blasts of rockets.

"Genuflection," Ginther muttered.

"An act that still has meaning," Carpenter said as they climbed out of the car.

"But no effect."

They walked a few steps into the field and stopped. They watched the hills. They waited while the thunder of the genuflection grew louder and more desperate.

They didn't wait long. As the clouds gathered strength and turned the day from the last light of joy to the first grey of the end, the beast surged over the hills. Ginther's eyes widened. Awe shot his chest with agony. He looked up and up and up, and he thought, *Forever*.

Carpenter said, "It's all true," and the words were a sob of holy terror.

The beast crossed the hills in a single stride. It was bipedal. Though its shape suggested a towering carnosaur, it had the chitinous exoskeleton of a crab, even to the ends of its four great, clawed hands. In the shape of the head, Ginther saw a dragon, but perhaps because of the eerie, translucent blue of its eyes, he also saw a wolf. Its jaws were immense. When they opened, they did, as they should, look as if they could touch earth and sky. Its tail, covered in the same armor as the rest of its body, doubled its already staggering length.

Its coils were ready to embrace the globe.

"The horns," Carpenter whispered. "The horns."

Yes, the horns. The beast had one head, not seven, but it had ten horns. They surrounded its skull like a huge, twisting, iron crown.

With a second stride, the beast was halfway across the field. The earth shook and cracked. The next step would bring the finish to Ginther and Carpenter. Though his terror was mounting to new heights, Ginther had no will to run. He accepted what was coming.

So did Carpenter. "The name is right," he said.

"Yes." Ginther could barely hear his own breaking voice. "Yes, it is."

He stared at the monster of many mythologies, and beyond them all. He stared as it took that fatal step. He stared to the very last as the crushing shadow came down over him, and he joined Carpenter in a cry that was only possible in the presence of the end of all things.

The Eschaton had come.

And did the Countenance Divine,
Shine forth upon our clouded hills?
And was Jerusalem builded here,
Among these dark, Satanic Mills?

EVANS POKED HIS HEAD IN the command tent, looking both sheepish and irritated. "Sorry to bother you, brigadier," he said. "Bit of a problem at the gates. That clergyman who's been in the news insists on seeing you. Won't take piss off for an answer."

Joyce Caldwell sighed. "Show him in, captain." Better get this over with.

Evans was surprised. "Are you sure? Brigadier, we could—"

"He's family."

The captain's eyebrows were high on his forehead.

"Oh," he said.

"Right," he said, and managed to swallow his questions. He withdrew.

Caldwell walked out of the tent to wait. Around her, the playing field of Old Trafford was an armed camp on the move. The Eschaton was approaching. The best was within a few kilometers of Manchester's western suburbs. Troops, tanks, self-propelled artillery, and multiple rocket launchers headed out from the mustering grounds. A large contingent remained. If the Eschaton broke through the lines and entered the city, Caldwell hoped to draw it to the stadium, where a high concentration of firepower might make a difference.

If. Hoped. Might. She knew better. Everyone did. But duty demanded acting as if they didn't. She held tight to duty. There wasn't much else to hold, as city after city, and nation after nation, burned in the Rage.

Seven years ago, it would have been an honor to be charged with Manchester's defense. Seven years ago, she would have been laboring under the blessed illusion that her efforts might bear fruit, and that she might save the city. That was before American East Coast, and the holocaust in the Mid-West, and the end of California. That was before Tokyo, before Moscow, before Mumbai, and Sydney, and Lagos, and Berlin, and Paris, and Shanghai, and… The list was endless, a Domesday Book of annihilation. Was there any reason to think that her very conventional forces would succeed where much vaster armies, and measures far more extreme, had been swatted aside? No, there was not. Nuclear craters marked the failures of the most desperate moves.

There was no order to the devastation. The path of the Eschaton's march followed no pattern. There was no way to predict which city would be next. The only true certainty was that the time would come to every major population center. That hadn't stopped the rise of some false certainties. For seven years, the Eschaton had not approached the British Isles, and Caldwell had seen the belief grow, among those who sought comfort in the nurture of intolerant myth, that this was the result of divine intervention. Albion, said the men with minds like fists, was Chosen. To keep it safe, to keep the protection of the Almighty, it was necessary to expel the people who did not look or think or love like the men with minds like fists. And if the tottering government did not expel them, then it would be necessary to hurt them very badly. In the last few years, Caldwell had spent so much time quelling or clearing up the aftermath of humanity's worst impulses that the arrival of the Eschaton had almost been a relief.

Almost.

Maneuvering through vehicles and soldiers, Evans delivered Sam Bickford to Caldwell. "Thank you, captain," she said. "That will be all." Evans saluted and left.

"Thank you for seeing me, Joyce," her brother said.

"What do you want?" She could guess, and she had little desire to waste what time remained to her. Given a choice, there was somewhere else she would much rather be.

"I want salvation," Bickford said. "For all of us. Isn't that what we're both trying to achieve?"

"You could say that, but I'm not going to achieve anything standing here with you."

"Do you honestly think you can destroy the beast?"

"I'm going to try."

"That isn't what I asked."

She sighed. "Where is this going, Sam? Because I have better things to do than have another circular conversation with you."

He looked at the ground, and there, nervous before asking a favor, was her younger brother. Dark hair and beard graying now, though a long way from the iron her own hair had turned years ago. Still as slight as he had been in adolescence. There was little sign of the powerful speaker.

"I need your help," he said.

"With what?" She was at a loss.

"I need your belief, first."

"You won't have it."

There was great pain in his eyes. "When you were younger, you gave it to father."

"Who didn't deserve it." That petty tyrant and hypocrite had deserved her fist. If he had lived long enough for her to reach adulthood, she would have given him that gift. Oh yes, she most certainly would have. Instead, she had to content herself with rejecting the patronym, and taking their mother's maiden name instead.

"But what he represented *did* deserve it," Bickford said. "He was a poor churchman. That isn't the fault of God."

She said nothing.

He smiled gently. "You do have faith," he said. "Even if you don't think so. Think about what you're doing. Can you truly believe you're fighting something natural?"

"It isn't a god, if that's what you mean."

"I don't mean that. Not a god. Not God. But it is proof of His coming." His smile went from kind to beatific.

"Odd proof, killing hundreds of millions."

"They are safe at His side. Use your reason. It will bring you to faith. Consider the beast's name…"

"Not surprising it's been called that. Given everything."

"We knew it as the Eschaton from the day it first appeared. All of us did. Everywhere."

She wanted to tell him he was wrong. She couldn't.

"And look at it!" he continued. "It makes no evolutionary sense whatever. An exoskeleton *and* an endoskeleton? A biped with four arms? It comes from the sea, and yet breathes—"

"I know all this," she said, cutting him off. Her brother was wrong if he thought this litany of impossibilities was going to bring back to God. It *was* undermining the faith she needed in the value of her actions. It was destroying her hope that, even if she died today, she might, through her sacrifice, save some of the people of Manchester. Keep more of them safe than there would be without her. Keep Sandra safe. A bit longer anyway. Just a little bit longer. She didn't think it was too much to ask to be allowed to fight for that illusion.

"How can you consider something so unnatural and not see evidence of the divine?" her brother asked.

"What it did in the Middle East, was that your idea of the Second Coming?"

Bickford winced. "No," he said, and she saluted him for his intellectual honesty. "It wasn't. That was a time of revelation for me."

"I'm sure the people who died would have been glad to know they served a purpose."

His personal logic had too much momentum for him to notice her gibe. "We cannot be passive before the challenge of the Eschaton."

Caldwell stared. She swept her arm around the stadium, taking in the full panorama of the machinery of war. "How can you call this passive?"

"It's only a half-measure, and that's why it's failing. This has to be a crusade. We can't just hurl a spear at the beast. The spear has to be blessed."

"Are you trying to tell me that there were no believers who took up arms anywhere else in the world? Or here, for that matter?"

"Not in the way I want to fight."

And there it was. The Bickford hubris. *Unlike the father, it was tempered in the son by kindness, and a generosity that sometimes tipped,* Caldwell believed, *into naiveté.* She liked to believe the yokes she had borne through her childhood and then her adult life had purged the worst of that inheritance from her. But in Bickford, in this moment, the legacy was huge. Still, she was curious now. "And what way is that?"

"I am leading a prayer service in Manchester Stadium."

"I'd heard. Quite a gathering of political extremists turned out for you, or so I understand. The same crowd that was still declaring England immune a week ago."

That made him squirm. "There are some—" he began.

"The same crowd that would curb stomp the likes of me, given half a chance."

"That isn't what I'm preaching," he said, almost pleading now. "You know me better than that. But the doors are open to all. How can I turn away anyone who has the genuine need to pray?"

"Prayer and spiritual help. That's all you're doing? I'd assumed you had ironic symmetry in mind."

He looked hurt. "Symmetry, yes. I would never feel scorn for what you're trying to do."

"Even though I'm wrong."

"Half-wrong," he corrected. "And so are we, without your help."

Finally, she thought. *The point.* "Which would involve what?"

"I need one of your vehicles. A rocket launcher."

"Just one? Is that all? Will an M270 do the job?"

He nodded. He never had been good at irony. "I don't know anything about the different kinds. I trust your judgment."

"And you're going to drive and operate it yourself?"

"Of course not. We'll need a crew, too."

"And this is going to make a difference how?"

"Its rockets will be blessed. The prayers of thousands will speed them on their way. Their flight will be true."

"This will kill the Eschaton." Her voice didn't hold quite as much disbelief as it should have. Her command was also an act of faith, and she couldn't utterly dismiss Bickford's hope without hurting her own.

He was impervious to all doubt. He was still smiling, and this time, he raised his eyes to the sky. "Once you admit the nature of the

Eschaton, once you see the proof that it embodies, then you know that what I propose cannot fail. The Hand of God Himself will strike the beast down." He tilted his head back and closed his eyes, as if basking in the light of Heaven. Overhead, the evening clouds were dirty with the smoke of distant fires.

Caldwell waited, silent, for Bickford to finish his moment of communion. When he looked at her again, she said, "Go back to the stadium, Sam. Do what you can for that flock of yours."

"Please don't dismiss this out of hand. Will you think about it? After all, what difference will one launcher make?"

What difference would a thousand make? He didn't have to say it. The thought came unbidden. "Go back to the stadium," she said again. "I have work to do."

In the distance, but not nearly far enough, came the sound of explosions and the earthquake-deep boom of immense footsteps. And then the roar. That roar.

The roar of the end of all hope.

Bring me my Bow of burning gold;
Bring me my Arrows of desire:
Bring me my Spear: O clouds unfold!
Bring me my Chariot of fire!

SHE HAD THOUGHT SHE WOULD ride out for the front lines. No, that was wrong. She had *hoped* she would have to do that. That would have meant the lines held long enough for her to reach them. That would have meant they held at all.

They didn't.

The explosions, the footsteps, and the roar approached with all the mercy of a storm surge. The stadium defenses had time to make ready, and then, lit by the spotlights, the Eschaton appeared. Caldwell felt her eyes widen. The monster loomed high above the outer walls of Old Trafford. The field shook with the simultaneous fire of dozens of cannons and rockets. The bombardment, apocalyptic at ground level, was reduced to insignificance when it hit the Eschaton.

Streaks of fire became tiny blossoms against the articulated shell of the beast. With its next step, its lower leg smashed through the walls. As if kicked, Stretford End blew apart, its mosaic of red and white seats flying like confetti. The steel from the superstructure became a rain of javelins. Concrete chunks as big as cars catapulted across the field. Caldwell leaped aside to avoid a piece that hit the ground and rolled towards her, crushing the command tent. The Eschaton waded into the stadium. It stood on the wreckage of Challenger main battle tanks and AS-90 self-propelled Howitzers. It lowered its head, taking in its foes with eyes whose judgment was clear, alien, and absolutely frozen. It opened its jaws wide. Its chest rumbled, and there was the sound of a great wind being sucked away.

Caldwell knew what was coming next. Everyone in the stadium did. They had read the intelligence. They had seen the footage. But the mythic could not be understood until it was experienced.

Infantry ran for mirages of cover. Caldwell crouched low behind the rubble that had destroyed the tent. The heavy armor fired one last time, a gesture of defiance as brave as it was useless.

The Eschaton breathed death on Old Trafford. The doom took the appearance of a beam of braided impossibility. It was white, crystalline flame. The beast turned its head from left to right, spreading the blast across the entire field. Behind her shelter, Caldwell felt the horror pass just over her head. She bit back a cry of agony as frostbite and incandescence reached through her fatigues.

Silence fell, ghastly with anticipation. Caldwell raised her head. The Eschaton stood there, cloud-breaker, sky-killer, looking down on its work. The fallen walls of the stadium and everything within them were encased in flames of ice. Human, vehicle, and ruin were twisted into immobilized writhings of absolute torment.

For a few seconds, Caldwell stared at a tableau. Hell was motionless. It had a grace that came with perfect extremity. Then the explosion came, the ice becoming motion, becoming a solar flare. The heat forced Caldwell down again. She was surrounded by wall of flame thirty meters high. The Eschaton raised its arms and roared. It drowned out the firestorm. For a moment, she expected to see chunks of the sky fall earthward, smashed by the Jericho blast of the roar.

The beast strode onwards, leaving the burning, broken toy of the stadium.

Caldwell watched it go. *Beast*, she thought. *That's what it is. A beast. One we can't kill, but it isn't anything more.* She was holding back something profound. She knew what it was, and at the same time refused to acknowledge it, even as a false possibility. She refused to let the impulse turn into a thought that might defeat her.

The fire kept her trapped for a quarter of an hour. When it died down enough that she could leave her shelter without being incinerated, she made for a gap in the flames. It had once been the East Stand but the Eschaton had gone this way. Evans and a few other survivors joined her in escaping the burning stadium. Very few.

Smoke rolled through the falling night. The city was lit by the glow of its own pyre. Where the Eschaton walked, it left a spreading wake of ice, then fire. The burn was already a kilometer wide. The beast wasn't following streets. Caldwell watched it head northeast, roughly parallel to the canal, smashing its way through the city blocks. Buildings toppled at its touch. Its tail swept back forth behind it, bringing down the few towers that survived the initial moment of its passing.

Caldwell tasted the bile of failure. It was a failure she had known was coming. That didn't make it any easier to accept. She had lost her city. Thousands were already dead. Soon, the casualties would number in the tens of thousands. Then the hundreds of thousands. There had been no evacuation. There had been no time to move over two million people and nowhere to send them. Those who could had taken refuge in basements and underground car parks. Most people had no choice but to hide in their homes. Now those homes burned and fell. Some, that the Eschaton smashed with its fists, flew as they disintegrated.

She saw the world ending at the hands of a being so huge that to see it was to know it as the source of awe. She knew that Bickford was right, but still, even now, she held back the full realization. If she followed her thoughts to their inevitable conclusion, she might not be able to fight any longer. Perhaps her brother was also lying to himself.

She headed south, dodging flames and climbing over wreckage until she reached an area that was still undamaged. She found more fragments of her battlegroup there. She commandeered a Panther Light Multirole Vehicle. Evans drove.

"Manchester Stadium," she told him, then got on the radio. It took her a few minutes to contact the crew of a viable M270, but she found one, and directed the launcher to meet up with her at the stadium. She would give Bickford his holy weapon. "Do not engage," she ordered. "Am I clear? Your arrival on-site is the priority."

The streets were clear of civilian traffic, and they made rapid progress up Stretford Road. Caldwell looked out the passenger window of the LMV. In the gaps between blocks, she watched the Eschaton's progress. When they reached the open area at the intersection with Princess Road, she asked Evans to stop.

To the north, she witnessed the Eschaton reach Beetham Tower. The sleek glass monolith, the tallest skyscraper in Manchester, was gossamer-thin before the monster. The Eschaton looked *down* on it. Its four arms grasped the building. The monster ripped the upper two-thirds of the tower from their base. It raised the building over its head, then hurled it to the ground. The impact shook the city. The Eschaton turned then, breathing annihilation around a full 360 degrees.

Caldwell looked away when the flames rose. Sandra's apartment was just off St. John's Gardens. The neighborhood had just ceased to be.

"Let's go," she told Evans. She tried to take comfort in the knowledge she wouldn't have time to grieve for very long.

The Panther arrived in Sports City. The M270 was there less than five minutes later. Caldwell stood beside the LMV and listened to the prayer rise in waves from the interior of the stadium. She felt her jaw clench. The old anger was still there. Bickford's faith would never be hers. The best she could do was hope his was well-placed.

Inside the stadium, the lights were on, and Bickford's amplified voice resounded. He had managed to have generators installed. The stands were full. There was barely room on the field for the vehicles to maneuver. Bickford was on a stage before the north stand, leading a choir of fifty thousand in hymns of praise. Caldwell had never seen her brother in full flight before. She had known he was successful in his calling. He had been leading his own army for years now. But on those rare occasions they had crossed paths during their adult lives, he had still been the quiet, kind brother who was too willing to defer to authority.

She wondered whether anything was different now. As he worked the stage, she saw power, confidence, a commanding ecstasy, and all of it was in the service of another Authority. The enveloping rush of tens of thousands singing in unison was intoxicating, and it was easier for her to believe, in this moment, that hope could be real. She clung to her duty to try anything to save the city. It was her shield against despair, against mourning, and against a darker belief that, as it threatened to emerge from the darkness, had the terrible contours not of faith, but of knowledge.

Bickford stopped in mid-prayer when she reached the stage. He beckoned for her to join him. She shook her head, refusing to be part of the spectacle. She knew her brother was sincere in his desire to do good, but she distrusted an instinct for glory that was another inheritance from their father, even if he didn't seem fully conscious of it.

He came down from the stage to greet her. As he did, the stands quieted, but only for a moment. When the noise of Manchester's death rushed in from beyond the walls, the crowd launched back into "Bread of Heaven" with redoubled fervor. If the song was loud enough, the people could hide from what was coming.

"Thank you," Bickford said. "I knew you would feel the touch of the—"

She cut him off. "I didn't feel anything." That was a lie, but she was suddenly afraid of hearing the word *divine*. "Prove to me that I should, Sam. Make this work."

"It will work, but not because of me." He hugged her, then turned back to the stage. One foot on the stairs, he paused and looked at her. "It will come, won't it?"

She almost laughed at the horrific irony of his question. "How could it not?" she answered. "Have faith."

He smiled. "Of course. Please wait for my signal before launching." He bounded up the stairs. In the center of the stage, he raised his arms and spread them wide. The people stopped singing. "Our deliverance is at hand!" he shouted, and the cheer washed over Caldwell like a tidal wave.

It chilled her. The cold came not because of the belief of others, but because of her own. Denial became slippery. Faith was contagious, and it terrified her as the battlefield never had. The fear was worse than the terror she and every solider under her command had experienced at the first sight of the Eschaton. The fear was worse because it sprang from that encounter. Seeds had been planted at Old Trafford. They had sent roots down to the heart of her identity. As the futility of all her training, of all her decades of experience was revealed, something grew. Now the hymns were bringing this thing to the point of its malignant bloom.

Explosions drew closer. The doom-rhythm of the Eschaton's footsteps drowned out the crowd. The people faltered. Bickford did not. "The Lord is our Shepherd!" he reminded them. "We shall not want. Now, especially now, we shall not want."

The Eschaton appeared, blotting out the night sky visible through the roof of the stadium. As distant as its cold eyes were, as minute as humans must be from its perspective, Caldwell felt as if the monster saw and passed a verdict on every soul present. The Eschaton stepped on the west stands, crushing thousands to wet ruin. It was amongst them now, the mountain that had come with fury to destroy the city. And then it waited, as if its actions and those of the insects before it were a form of dialogue.

Or the call and response of prayer.

Bickford began to sing. His voice carried over the screams of the injured and dying. The people, embracing the hope he promised and the faith he provided, joined in.

Tens of thousands strong, the choir sang "Jerusalem."

> *I will not cease from Mental Fight,*
> *Nor shall my Sword sleep in my hand:*
> *Till we have built Jerusalem,*
> *In England's green & pleasant Land.*

"NOW," BICKFORD SAID.

Caldwell couldn't tear her eyes away from the Eschaton. How could she be reading something beyond the animal, however immense, in its posture? How could she be seeing *intent?* Yet she knew that she was. The blossoming inside her began. Even so, she was able to give the order to the crew of the rocket launcher.

Bickford shouted, "Behold the Hand of God!"

The hymn reached its climax. The faith of the thousands was tangible, and Caldwell felt it fly upwards with the rockets. As the fragments of seconds stretched to aeons, she could well believe she had helped forge a holy weapon. She could well believe her brother spoke the absolute truth. She could well believe it was the divine hand itself that rose to strike the abomination that had dared lay waste to the world.

She could believe all these things. She did not, because the far greater belief that she had been fighting was now upon her.

The Eschaton reached an arm forward. With sovereign contempt, it batted aside the Hand of God. The explosions were the sad dissolution of faith.

For a few seconds more, the Eschaton did nothing else. It seemed to be waiting for the full significance of the moment to fall upon the assembly. Beside the Panther, Evans had collapsed into a ball, his head to the ground, defeated. Caldwell looked back at Bickford. Bereft of his illusion, he had fallen to his knees. The full truth of what he had been telling his sister was hitting him. There was a divine force at large in the universe, and he was looking at it. His mouth hung open in an agony of awe.

Caldwell faced the immensity. The Eschaton rumbled. The terrible sucking sound began once more. The fullness of epiphany rocked Caldwell. She was battered by the belief that was knowledge, the knowledge that this was the only deity her world would ever know.

Caldwell didn't fight the truth, but she didn't surrender. She flew beyond grief and despair, and seized the only weapon left to her: defiance. Standing upright to the last, she howled at the Eschaton. She shouted into the dread second of final silence.

She was roaring still when the Eschaton opened its jaws wide and gave them all their baptism.

THE LIGHTHOUSE KEEPER OF KUROHAKA ISLAND

Kane Gilmour

THE GRAY LIGHT OF THE morning merged with the steel color of the waves, giving Shinobi the feeling he was being tossed around in the air. He stood at the bow of the freighter, his young hands gripping the rail tightly—he'd been told and he remembered, 'one hand for yourself and one hand for the ship, at all times'—and he peered into the murky shades of concrete that filled the sky and the sea. He couldn't determine where one began and the other ended.

Thick fog shrouded everything, and his one thought over and over was to wonder where all the brilliant blue had gone. From his home in Wakkanai, at the northern tip of Japan, the sea was always blue, even on stormy days. But here, in the no man's land twenty miles northeast of Hokkaido, everything looked hostile to the boy. But then, everything in the world now looked that way.

"Shinobi," he heard his father's abrupt voice from behind him. Mindful to keep one hand on the damp railing, as the massive freighter bounced in the invisible troughs of the cold waves, he turned to see his father approaching him from the starboard side of the ship. "Come inside. We are nearly there."

Shinobi walked along the railing, moving hand over hand, lest

Illustration by **ROBERT ELROD**

some rogue wave slap the big ship and send him headlong into a never-ending drop through the gray moisture. "Almost where, Father? I've checked the maps. There's nothing here."

His father, a stern man named Jiro, remained quiet until Shinobi reached him along the rail, skirting the massive multi-colored metal containers that filled the center of the ship's broad foredeck. When Shinobi looked up at his father, he realized the man was not simply waiting for him or being his typical quiet self, but rather he was peering intently past the bow of the ship and into the gloom.

Shinobi knew to stay still and be quiet. His father was either deep in thought or looking for something in the fog. The man would speak when he was ready to, and not before. With nothing else to do, besides hold the railing, Shinobi studied his father's face. He quickly determined that the man was actually looking for something in the thick mist that shrouded the ship. He was just about to turn, when his father spoke.

"There," the man pointed past the bow, "Kurohaka Island."

Shinobi turned and momentarily let his hand drop from the railing in surprise. In a part of the Sea of Okhotsk he knew to be empty of any spit of land, a jagged dark shape was rising from the sea and the fog. The island looked to have strange curving towers near the center, and rough rocky shores at the edges. Finally, his eyes sought out what he was looking for—the lighthouse. It was on the end of the island, on a high rocky promontory, but its lifesaving light was absent, and its white paint made little difference in the thick fluffy coating of whitish gray that filled the air. The spire could barely be seen in all the mist.

Shinobi's father was a lighthouse keeper in the region, being paid by the governments of both Japan and Russia to ride whatever available ships were in the area, and to frequently visit and maintain the ramshackle lighthouses on the islands scattered around Hokkaido and the giant lobster-claw tips of Sakhalin, around the Gulf of

Patience. Shinobi had travelled with his father to Rebun Island and Rishiri Island. He had even gone on one memorable camping trip with his father to the abandoned Russian island of Moneron, northwest of the Soya Straight. He had listened attentively to his father's few descriptions of his work on the lights. Shinobi was meant to take over his father's work some day, first apprenticing in two year's time, when he turned fifteen. He had studied hard in school, and paid special attention to the nautical maps in the library and around the house. He knew the names of every jagged rocky islet in the area, but he had never heard of Kurohaka Island.

True, his attention of late had not been on maps or studying. Instead he had been seeing things, and hoping he wasn't losing his sanity. But he had kept that information hidden from his father.

"Kurohaka?" he asked.

His father nodded grimly. "A dark place, but still part of the job. Let's go in."

Shinobi followed his father back to the ship's forecastle, wondering at the name of the island. Kurohaka. *Black tomb*. He wondered if sailors had named it that because it was such a rocky shoreline. Many times islands were given fearsome names to warn sailors off the reefs. But the name might actually stem from a true tomb.

He wondered who was buried there.

Or, considering what he had been seeing lately—*what* might be buried there.

THE FREIGHTER HAD LOWERED THEM in a small speedboat with winches from the high sides of the rusting gunwales. Once in the choppy water, they had made quick time to the dark island, and his father expertly navigated them past some treacherous headlands and into a tiny sheltered lagoon. Any boat larger than their speedboat would not have made it into the small inlet. They pulled the boat up to a concrete pier that jutted an absurd four feet into the water from the wet rocky land. The lagoon looked to Shinobi to be a popped volcanic bubble more than a sandy beach. The shoreline was all dark rock, but at least here it was smooth.

Shinobi helped his father tie up the small boat to the two rusted metal cleats sunk into the concrete pier's rough surface and carry their gear ashore. When he turned to the gray sea, he could watch the freighter moving away into the distance. A different boat would swing by in two days to collect them.

"How can this island be here, Father?"

Jiro Yashida hefted his pack and began walking up the rocks, toward the interior of the island. He spoke over his shoulder to his son in short bursts. "You know the maps. Think of the shapes. A long chain of islands connects Hokkaido to Russia's Kamchatka peninsula. And Wakkanai points at the western tip of Sakhalin. Is it really so surprising to you that an island lies midway between Hokkaido and the eastern tip of Sakhalin?"

Shinobi considered his father's logic, and found that geologically, the location of the island made perfect sense. "No. I understand, but the island does not appear on the maps."

"Many don't," was all his father said.

They turned left and followed a coastal trail up along the rocks, twisting and turning through switchbacks, until the base of the white lighthouse was visible overhead. Their path, keeping so close to the shore as it did, kept the rest of the island hidden from Shinobi's view, even as the fog began to lift. What little he could see was dark brown and black rock, most of it volcanic, and fitting with his initial assumptions about the geology of the island. Shinobi was not fond of math at school, but when Earth sciences came into things, he paid strict attention.

With the base of the lighthouse just thirty feet overhead now, their path narrowed, and they needed to rely on the artificial railings made of thick heavy chains. They had been bolted into the side of the rock and painted in so many layers of heavy black paint, that even when Shinobi could see the outer layers had chipped, all he could see in the remaining holes on the links were more and more layers underneath.

Shinobi watched where his father stepped, and how the man moved his hands along the chains, as if they were the railing on the freighter—*one hand for the ship*—and he did the same. They were nearly to the top of the path, which would bring them right to the door of the lighthouse, when his father spoke.

"When did you plan on telling me? Or did you think you should keep it to yourself forever?"

The man didn't pause in his ascent, nor did he look back at his son.

Shinobi knew what his father was talking about, of course. There was just the one thing he had kept from his father in his whole thirteen years.

His father was talking about the *monsters*.

Shinobi could see them, and no one else could.

He stayed quiet, thinking how best to answer the question, as his father made it to the top of the climb and lowered his pack to the ground, just outside the door to the lighthouse. Finally, as Shinobi neared his father and the pack, he spoke, while removing his own heavy pack.

"Have I done something wrong, Father?" Shinobi hung his head as he spoke.

His father reached down and tenderly lifted Shinobi's chin, so he was looking his father in the eyes. "You have done nothing wrong, *Shino*."

"How could you have known?" the boy asked, his eyes beginning to water.

His father quickly turned, allowing him to save face, as a tear sprang from the corner of his young eye and ran down his round cheek. The man worked a large brass key into the lock on the lighthouse door, and entered. Shinobi followed.

"The haunted look in your eyes, son. I had the same look, when I first saw the creatures."

That his father knew about the monsters was a surprise to Shinobi. That his father had seen them, as well, filled the boy with a relief he hadn't known he needed. He followed his father up the twisting iron staircase. The lighthouse was close to a hundred feet in height—Shinobi could tell by counting the stairs as they ascended in silence. He wanted to ask his father more, but he knew the man would tell him when he was ready. Probably at the top of the tower, since speaking while ascending the steep steps would require an excess of oxygen, and Jiro Yashida was a practical man of economy. Shinobi hoped to be as sensible when he was an adult.

As his father came close to the lantern section of the tower, a good twenty steps ahead of Shinobi on the cast iron stairs, he began speaking again, but softly. "Every first-born child between the ages of thirteen and eighteen has the sight, *Shino*. But only first-borns. Your brother, Naro, will never be able to see the beasts, as you do. Unless you were to die, before he grows to adulthood. Most teens lose their vision as adulthood approaches, but in our family, we are unusual. We retain the sight as adults. I still see the creatures today, son."

The man stepped up off the stairs and into the service room of the lantern. Then he ascended a straight ladder to the optic section of the tower. Shinobi hurried after him, as the man stepped off the ladder and opened the door from the optic room to the gallery around the tower's top. Wind rushed into the structure and flooded down toward Shinobi. It was cold and, of course, he could smell the briny aroma of the sea, but there was something else on the wind. Something old, like dust.

Jiro walked out the open door to the catwalk and waited against the railing, as Shinobi caught up with him at last.

The fog had lifted as the day's sunlight burnt it away. The cloud cover had receded to a low blanket hovering over the land in patches and threatening possible rain, but not until later. For now the morning sunlight was piercing through the covering in spots, like samurai swords thrust downward through pillows, toward the green land spread out before them.

But the clouds did not hold Shinobi's attention.

His eyes took in the many shades of green across the central part of the land of the island, and the things that pierced the green, reaching up like clawing hands to the sky—a reverse of the angle of the beams of light slicing down from above.

They were bones.

Hundred and thousands of *bones*.

The slim graceful towers Shinobi had seen from sea were giant rib bones, arching into the sky as high as the lighthouse. The carcasses of giant hundred-foot and two-hundred foot long strange beasts Shinobi could not recognize littered the island, and stretched as far as he could see. His father had said the island was approximately three miles long, and from his position near the top of the lighthouse, Shinobi could see most of the way to the far shore, where the green gave way to the dark volcanic rocks again. There were unnatural mounds and low hills in places, and the boy guessed they were the covered graves of yet more of the massive creatures. At the center of the island was one huge rounded hill with some irregularities and lumpy tufts of bushes and trees on it in places.

Shinobi spotted massive lobster-like claws, and desiccated snake-like twisting bodies, piled high on tangled horns and bulbous bones. Most of the creatures had decayed to the point of little more than skeletons—even though the bones were impressive at their immense scale. A few of the dead monsters still contained eyes in unusual locations, or mouths full of teeth taller than the apartment buildings back in Wakkanai.

"I see them all. This island has been a place where they come to die for centuries. Whenever one of them is injured, it comes here of its own volition. We don't know why." Shinobi's father looked gray and ashen, as if the sight of the boneyard was still unnerving to him. It did little to ease Shinobi's own tension at the sight, but the revelation that he was not going crazy and he was not the only one with the sight helped him some.

"H-how many?" was all the boy could stammer.

"We don't know. When those few of us with the sight have found these mega creatures dead in other parts of the world, it has become a tradition to bring them here. I will tell you how it began. I will tell you what happened. You are one of the rare ones, Shino. You will have the sight all your life, and like me, you must become the caretaker of this necropolis. We guard more than just the bones."

The older man fell silent as the wind ripped past the top of the tower, bringing the scent of the water and what Shinobi now suspected was the smell of the dead.

"First we will fix the light, son. It warns sailors to stay away, and that is a very good thing. Then we'll go down and have a talk. Our family first took on this bizarre appointment with your grandfather, Haruki. He was the first in our family to see that the world is truly full of monsters."

HARUKI YASHIDA RAN FOR HIS life.

The bombing of the city had ended a few days earlier, but he knew what would come next. He had seen the hideous monstrosities with his own eyes. The war had gone on for far too long, but this new twist? He didn't know what to think. All he knew for sure was he would need to be far from Nagasaki on a ship, before they came here and did what they had to Hiroshima. The world was talking about American weapons that could level a city, but Haruki knew better.

This hell was not from the West.

The storm was approaching. Massive clouds had formed at the northern edge of the city. As the residents of the battered outskirts took shelter underground in grubby dirt tunnels and cramped wooden bunkers, Haruki raced along the broken, rubble-strewn streets, leaping trash heaps and scrambling over fallen walls, tumbled wood, shattered plaster, and the ever-present terra cotta tiles that littered the ravaged city. He had been to Nagasaki once before, and loved that the old ways were still intact with regard to architecture and design. But after what he had witnessed in Hiroshima, he knew that even concrete and steel would have offered little protection from what was coming.

It had taken him two days to get here from the ruins of Hiroshima on the last of the three packed, refugee trains that had made it out. He had seen the final devastation, with the terrifying pink rays of death spewing from the snake-like creature's mouth. He had watched out the windows of the train, from a distance. A distance of miles, but even from that far away, he had felt the heat of the blast. Haruki understood that few would have survived the snake-beast's frantic battle with the gigantic, squid-like monster. He and the others had all fled—all the way here to Nagasaki, but Haruki was one of the only people to have *seen* the beasts. The others all spoke of bombings and of some American super-weapon. Or they spoke of earthquakes and floods. Even of American troops invading.

Haruki remained silent, listening to the conflicting versions of the event. He understood that these people had seen the devastation and the destruction, but he knew they would all have different interpretations of what exactly it was that had murdered an entire city. He had lived with that discrepancy since he was a child, when he first saw the *monsters* in the world, and he had realized few others could. He came to know that only first-born teenage children could actually see the world the way it truly was. Like other teens, he should have lost his ability to see the creatures when he became a man, but for some reason, with him, the sight had never faded.

As the train pulled in to Nagasaki, he overheard some teenagers whispering quietly near the rancid stinking lavatory, which was little more than a closet with a hole in the floor of the train and the rails rushing by below. They were comparing their events of what had happened—and pouring derision over the multitudes of conflicting versions of the story they had heard the adults tell. They had seen the giant beasts, just like he had. Haruki had gone over to them and spoke softly.

"I saw what you saw. You're not crazy."

The teens had been startled by his admission, but nodded, grateful for it.

Haruki understood the haunted look in their eyes. He'd had it in his own since he was fourteen. He'd tried to find the teens again in the throngs of packed humanity swarming off the train and into the station, but he lost sight of them in the sweaty masses.

He was going to try to find a ride to the harbor, but the roads were blocked pretty heavily to the north of town, from the damage sustained days earlier by Allied bombing raids. Looking north to the approaching gray storm clouds, Haruki had opted to run for it instead. He needed to move rapidly south through the shattered residential neighborhoods, before he would pass through the industrial factories and the Allied prison camp, on his way to the southern harbor. He knew if he waited too long, any sea-worthy ships would be gone.

An underfed dog with patches of dark fur leapt out of a trash pile, snapping and barking at Haruki as he ran, but he ignored the noise, one of many sounds all blending into the hurried roar of a wartime city. As he came closer to the fence-line of the prison camp, he felt a hot breeze rip into the city from behind him, and he turned to see he wasn't going to make it to the harbor in time.

The wind had blown the gray clouds filling the horizon into the city, spraying dust and small specks of debris. Flashes of pink and golden-green light erupted from within the clouds, as if mystical lightning were threatening to attack the northern edge of the town. Haruki knew that wasn't far from the truth. He turned to run again, but a shouting voice halted his run.

"Hey, mister! Over here! Quick!"

Haruki turned away from the fence line of the camp. Two of the teens he had seen on the train were hunkered down behind the low wall of a dwelling that had partially collapsed in the last bombing. Just below the line of the crumbled wall, he could see the top of a third head, with peculiarly light colored hair. The teens he recognized waved him over, as another gust of wind carried a choking cloud of dust past his face, and he detected the scent of rotten meat on the breeze. He raced across the street and leapt over the wall, just as the two teens ducked down below the shelter of the fragmented wood and cracked plaster. A shrieking noise ripped out of the cloud behind him, and Haruki instinctively ducked down lower behind the wall with the others, just as a far stronger gust of wind rammed into the structure at his back, shaking it. A wooden food cart flew overhead, crashing into one of the few remaining walls of the vacated house, splintering into fragments no larger than toothpicks.

The force necessary to do that! Haruki thought.

He squatted lower as the wind howled and the shrieking noise grew louder around him.

"The edge of the battle…the debris cloud… It's one of the first major dangers," one of the two teens shouted at him over the roar of the wind. The boy was probably no more than fifteen, with shaggy dark hair, like most Japanese boys his age, and thick-framed glasses. The other boy Haruki recognized as older, at maybe seventeen. He had a long thin scar up the side of his face, and his countenance was grim.

"Be prepared to run as soon as the wind dies down," the older boy shouted.

Haruki just nodded. He turned to the other side of him and was in for a shock. There wasn't just one more person next to him—there were three. One was an attractive girl, probably seventeen. She had long wavy hair, and a somewhat chestnut face. Haruki had seen women like her before. She was not pure Japanese. At some point in her ancestry, she had some Pacific islander in her. Haruki found her to be stunningly beautiful. She was hunched down like he was, and holding her ears against the shrieking of the wind, as the storm found its way to where they hid. Next to her was another boy, round and chubby, at least fifteen, but possibly older. He was blubbering and crying, covered in plaster dust, and his nose was crusted with old snot.

But neither of those two held Haruki's attention long.

The third person was an adult. A man, probably a year younger than Haruki's twenty-one. But this man was not like the others. He was the source of the lighter colored hair Haruki had spotted before he jumped the wall.

This man was an American.

Haruki stared at the man. He was wearing tan pants and a thick dark brown leather jacket. *A pilot*, Haruki realized. He was about to ask himself where an American pilot could have come from, when he realized that just across the street was the fence of the prison camp. *He must have escaped!* As Haruki scrutinized the man's face, he saw the boy inside. Then it became apparent. This pilot wasn't really an adult. He was still a teen. He had probably lied about his age to join the military. He wasn't as young as the others, but he couldn't have been much older than the girl.

The wind sped up, and more debris began to fly over the top of the small wall, crashing into the remains of the house, as Haruki hunched with the rest. He felt the wall shift behind his back, and realized how fast and strong the wind must be. Then the wind and the shrieking sound began to die down, but before it could stop completely, he felt a great tremor in the ground beneath him—not like the earthquakes he had felt near Kyoto as a child, where the ground would rumble and shake for even minutes at a time. This was an immense thud—a single impact that more closely resembled an explosion.

"Now!" the older teen with the grim face yelled.

All at once Haruki was scrambling up to his feet and running south again, with the four terrified teenagers and the brown haired pilot. The ground shook again with another impact before they had run even ten steps. "I was heading for the harbor," Haruki yelled to them.

The American just looked at him for a moment, then turned away. The older boy grunted an acknowledgement. Haruki realized the American man might not speak Japanese.

"We are running for a ship!" he told the man in heavily accented English.

The man, running hard, turned to glance at Haruki with a half-grin. "Good plan! Those things yours?" He asked the last part with his thumb cocked back behind him.

Haruki didn't spare a glance the way he'd come. "Not ours. We are in this together."

The American nodded. They ran with the others to the end of the street, then turned onto a wide avenue that would bring them past the last factories in the southern part of the city.

"Dakota Talbott," the pilot said, his breath coming in heaving gasps.

"I am...Haruki."

The other teens either spoke no English, which was likely, or they were too out of breath from running. The group was no more than a mile from the harbor, but Haruki knew they were out of time.

He chanced a look over his shoulder and was glad he did.

"Down!" he shouted in Japanese and threw himself into the American's back, knocking them both sprawling to the ground. The older teens all dropped to the cracked asphalt road, as a gasoline tanker truck flew over their heads. The younger, chubby boy with the snotty nose hadn't leapt down.

He had turned to see what the problem was.

Haruki saw the boy's tear-streaked face, and knew that the boy didn't even have time to understand the threat before the truck smashed into him and swept him up the street, before it slammed though the brick wall of an armor plating factory. A fireball erupted from the hole in the wall, sending a wave of heat and vapor back toward them.

"Stay down," he shouted. He didn't need to translate. The American had seen the fireball, too, and quickly ducked his head down to the asphalt and covered the back of his head with his hands.

Haruki did the same until he felt the wave of baking heat rip past above him.

Then he felt another stabbing thump in the earth from below, and another of the hideous shrieks occurred.

This time, he looked back.

The clouds of smoke and debris back up the street separated, as the mouth of the huge snake-creature blasted out of the center, its twenty-foot tall teeth snapping and gnashing. Its body slithered out of the cloud like a snake, but this close up, Haruki could see that only its movement resembled that of a true snake. Its back was ridged like the bony scales or plates of some dinosaur representations he had seen in a museum. Yet the creature's skin below the bony protrusions was smooth and shiny, like that of a whale. Its head was lumpy and misshapen, not sleek like the head of a viper. But when it opened its mouth and turned its long forked tongue back at the cloud of the oncoming storm, Haruki knew it had more in common with a viper than its skeletal structure hinted at.

He saw that the creature had short, fin-like legs along its length—three on each side. They didn't look functional, but as the long tube of the body, which was easily thirty feet in diameter and over a hundred and fifty feet long, slithered out of the debris and dust, it rolled on its side, and the fins scrabbled at the broken asphalt beneath the beast. Suddenly its immense bulk shifted sideways, and the creature pulled its head back to strike at the cloud.

The sharp impact to the ground came again, and then again faster.

Haruki turned away from the spectacle and saw the others all watched with him, standing limp and lifeless, looking at the gargantuan snake-beast.

"Run!" Haruki shouted.

His voice snapped the teen boys out of their stupor, and they sprinted away down the street. The American—*Dakota*—grabbed the girl's hand and ran as well, dragging her after him.

Haruki took five leaping steps, but something slammed into him from the side as the thumps in the ground increased in tempo. Then he was flying horizontally across the street, straight for a huge section of a traditional wooden wall. He crossed his arms in front of his head, as his body twisted in the air, and he saw that the giant snake creature had lunged back at the gray billowing clouds, its tail-end snapping away from the far end of the street and whipping into Haruki's body, as it crossed the road. But Haruki was confused, because the head had hit him, instead of the tail. He could see the long fangs of the creature's mouth retreating. The trail of ripped up asphalt on the ruined street left little doubt in Haruki's mind as to the true chain of events, though.

His crossed forearms made contact with the thin wooden wall of the partially destroyed home, and the surface of it tore under the impact like origami paper. His arms barely felt it, and then he was slammed into another wall. He slid down to the floor, broken slats of wood falling on top of his head. Small pebble-like chunks of plaster rained down on Haruki, and as he stood, wobbly on his feet, he found himself looking at a completely undestroyed bathroom wall, with the mirror over the wash basin still undisturbed. Covered as he was in plaster dust and dirt, Haruki looked like a ghost.

"Haruki! You're alive!"

He glanced over to see the pilot and the girl. They were standing at the door to the broken building. Then he ran to them, shouting, "Go!"

They turned just before he got to them, and they sprinted along the street, away from the mega-snake, which was hissing and striking at something unseen in the billowing soot and dirt. Now that Haruki shot a look at the thing, he could see where his confusion had come from. He *had* been hit by the tail end. It was just that the creature didn't have a proper tail. It had a head at each end! As far as he could tell in the quick glance he had of the beast, both heads were identical.

As he and the others got several yards away from the massive beast, they found the two surviving teen boys—the one with the glasses, who had called to Haruki, and the grim-faced lad. The boys were huddled behind a pile of rocks and construction sand, which had obviously been dumped in one of the war's few lulls, in anticipation of making repairs on the ruined neighborhood. The boys were peering intently over Haruki's shoulder at the ouroboros-like thing with equally dour looks, until suddenly their faces changed. The boys began to look elated.

Dakota and the girl skirted the pile of sand to the right and Haruki peeled left, then he threw himself down with the boys and heaved, trying to catch his breath from his recent sprint. As he looked back up the street, he could see what had given the teens hope.

"Kashikoi," he said, amazed at what he saw.

He had heard tales of Kashikoi when he was a teenager. Other teens spoke of the behemoth as if it was a force of holy good in the world. Most of the teens claimed to never have seen the creature, but those few who had, spoke with a glow in their eyes, always making Haruki think they were telling the truth. Most first-borns, when they had the sight for the few years before it faded, would spot all manner of unusual monsters and creatures that existed in the world. Things from flying monkey creatures the size of a loaf of bread to human-sized monsters like a horned cyclops, and bizarre hybrid things that could barely be called animals, like winged antelope and dogs with bones growing out of their bodies. But most of the creatures the Japanese teens had seen—or at least those Haruki had heard of—were of small scale. Only a few ever spotted an omega-class creature like the massive ouroboros, or the gigantic squid that had battled it in Hiroshima, shooting purple lightning from between its long pink tentacles, out of what appeared to be its ass. Haruki had spotted something once that was about the size of a dinosaur swimming off the shore of Chiba, but until he had seen the two gargantuan creatures trying to kill each other in Hiroshima, that had been it.

Now he was seeing the omega-size beast of all beasts.

Kashikoi was something akin to a mighty tortoise. Its shell was a steeply pitched mound with lumps protruding up in steeper bursts—as if the animal under the shell were trying to force its way out in pointy places. The legs were powerful scaled things that resembled a cross between a typical tortoise's tough limbs and the leathery clawed things to be found on a massive monitor lizard. Each scale on the monster's armor was larger than a man, and standing as it was on its hind legs, the beast must have topped over a hundred feet in height. It would have been taller if its heads—the two of them on individual necks, stretching from doughy folds at the front of the shell—had been pointed upward to the sky. Instead they angled down and forward. Toward the humongous snake beast.

Each head had thick bony horns and ridges, protruding backward along the jawline, and triple fins on top of the rounded head, giving the creature more of a dragon look. The gnarled bird-beak jaws opened wide and dripped a spattering pea green saliva that burned holes through the ground wherever it touched.

The ouroboros demon shot its head out, lancing its forked tongue at Kashikoi's belly, but the under surface of the shell was as thickly armored as the outer surface, and the snake simply bounced off, its twisting snapping body following the head in an arc through the air.

Kashikoi swung a powerful foreleg down, the jagged tips of the claws on its foot—snapped off in some long ago battle—still tearing a gouge down the snake's side, before the wounded ouroboros skittered away sideways on its stumpy side fins. As the snake-horror blasted through the brick wall of a factory, as if the wall weren't there, masonry and smoke shooting high into the sky, Kashikoi lowered its upper body down, until its full weight slammed into the ground with the same sharp booming thump that Haruki had heard earlier.

But now the impact was much closer to him, and he was amazed as the earth shot him upward into the air from the strike, as if he had been on a trampoline. He landed in the soft sand pile, and turned to see the others all hitting the ground as well. The noise from the impact was louder than the sound of a Mitsubishi jet roaring overhead, and the sheer weight of the creature blasted a wall of air and dust toward Haruki and the others that felt like a hurricane wind.

"We can't stay here!" he shouted.

They were picking themselves up when the air shook with a trembling vibration. A powerful shriek, like those Haruki had heard earlier, ripped into his eardrums. His hands shot to cover his ears from the hideous somewhat mechanical sound.

Kashikoi was roaring!

Haruki saw that the ouroboros had lunged again, and as it had had no luck against Kashikoi's densely armored shell, it struck a rear leg this time, sinking twenty foot white fangs deeply into the tortoise monster's scaly flesh. The blood that squirted from the wound in a gushing burst was a deep dark green. Kashikoi shrieked and focused the alien eyes of both its heads on the double-ended snake, where it was still clamped to the injured leg with one of those ends.

Golden fire ripped out of all four of Kashikoi's eyes, tearing into the snake fiend. The wave of heat rushed back at Haruki as the ouroboros instantly recoiled, releasing its grip and using its strange fins to wind its way sideways, back and away from the injured mammoth amphibian.

Kashikoi lunged fast toward the retreating two-headed snake, his immense size no impediment to his speed. The ground shook hard at each impact of the massive claws, and as Haruki fell to his side, he saw the immense tortoise creature's left head snap open and clamp down hard on the snake thing's neck, just behind one head. Steam rose from the ouroboros's body where the powerful jaw had snapped, and the snake tried to recoil, but Kashikoi's neck unexpectedly yanked backward, pulling the twisting snake into the air. As soon as its head at the other end had cleared the ground, Kashikoi swept a powerful foreleg at the monster and released his hold near the opposite head. The effect was the snake monstrosity being hurled through the air, as if it weighed no more than a fly batted away by a human hand.

But the creature was coming for Haruki and the others.

Haruki turned and moved toward the girl. Dakota was on the other side of her, having just gained his feet again. The other two teens had fled. Haruki ran into the girl and pushed her into Dakota, and the three of them tumbled down the side of the sand pile to the bottom, just as the top of the pile erupted in a spray of sand.

The ouroboros swept just barely over their heads. It flew further down the street and slammed through two buildings, twisting and winding all the way. Haruki and the other two struggled to their feet yet again, as the winding snake slithered out of the rubble and back toward them, retracting a head at one end, and then striking up and forward. It would clear Haruki's position by several feet, so his eyes naturally shot upward to watch the snake strike. Its tongue shot out, as it raced at an incline up through the air. It spewed a searing line of pink energy from its mouth, the jaws open nearly at a 180 degree angle, all fangs pointing forward. The energy beam shot across the sky and scored along the side of one of Kashikoi's two necks. The tortoise-beast started to fall backward.

Haruki turned back in time to see the other end of the snake was coming his way, and staying low, near ground level.

Dakota had seen it, too.

Haruki had just a split second for his eyes to meet Dakota's before both men were in action.

Haruki raced toward the American, but he moved instead for the beautiful girl. She was looking upward, as the mega-tortoise fell over backward onto its shell in excruciating slow motion. Haruki shifted his angle for her, as his eyes swept back toward the quickly advancing snake head. It shifted in mid flight, its oversized eyes—larger than trucks—suddenly twitching, as its inner eyelids closed vertically, before retracting open again. It twisted its head in mid flight.

It had seen them.

Haruki lunged, just as Dakota reached the girl and pivoted. Dakota shoved the girl, throwing her directly into Haruki's arms. Haruki wrapped his arms around her as they fell to the side. He twisted so he would land on his back, cushioning the girl from the fall.

But no one was left to save Dakota.

He tried to turn at the last second, one arm cocked back as if he meant to punch the monster in the mouth. But the jaws were wide open, the immense fangs all pointing directly at Dakota as several of them skewered him from behind, right along the edge of the creature's mouth. The long fangs ripped out the front of Dakota's body. Then the huge snake mashed its mouth shut, folding Dakota's pierced corpse in half and grinding him into several pieces, some of which fell to the ground as the beast's head flew past. Haruki saw a leg and part of the pelvis still jammed between the gargantuan teeth before the ouroboros passed over him.

The girl had not seen, as her face had been turned toward Haruki's chest. And her long wavy hair had flopped over to cover her face. Haruki turned to his side and twisted to his knees, dragging the girl up. He swiped his hand across her face, pushing her hair back. Her face was gaunt and pale. She was in shock. He bent down and put his shoulder into her waist, hefting her over him like he had seen firemen carry victims.

He ran down the street, focusing on his footing amongst the

rubble. When he was past the second building into which the ouroboros had crashed, he turned to catch sight of the battle one last time, before rounding a corner of a still-standing steel factory building.

Kashikoi had indeed landed on its steeply rounded bulbous back, but the beast kept rolling. Its giant back claws had dug in, the momentum carrying it around and up. The immense thing was now standing on its hind legs like a man. The ouroboros had fired its terrifying pink mouth rays again, but they appeared to do no damage to Kashikoi's armored belly. The rays shot past Kashikoi too, though, and when they did, they obliterated any man-made structure they found.

Just before Haruki rounded the building's corner, he saw the move that was coming. Kashikoi was bringing both its forelegs, and the jagged, scarred claws on their tips, inward to crush on the sides of one of the ouroboros's heads like a vice grip. The boom shook the wall of the building, as Haruki rushed past, the girl unconscious over his shoulder. He stopped only three times before he made it to the harbor and a ship that took him and the girl to Yakushima Island, south of the main islands of Japan.

"WHO WON THE FIGHT, FATHER?"

Jiro looked out over the landscape of bones in the distance, most easy to see from their new vantage, high on the massive grassy hill near the center of the island. It was late in the afternoon, and the sun shone brightly across the strange landscape. Shinobi had been frightened by the bones at first, but upon seeing them closer, after the two had fixed the light on the lighthouse, the ever-present thick carpet of green moss that covered much of the island and the ancient bones somehow charmed the lad. Jiro stood up and stretched his lower back, then smiled.

"Kashikoi dragged the ouroboros to the sea, but the beast was revived by the water and escaped."

Shinobi stood and pretended to stretch his own back, as he had seen Jiro do. The boy often imitated his father. Jiro smiled again.

"So…the world believes that the devastation at Hiroshima and Nagasaki was from Atomic bombs?"

Jiro grunted. "Most people. Even many with the sight have no reason to doubt history. But history is always written by those who win in conflicts, Shinobi. The Americans claimed the credit for the destruction—who knows what *they* saw as being responsible."

The man started down the grassy hillside, and he could hear his boy following him.

"What happened to Grandfather Haruki, then?" the boy inquired.

"He and the woman married. They moved north to Wakkanai, and he took the job as lighthouse keeper of the surrounding islands. But your grandfather never lost the sight, Shino. Like you and I, he kept his ability to see the creatures his whole life. Your grandmother—my mother—forgot what she had been through just months after it happened. They were both *nijū hibakusha*. Double survivors. Japan has officially recognized 165 hibakusha as having survived the destruction of both Hiroshima and Nagasaki, but your grandparents were actually 166 and 167. But they never told anyone. Your grandmother's memory of the event was muddled at best, and Haruki could never tell anyone what had really happened. He kept track of Kashikoi, though, as the creature moved north through the islands of Japan, in the days after the war. The beast was much more careful in its travels then, he said. Almost as if it was aware of the terrible destruction its battle with the ouroboros had wrought."

Jiro fell quiet as he descended the rest of the hillside. As Shinobi scampered down behind him, he looked again to the sky but there was no sign of another storm. Still, they would get inside the lighthouse to sleep for the night long before darkness fell over the necropolis.

As Shinobi reached the level ground at the base of the hill, he paused and tilted his head. Jiro could see that his son was working out how to phrase his question. He waited on the boy.

"Why are there so many bones here? Why *this* island? And why is Kurohaka Island not on any of the maps?"

"This is where he took the ones he defeated."

Shinobi's eyes widened.

Jiro nodded. "Kashikoi defeated many threats against Japan, and when he killed another giant beast like the ouroboros, he would bring it here. Remember, some of the corpses here are actually monsters that were dying and came here voluntarily. Some of the bones are from creatures that died and were transported here by teens with the sight."

Jiro started walking for the lighthouse. "My father tended the light that would keep most sailors away from this island, and he received a government check from both Japan and Russia to tend to the outlaying islands as well. I took the job from him, just as you will one day take the job from me."

Jiro noticed Shinobi's absence after another handful of steps and turned to look back at where Shinobi remained rooted to the ground, at the foot of the steep hillside.

The boy had a perplexed look on his face, until he finally asked his burning question.

"What happened to Kashikoi?"

Jiro looked at the boy, then raised his eyes to the immense hill behind him. Then he lowered his eyes back to the child and raised one eyebrow.

Color drained from the child's face as realization sank in. The boy turned to stare at the side of the hill, upon which they had been perched all afternoon. The hill which was not a hill. Jiro chuckled and turned toward the lighthouse.

"We tend the light, and we protect the protector. Come now, Shino. It will be dark soon."

OCCUPIED

Natania Barron

:: Maker

JULIAN MOVES THROUGH THE NARROW sewers and drainage pipes without hesitation. More a mole than a woman, she navigates with perfect precision, her thick boots trudging through every kind of detritus provided by the city. She is immune to the bloated rats, the stench, the slimy mold crawling up the side of the glistening brick. It's only the things out of place—the sound of a small gator slipping into a stream, or an unanticipated moan—tthat would stop her. And nothing does for quite some time.

Then, just as she is about to take the final twist toward her own alcove, near Berfa the Engine, she stops cold. Something glows. Not the light of a lantern or candle, not even the odd luminescence of the mushrooms that sometimes grow in the depths. It is something blue and cold and frosty.

:: Creature

WE HAVE BEEN ASLEEP FOR so long; so long that all is dust. Our tongues. Our eyes. Our bodies. Our shrunken phalluses. These sick and sad reminders that we had bodies, once. That we felt the power

Illustration by **CHUCK LUKACS**

of blood, felt the coursing of the Holy Spirit within us. Tasted and rutted and blazed. We were passion and power and knowledge. Too much knowledge.

A thousand thousand years, and we have suffered in the miasma of loss and excommunication and forgotten our names. Once, we were feared, favored, loved. Now, we only whisper to ourselves, with no knowledge of our names or our purposes. One among us was a healer; another a poet; another still a guardian and warrior of a kind rarely seen. We were astronomers and visionaries and, for no reason other than our lust for life, we were cast aside. Forgotten.

We have lived without hope. What power made up our bodies has been dispersed so far and wide that we have given into the monotony. The pain. Suffering gave way to anger and back again to suffering, and it has gone on so long that we had forgotten that once, before we had been reduced to such nothing, we had plotted. Planned. Planted seeds, however far-flung, of the hope of rebirth.

A sword. Forged from the heart of a star. Melted down and changing hands, century after century, passing borders and oceans. Coveted, cursed, stolen. Our last hope.

:: Maker

JULIAN CURSES. SHE CANNOT HELP herself. The sudden disruption causes her to stumble, losing her footing, twisting her ankle. It cracks under her weight, sending bright sparks of pain up the side of her leg and she gasps in spite of herself, wishing she had opted for another route. The last thing she wants is discord. Her routine is all she has—it's what keeps her from losing time and whatever else precious she has left to her.

Part of her is sensible and says that she ought to keep moving, albeit slowly, back to her enclave. It is the safest option, and safety is one of Julian's most intense concerns. She knows how difficult it is to languish in pain and suffering after safety has been ignored. With a gloved hand she reaches up and touches the stump of her ear, feeling the ragged bumps and twisted skin, hearing the strange scratching noise such a motion produces.

But the light. That blue. As she braces herself against the wall and finds her way toward breathing more regularly, she notices that it flickers and dissipates with a certain rhythm. Not quite a pulse, but it is regular. And there's a smell, too. She feels as if she can remember the scent, but not entirely; it's a distant memory. A part of her brain fires, but she can't attach any strings to the thought. It just floats a moment, and then is gone, no connection made. But the memory is not a warning. What's left in Julian's mind is something burning and bright, something strong and dangerous.

Julian slides across the grimy bricks and twists her head to get a better look. Her glasses are dirty enough as it is, but it doesn't seem to matter. Her eyes are still dazzled by what she sees. The luminescence emanates from a small object, half buried in the mud and mold at the base of one of the drains. *The color is cold,* she thinks, even though she hasn't touched it yet. As if it were ice. Which is strange, she realizes, because she is very hot and very sticky. The room is not cold. The color is cold.

Why would it be here, she wonders? Perhaps there was a deluge above and it got knocked clean. Perhaps someone threw it down here to hide it. Or to get rid of it. *Such a beautiful thing should not be let go of,* Julian thinks.

Either way, Julian doesn't think much as she lunges forward to grab it. Every muscle in her crooked body twists as she moves— faster than she has moved in a decade—and as she tumbles forward into the muck, she wonders for a moment if it is pulling her. If the cold and light is reaching toward her, desiring her touch as much as she desires its.

She gasps, seized with a strange concern that someone else will take the object, and in a moment, she holds it in her hands, blinking down through grimy lenses, dazzled.

Scissors. A pair of scissors. When she touches them, whispers rise around her like steam.

:: Creature

WE ALL SHOUT OUT AS ONE. That touch! The touch of a human, but not entirely human. We feel her body, know her immediately as a descendent of ours. One of our children, a thousand generations removed from the perfect babes we birthed upon the earth. She is a broken, weak thing, and has no idea what she has in her hands. No concept that we, the Watchers, are rising up from the depths in ecstasy—have waited nigh a million years for this moment.

It is pain and anguish and love and grief we all feel in that moment. Through that cursed, magic metal, that single touch is as powerful as the breath of life we were once given. How small it has become. How simple. What was once a flaming sword, wielded by the greatest among us, has now become a tiny thing.

The touch is enough to wake us, to rouse us, but she must do more. She must remember what she is. She must awaken, herself.

We wait. We have waited long, it is true, but we would not exist if we had not waited so long. So, again, we pause. We draw breath. We poise on the edge and anticipate.

:: Maker

THE SCISSORS ARE SO COLD, so perfectly cold, in her hands. Julian smiles, tries not to laugh as she covers them up with a piece of burlap to dampen the light. They are so beautiful. So ornate. So delicate. It reminds her of the kit her mother had, back when she lived Above. The scrollwork looks almost Eastern, and she runs her fingers along the side and smiles. She loves the cold. It's a welcome cold. A bright cold. The cold of stars in the firmament.

We are a many. We are a waiting. We are a hunger. We are a watching.

She has heard the voices before, and she is not afraid of them. In a way, she is relieved. That the whispers have intensified means she's less mad. It means that something—this pair of scissors—has been waiting for her all these years. It means her work has not been in vain. It means the years of ridicule and scorn…

But no one has ever understood Julian, not even Brother Barrier. No one except her companions, all awaiting her in her nook. And that is where she goes, her breath caught in her throat as she makes her way without hesitation, the scissors pressing against her breast as she navigates the sewer to the place of her own.

There are half a dozen locks on the door of her space, and she quickly goes about releasing them, though she fails twice on the third lock. When she finally makes it inside, she is breathing so heavily her spectacles start fogging up. Julian won't let go of the scissors, even though they bite into her hands with their unearthly cold. Her whole arm is numb now, up to the elbow, and she takes a quick stock of the room.

The specimens line the room from floor to ceiling, in jars and boxes and cans, depending on the individual situation. Arms, legs, fingers and toes are the uppermost tier, while the most easy accessible drawers and shelves are lined with the more delicate matter: eyes, tongues, and silvery webs of nerves and veins. Most are preserved, thanks to Brother Barrier's help attaining ingredients and fluids from Above.

He has always been oddly fascinated with her work, even though it has nothing to do with the steam pumps. The day he stumbled upon her, she was terrified he would judge her, make her stop. He wore the robes of a priest, after all. But instead of fear, he was full of awe. Awe and support.

What specimens aren't preserved wait in the experimental section, one level below. As Julian takes the burlap off the scissors, something miraculous happens.

The light from the scissors brightens the room, bouncing off red, wet brick, and trembling through the formaldehyde, ethanol, and methanol solutions. Brilliant blue flashes across the surface, like an electric charge, and every eye turns, every finger points, every submerged ear and floating brain matter turns to focus upon her.

We are a many. We are a waiting. We are a hunger. We are a watching.

:: *Creature*

TO BE AWOKEN IS AN experience akin to no others. To see, however dimly, after thousands of years blind and hungry. To hear. To sense. To know. We tremble and cry out, lips making no noises, choking and drowning and screaming at once. At first, we are jubilant, in spite of the pain—or perhaps because of it, for pain means life. But we realize, quickly, that in this moment of pain and awakening is confusion. Broken. Not as promised.

We are further shattered. We are fragmented. Some of us see—some of us hear—but none of us can do both. When once we suffered and dwindled as one, now we each remember and splinter. Our names come back to mind, our knowledge, but not complete. Uriel. Azazel. Samyaza. Baraquel. Kokabiel. More.

And my name. My *name*. I want to speak it. But all I am is an eye. The eye of a goat. The light from the metal of that ancient sword—no longer a sword, and much diminished—makes my existence a misery. I cannot look away from the cruelly misshapen Daughter of Nephilim, and she stares back at me stupidly. The voices of the other Fallen pulse around me, filling the water in which I'm suspended. They are mad, trembling. Their fury will ruin this for all of us.

I panic. I am nothing but an eye. A mad, wide-seeing eye, slowly losing the only chance I have had in an eternity to breathe the air again. I do not want destruction and death. I do not want revenge. I want escape.

I know what I must do.

:: Maker

JULIAN FALLS TO HER KNEES, and one cracks and shatters against the white tile. But the numbness has moved through her body so completely that she merely notes the sickening snap of cartilage, distantly. One moment her body is filled with a vibrating, orgasmic pleasure, and the next she is crawling toward a jar in the middle of her collection. She holds up the scissors and looks through the holes, as if they were another pair of spectacles. And indeed, she does see better through them. She notices that each of her specimens, now following her every breath and movement, glow different shades. Some are the red of fresh blood; others shimmer silver and gold, tendrils of light refracting across the glass surfaces. Every color in the spectrum.

Dazzled, Julian stares for time out of mind until she notices one different than the other. One of her favorite specimens. Not human, this one, and a rarity for that. It is the only specimen she killed with her own hands. Perhaps that is why she glances at it longer than the others, why she notices the blue hue of the dappled light. It is the only one unchanged by the view through the scissors.

She leans forward. She raises her fingers, scraped and bloody. The wide pupil regards her intently. It swims forward and backward within the glass, but it never loses focus. Julian has been a master preserver for years, and the golden goat eye is one of her favorites. She remembers well plucking it from the skull of the so recently expired creature. She'd roasted the other one. But it had been blue. This was gold, and too beautiful to be eaten.

We are a many. We are a waiting. We are a hunger. We are a watching.

Now she wants to eat it. Now she wants to touch it. To listen to it. To know it. It tells her things, whispers her name again and again.

Julian does not lower the scissors, but with her free hand she presses fingertips to the glass. She tries to recoil for the heat is overwhelming. Her skin immediately bonds to the glass, and she smells burning flesh though feels nothing. A heartbeat more and the glass shatters, impaling her hand with a thousand tiny lacerations. Blood drips freely, filling the room with a coppery, burnt scent.

She picks up the eye with her bloodied fingers and writes the word it commands her to, pressing the soft organ to the floor. On the bright white tile, Julian weeps with joy as she writes a single name: *Penemue.*

:: Penemue

MY NAME IS SPOKEN, AND I arise. Unlike my fallen brothers, I am released from the nightmarish hold between life and death, animation and oblivion. It is bliss. Joy. Fury. To know my name at last is a pleasure beyond all memories. And there are so many memories.

My first thought is to take our Maker's body from her—it is not holding up well, and she may not have long in this life—but I cannot. I have ever believed in my own innocence, having been damned to eternity for loving a mortal man and bringing the gift of writing to him. Every living human being owes me a debt of gratitude for my so-called sin, but I will not make more sins out of my own hatred of God. I will not. If I am to live again, I must do it purely and without trespass. I have learned…

Our Maker stares at me, and I can see myself as a pillar of blue fire in her eyes. I am beautiful and horrible, but I am weak and frighteningly vulnerable in this state; this she does not know.

My brothers know. My hesitation to do her no harm has given them space to call her back. And I, bodiless, am powerless. I try to blaze brighter, but the voices of my brethren rise louder and louder, a dissonant clamor of commands and cries, and our Maker is frozen. Her body twitches, her neck twists, and with those delicate scissors in hand she starts to make her way toward her macabre collection, the collection she has been putting together for so long, for this purpose alone.

:: Maker

JULIAN KNOWS FEW THOUGHTS OF her own except a sense of gladness. A sense of purpose. The blue flame creature burns brightly, but it no longer speaks words she knows. It can no longer command her. The others, the Watchers, for whom she has waited her whole life, dictate her steps now. Command her movements. She understands now, yes. She understands that collection around her has not been only to keep her company, it has been part of a grand plan. A plan to make her more. Greater. It's what Brother Barrier has told her, time and again. She is part of a bigger, more divine plan. And the awakened specimens, her friends, have come at last.

The scissors. She understands.

This is the blade that binds, no longer the blade that sunders. Cleave and join, Daugher of Nephilim, and give your body new life.

The first cut is the hardest, even though there is little pain. Julian has spent so much time cutting and dissecting other things, that even in her dimming consciousness, it seems wrong. But she needs another arm to do this task, and the only way she will be able to add another appendage is to make room for it on her chest.

She picks the corded arm from the sewer worker she'd harvested two months before. Or, rather, it picks her. Its container falls to the tiles and shatters, the limb climbing its way up her soiled petticoat and leather vest as she leans back to accept it.

That moment of connection is a black terror, but Julian has dreamed of this her whole life. She has only not remembered the dream. Now, as it's happening, this moment of rebuilding and transformation, she recalls every detail. Of her dying. But not dying. Her ecstasy.

Again and again she plunges the scissors into her body, through cloth and skin and muscle, and again and again the specimens come to her, merging with her body. She is their mother and Maker, giving them blood and life again—saving them from death. Every step in her life has been leading to this moment—every spewed word of hate, every uttered curse below her breath. She has never believed in God, no. Julian has only relied on herself and her connection to a greater, wilder, madder design out there.

Julian plunges the scissor blades into her heart, and it is done.

And now she is all greatness and power, and mad beauty. Her body swells and grows to accommodate the appendages of her new friends, roiling and undulating, filling up the small space, pushing out that blue fire into the passageway beyond. There comes the sound of feet, but it is distant and unimportant to her now. For she is a creature of a thousand eyes and arms, a thousand voices, a thousand terrors.

And she is hunger. She is wanting. But she is no longer waiting.

:: Penemue

IT HAS GONE WRONG. SO wrong. I should have known my brothers would never manage a peaceful entry, They are too full of fury. She has welcomed them, but she cannot see what I see. It is not that they are granting her power, but that they are fighting for it among themselves. Her humanity is swallowed up in moments as she grows beyond imagining, her form undulating like the long body of some many-armed creature of the deep, or monstrous arachnid.

My brothers fight among themselves for control of the body. Arms and teeth rend one another, and by virtue of blood and filth birth more, grow even more repulsive.

Penemue. My name still lingers on my mind and I taste something I have not in centuries: fear. I am afraid. Who am I? I have never been like my brothers. I have been outcast from Heaven and Hell, and now moments from my freedom, I am shoved out into the strange, dark corridor from where I was awoken, and my flame begins to diminish. Without a host, I know I will fade to nothingness. True nothingness. Perhaps that is better. I am sinless, now. I am reborn and perfect.

But I cannot. I know their hunger. Finding a host means a harsher judgment, but only I know how to stop the creature, the many-eyed beast growing fast along these strange hallways running with filth.

He stands there, clutching his heart, my blue flames flickering in his eyes. There are tears coursing down his cheeks, and his lip trembles. A priest, I can tell, even in this strange place. He wears black with a swath of white at his collar, and his bald pate reflects. He whispers ancient words familiar to me, an invocation of an angel. Of Gabriel. I remember him well. A friend in brighter times. That this man thinks I am Gabriel is a balm to me, a moment of strength in this weakened state.

"I must welcome you, messenger," the priest says, bowing his head and going down to one knee. "I am your servant, all body and soul."

I enter him in an instant. I do not think beyond that, for I can hear the walls around me shaking as the creature expands. It groans, as well, this leviathan of the deep.

I become the priest, and the priest becomes me. He is not gone, but he is no longer. I take from him his life, his memories, his intelligence, his faults. To the human eye this priest, this Brother Barrier, is like all others save for the gentle glowing of his eyes and fingernails. He tells me what I need to know of this world that has grown in my absence. I am in a sewer, where all the filth of humanity flows. Julian, the name of the Child of the Nephilim, has lived here for thirty years, since she was but a newly flowered girl, and has collected these specimens for her own pleasure, to quell the voices in her head. Brother Barrier found her fifteen years before and helped her out of pity but also out of understanding. He, too, has heard our voices. Not through his blood, as Julian has, but through his own preternatural abilities.

The body I have now is painfully human. The muscles are atrophied in places, the stomach soft. The heart trembles with some sort of ailment. I can heal what I am able, but there is little hope he will last beyond this task.

:: Creature

THE CREATURE OF A THOUSAND corpses cries out in agony and joy, feeling the pulse of humanity above and sensing the waters not far. The cleansing waters of the ocean. Food and drink. Revenge and lust. With nothing more than the stars to guide, the creature looks up with a thousand eyes through grates and slits in the ground, pulled toward the center of the city, along the great bend in the river.

Sliding up through the sewer, its shape changes a dozen times, rearranging its girth. Arms and legs, paws and muzzles, teeth and hooves, all slither against each other to slip through the narrow space. Up and up in an endless ladder of bodies and bones, snapping and mending over and over, dim eyes lighting up and down each unfathomable arm.

Toward the whitest, tallest, building, pulled as if by magical impulse. The most holy place in the city. It must be taken down before the feeding can begin, this alone the fallen brothers agree upon. The creature of a thousand corpses knows the dark memories of their host, knows the way she had been turned away as an abomination. It feels the dead beneath the streets, smells the murder and chaos. All these beautiful and horrible gifts they, not God, have given to mankind. And now, it is a great reckoning.

When the creature's full girth meets the air a great fog begins, as something in the smoky atmosphere reacts against the living dead. The many fallen brothers begin to argue, surprised by the sudden pain. The creature lunges north, spilling white smoke throughout the streets in huge, stinking pillars. As the brothers disagree, the mass of the beast smashes left and right, crushing buildings beneath it and smothering all living things in its wake. Brick and wood and steel crumble as if mere afterthoughts, and those caught below see nothing but the massive arms casting shadows. Hands and mouths reach for any useable weapon, and so the seething creature becomes sharper and more deadly.

:: *Penemue*

I AM SLOW IN THIS body, and breathing—something I had dreamed of doing so long—is an abysmal pain to me. I know where the creature is, where my fallen brothers move, but I cannot catch up to them fast enough. I pause as I exit the sewer, feeling something digging against my hip. I had not noticed it before, and I have to listen to Brother Barrier tell me about it before I throw it away. It is a weapon, which he calls a *firearm*. It is intended to kill others, though I cannot imagine how. He explains it is full of ammunition. I still do not understand, so he shows me. Turning it over in the moonlight I feel the cold metal and understand better. There is a charge within, and with the proper aim, I could send a menacing bolt.

But not to the creature. Not to my brothers. Only one thing would undo them, and likely me. I pause to catch my breath and renew my focus. At my feet, fog swirls, smelling of sulfur and decay. I see better than the other humans running past me, away south. Some carry bodies, severed in unspeakable ways. Livestock knock over humans in their terror, trample them.

Trying to keep a distance, I make my way slowly north. I can see straight through the strange square buildings and know immediately where the fallen brothers are going. Even though they continue to squabble, and through their squabbling grow and absorb all around them, they seek a holy place. A high, holy place. From there, they will fight. Or they will seek to storm Heaven. Or they will seek more blood until they have summoned the Devil himself. Or all at once.

The skies crackle with lightning, and the fog rises. In the

distance I can see the arms of the great beast limned against the dwindling starlight.

"She buried the blade in her breast," I tell Brother Barrier. He is rather quiet, and does not seem to understand. "I must reach it, must remove it."

"Don't angels fly?" he asks slowly.

"Sometimes," I tell him. "I mostly burn."

"Seraphim," he says.

"Once," I reply.

"You were close to Heaven."

"I thought I could go back. But I see now I cannot."

I run, now. The air smells of blood and fire. Shrill noises—sirens, Brother Barrier tells me—whine in the distance. The salt air from the sea drives tears to my eyes, remembering a life for which I earned a thousand centuries of torture. Remembering a face. Remembering hands, perfect and strong feet. A perfect human, touched by none of this terror. What became of him? We bore no children—how could we?—but his love cost me so much. Those perfect ebony hands, which I loved and taught the holy marks upon paper.

The cathedral rises before me, three steeples stretching to the skies, but darkening against their white sides as my fallen brothers rise. There is no time to marvel in this creation of humanity, for I hear voices in the air. My fallen brothers. Hear their wailing cry, their furious oaths of destruction and death. Destruction of humanity, destruction of each other. They loved once, as I did, but they birthed the Nephilim. I was merely caught up.

And now, I watch in horror as I hear the side of the cathedral snap. One long tendril reaches up and squeezes, working as leverage so the fallen brothers can climb higher, that the massive creature may get a better view of the city.

In the distance I sense the waters rise from below, Julian's steam pumps are failing. Soon the city will be submerged. What does not die from the hand of my brethren will drown.

I can see the beast better, now, as I come around to the square behind the cathedral. It arranges itself over and over again, the center glowing blue where the scissors lie, but never rids itself of the massive tentacles. Sometimes six. Sometimes thirteen. They lash and break and bend all around them.

I approach the cathedral at a dead run, ducking as debris falls down. There are still people inside. Many of them. No doubt they came here seeking refuge. I can smell their fear mingled with incense. The closer I get the more I see the muck and sludge the fallen brothers have dropped over the building. It hisses and oozes, stinging my face as it drips on my skin. I wipe it away, and with it some of my flesh. I cannot even imagine what it would do to a mortal.

THEN, IN A MOMENT OF sudden inspiration from Brother Barrier, I stop. I look to the heavens in between a swath of cloud. The stars blink at me. I wonder… the other angels. Would they hear me? Did they forget me? In this moment of need, would they heed my cry?

No. I am too afraid they will not answer. As the beast rages above me, I move through from pillar to pillar around the cathedral until I find a door unobstructed by bodies or debris. The sound from inside is somehow worse, though dampened. I do not have time to wonder at the strange symbols and drawings, so alien to me. The straining of the building rips my breath from my body, but I keep the pace while Brother Barrier sings strange hymns I do not know.

The center tower is still holding, and that is where I must go. I pass humans, many of whom recognize me as Brother Barrier until they see my eyes. Some scream, others fall into a sort of silent reverie, giving me knowing smiles. He tells me their names, and I say them aloud, and they are blessed by it.

Up and up I go, pushed ever onwards by the passing of time and the groaning of the building. On top of it all, I hear the keening of the tower bell, straining with the cries of the creature. The fighting, rending battle. It grows. More and more it grows as the fallen brothers continue their squabbling. And it will continue to swell with hatred and fury until not only this city is swallowed, but the entirety of humanity is black with the creature's insatiable search for blood.

Just below the bells, I make my exit into the night air. My brothers feel me, but they do not yet understand where I am. Brother Barrier's body is like a blanket across their eyes. From where I stand, I can see down into the gaping maws of the beast, faces and mouths open in anguish, eyes spinning in invisible sockets. They sing a thousand curses at me, but I search for only one thing. That glittering metal, stuck fast in the heart of what was once a woman.

I have never been the brave one among my brothers. My hands have rarely wielded swords, and instead have written poems and ballads and songs of old. I hesitate again, up on the ledge, and it nearly does me in. A thick cord of sinew comes up and around my ankle, snapping but not sundering it. The pain is strange and welcome, burning with my heartbeat and the searing in my face.

Now they know.

I am a Seraphim. I am a creature of flame. With one hand I steady the pistol. With the other I draw a word in the air with blue fire: thunder. I shoot the bullet through the word as it still lingers in air, and when it hits the creature, a sound erupts from its center and shakes it to its core. Another sinew shoots out, this time around my middle, but it is with less precision. I am able to shake it off, and I can see a new fire alight down the impossible monster's gullet of a thousand mouths. Some of the pieces begin to fall, mostly those which were acquired during the creature's journey from below the city. The weapons fall, too—long metal poles, broken iron doorways. They clatter and spark as they hit the rocky ground below.

"There are only two more bullets," Brother Barrier whispers to me.

I do not hesitate with my second spell. I mark the word "silence" in the air and shoot through it again, and the whole beast shudders and stops its wailing. Now I can hear the screams from all around the city. People are dying everywhere. But if they are screaming, it also means some are living.

We are a many. We are a waiting. We are a hunger. We are a watching.

"No longer," I shout down. "Release yourselves and return to the darkness! You will win nothing by your madness!"

We are a many. We are a waiting. We are a hunger. We are a watching.

I remembered that strange liturgy. I had escaped it, but I had held out hope. That was my greatest sin. I had held out hope for myself alone, and I had abandoned them. After a hundred thousand years of suffering together, I sinned before I had even begun again.

"I am so sorry," I tell them *and* Brother Barrier.

It is with that I draw the last word. I drop the gun and close my eyes. With a final, blessed breath, I dive through the word "brother" and plunge into the belly of the best to withdraw the key to our salvation, and doom us all back to oblivion.

THE SERPENT'S HEART

Howard Andrew Jones

FOR A NIGHT AND A day we had drifted, and we five had but two sips left in our waterskin. The calm waters stretched to every horizon, lapping gently at the side of our boat, now green, now blue. The tropic sun blazed down.

We spoke sometimes of the hope for a ship, for we floated along one of the caliphate's most frequented trade routes. Mostly, though, we were silent and morose, thinking of the friends who had drowned within sight of us, and wondering if we would live to set eyes upon our homes. I'd always thought it likely I'd perish at my friend Dabir's side, but had expected to meet my end warding him from some enemy. All of my skills were useless against thirst and the relentless sun.

The temperature finally eased a few degrees as daylight died. And then the black ship sailed up out of the twilight gloom.

It was a long, high vessel with four square masts. I had never seen its like, and felt a strange foreboding. The cook swore under his breath and whispered darkly of evil djinn.

The first mate, a sturdy black by the name of Ghassan, cursed him to silence. My friend Dabir, in his calm, reasonable way,

Illustration by **ROBERT ELROD**

explained this must be a vessel from the land of Chin. He pointed out the even horizontal lines that divided the sail, which he said was typical of their "junks," though he admitted he'd never imagined they were this large.

"Still," he said, his blue eyes twinkling, "so great a ship should have plenty of extra water."

His good spirits soon had all of us waving our arms and shouting in joyous anticipation, even the surly cook, who'd sprained his ankle when he dropped into the boat.

The vessel tacked towards us and our laconic helmsman spoke at last, joking that even foreign fare would be better than our cook's, which provoked a round of nervous laughter. It being near to the evening prayer, I led us in hurried devotions while that black ship drew ever closer.

My apprehension grew stronger as it neared. Though the ocean had never been my home, I was, by those years, no stranger to sea craft. Yet I'd never seen one with such a high rising stern. Huge red eyes were painted on the pointed prow, which lent it a monstrous aspect made all the more disquieting because of the steady metallic clank somewhere deep within the hull. As its ebon shadow fell over us, the craft seemed less a ship than a predator with a steel heart.

I counted fifteen silhouettes along the high rail but couldn't make out any faces. The helmsman wondered aloud whether they thought us threatening. Surely so many men would not worry over so few. It is true that we looked a little rough. In the mad scramble to abandon ship we'd lost our turbans, and so many hours in the rowboat had left our robes disheveled and stained. The cook was a bit paunchy, but helmsman and mate were hardy sailors; and Dabir and I were both in the prime of life. Though Dabir was a lean scholar, and some gray had touched his spade beard, he did not look a weakling. And as for me, well, as my wife would have told you, I was a striking figure of a man. But we were clearly in need of assistance.

Besides, if those aboard meant us harm, we could make little but a brave noise, for I alone had retained my sword. The others carried only knives

A broad figure leaned against the rail and called down to us, his voice deep and clipped with the accent of Chin folk. "Who are you, and what are you doing?"

Even I knew this was not the customary way to hail a vessel at sea and our sailors exchanged worried looks. The speaker sounded inordinately suspicious, as if we might somehow conceal a horde of pirates in our open boat.

Dabir lifted his hands to his mouth, forming a speaking trumpet. "Our own ship was destroyed," he called up. "We are the only survivors. Can you help—"

The man's voice remained wary. "Destroyed by what?"

Dabir hesitated only a moment. "A great fish."

I would have described it as a vast demon serpent, although I suppose Dabir was accurate to a point. He likewise neglected to mention how the monster had smashed our vessel with its huge armored head until the ship buckled, like a warrior with a broken back.

At Dabir's words excited chattering broke out all along the rail, but as I do not speak any tongue from Chin, I could not understand them.

"What are they saying?" I asked Dabir

Even in the dimming light there was no missing the droll look he gave me.

"Well," I said defensively, "you speak all sorts of languages."

"Aye, and you eat all sorts of foods. That doesn't mean you can cook them."

I would gladly have retorted with something clever, save that nothing occurred to me. Besides, a new figure had thrust past the others and now gripped the rail. Someone slender, and my suspicion was confirmed the moment the woman leaned out and addressed us. Her accent less pronounced than that of the man.

"How long ago did the monster attack?" Her voice was tense and commanding. "Is it near?"

"A day and a night past," Dabir relayed. "We may have driven it off," he added, for she was looking now to her ship's stern, almost as though she expected the great beast to pop up from the waves and start gnawing. "We wounded it severely."

Those words gained her full attention. Though I could not see her eyes, I felt the strength of her gaze fasten upon Dabir. "How did you do that?" she asked.

"If you wish to hear more," my friend answered, "perhaps we could discuss matters aboard your ship."

A bare pause was quickly followed with warmer tones. "But of course. We would have welcomed you in any case. Dewei, put the ladder overside so that our guests may join us. We will haul up your boat as well," she added

She stepped from the rail, and the fellow she'd named as Dewei began barking orders to the rest of the crew in the language of his people.

"I'd have liked it better if she'd been swifter to offer help," I said.

"I'm surprised she wasn't more skeptical of my claim," Dabir told me quietly. And at my questioning look he explained: "She knows of the monster."

I wasn't entirely sure how he knew that, but before I could ask, the lanky helmsman interrupted.

"For myself," he quipped, "I'd have liked it better if her ship didn't look like it'd been coughed up from hell and painted by Iblis, but I'll take what I can get."

Ghassan shushed him.

Dewei let down the rope ladder. I sent the cook up first, and Ghassan went close behind, to steady the fellow should he have trouble with his bad ankle. The helmsman went after, and then me.

My legs were stiff after sitting so long within that boat, and I stretched as well as I could whilst climbing the high side of that black ship. Now that I was beside the hull I heard not just one loud clanking, but others besides, as though mad musicians, bereft of drumskins, kept time by beating pipes together.

The weather deck resembled none I had ever seen. Long metal tubes projected out from various holds, and some of them moved up and down, letting off puffs of noxious steam that smelled of foul eggs. Also there were sharper chemical odors, and chains affixed to clanking winches. Lanterns hung upon masts and dangled from the nearest spar, and by their light I discovered that the majority of the crew were folk of Chin, although their numbers were sprinkled with a few Arabs and Indians. In amongst all the strangeness was the faint cluck of chickens, for the crews of ocean going ships cannot subsist solely on preserved foods.

Dewei proved a massive fellow who wore his hair tied back from his broad forehead. His narrow eyes fell immediately to my sword, and he demanded I relinquish it.

"Nay," I told him. "I guard Dabir."

"You will give up the sword," Dewei instructed me imperiously, "or die."

I smiled at him. "Then we will die together."

At that moment Dabir reached the deck. I would have stepped to offer him a hand, but Dewei and I were gauging one another.

"If he is the captain's bodyguard," the woman's voice said from somewhere in the gloom, "let him keep the sword a while longer."

This sounded reasonable enough save for that final phrase. Dewei bowed his head to her and she drew closer.

The woman of Chin was petite and spare, wrapped in a scarlet robe, and lovely in a severe way. I would tell you of the beauty of her almond eyes, but their fine form was undercut by a calculating coldness. Do not think I demean the wit of women, for Dabir's wife could talk rings around me, and my own Najya was shrewder than

I in many affairs. What I mean is that she was one of those who gauged everything in sums and balance sheets, be it beast or man.

"I am the Lady Xin," she told Dabir. "You will dine with me, Captain, and tell me how you wounded the monster. Your man can go with the others of lesser station. They will be cared for, I assure you."

"Captain Asim's station is as high as my own," Dabir told her, and for a man with untamed hair and a bedraggled robe he managed a great deal of dignity.

"He is captain? Not you?" she asked.

"He was captain of the vizier's guard," Dabir continued, "and has often sat at the right hand of the caliph himself. I am the scholar Dabir ibn Khalil, and it has been my fortune to be likewise favored."

Once more her eyes fell to me, and then back to Dabir. "So the ship's captain…"

"Drowned or devoured, Lady Xin," Dabir told her.

"It was Dabir's plan that lured, then harmed the monster," I told her. "The ship's captain but followed his orders."

"Very well," she said. "Dewei, have the others tended below, then join us. And get under way as soon as their boat is pulled aboard."

Dewei bowed formally to her, then moved off without so much as another glance at me or Dabir.

Ghassan and the others looked a little nervous, but Dabir advised them to stay together, and go with God.

"Yes, honored one," Ghassan said. "Come on lads." He made a brave show of following a beckoning sailor, and the helmsman lent a shoulder to the cook. I did not like this but had grown accustomed to the separation of folk by class and station when nobles were involved.

A wizened Chinese servant led us after the woman and up a long gangway. We passed a burly helmsman, and then Dabir and I were directed into a tiny cabin back of him. The ship rose higher yet, at least two decks, to that ridiculously high stern.

We found ourselves in a dainty water closet, complete with a cushioned toilet and a wash basin and two large pitches of water. The servant mimed for us to wash hands and faces and gestured likewise to some scented soaps lying upon a shelf before he left us.

Dabir and I cleaned up as best we could. We might have accomplished more had we not simply drunk two thirds of the water before we even set to our efforts. He and I were both men of discipline, but we had a great thirst, even if that water tasted of long storage in wooden barrels.

When we finally decided we had done our best, the servant outside led us through a door beside the water closet. We found ourselves in a paneled cabin hung with beautiful silk paintings of strange pointed buildings and misty mountains. Two quiet guardsman, all in black, girded with swords, waited against the wall, swaying alike with the three paper lanterns hung above the table. A pair of wizened Chinese servants placed covered dishes in the table's midst. Some other must recently have set the stunning white and blue plates.

Lady Xin already sat at the table's head, and she gestured to empty places two chairs down from her. "The cooks were preparing the evening meal just as your little boat was sighted," she told us.

Wine was brought, but I demurred, and Dabir explained to Lady Xin that such was forbidden. I had seen Dabir imbibe wine many a time, but I think this night he wished to keep things simple, and perhaps keep his mind clear. Thus were we served more of the stale water.

Strange delicacies were laid before us, and it was to my sorrow that most were fish of different sorts. I do not care for fish, be it fried or broiled or steamed or sliced into tiny pieces and smothered in sauce. Truly, I had a great hunger, but there was nothing for me but rice, fresh fowl, and a platter heavy with dried peaches and apricots.

The woman sipped at her wine, nibbled on the fish, and watched us closely.

I had lived long in Baghdad and ventured far, so I had seen folk of Chin before, but never a woman such as this. I had judged her a noblewoman, and wondered whether many noblewomen of Chin commanded ships. I did not think so. Under her loose silk robe she wore a stiff collared black blouse parted just at that lovely feminine juncture between her collar bones, where she displayed a petal cinnabar necklace. Her fingernails were scarlet, long almost as the talons of a beast, though her manner was extremely refined. Indeed, she held herself with the stiff dignity of the caliph's chief wife.

"You say that you harmed the serpent," she said at last. "How was it done?"

"I did not say it was a serpent," Dabir answered.

The two stared at each other. She tapped the rim of her goblet. "Very well, scholar. I know of the beast you described, and I would very much like it dead. Do you believe you killed it?"

"It is possible," Dabir told her. "But unlikely. What do you know about it?"

She answered his question with one of her own. "Why are you after it?"

I could not guess what Dabir was thinking, for his expression was unreadable. Likely he debated how much to reveal. In the end, he apparently decided upon frank disclosure.

"The monster's been harassing merchants of the caliphate for the last two months, all along the main sea route between Basra and India. It followed two or three of them for long hours, and a half dozen others have disappeared entirely."

"And so your caliph sent you to hunt it?"

"Yes," Dabir agreed. We had actually left under orders of the vizier, who dispatched us whenever some strange issue vexed the caliphate. He did this in part to please the caliph and, for reasons too complex to relate here, in partial hope that we would fail to return.

She lifted her fine goblet to ruby lips and took a dainty sip before returning it to the table. "So how did you attack it?"

Dabir then related how we had gone out in one of the fastest of the caliph's ships, with a trained regiment of spearmen, and told her how the barbed spears were tied to weighted drogues, which he hoped would drag against the beast's weight and tire it.

"Alas, the monster proved even larger than I had been told." Dabir smiled wryly. "And I'd hoped there had been some exaggeration. We pierced it with at least a dozen spears before it destroyed our ship. It was so enraged that it set upon the men amongst the wreckage. It was swimming after our boat until Captain Asim plunged a spear through its right eye."

He omitted the following moment where I tumbled backwards and struck my head against an oarlock.

She considered me without any great interest as Dabir spoke on.

"The creature thrashed about in the water before diving deep. We thought it would rise up and chew our boat to splinters, but never returned."

The woman tapped the side of her goblet. "I had hoped you had something more clever."

"I do," Dabir said.

Her eyes snapped up to him once more, but neither spoke. There was nothing to be heard by the creak of the ship upon the waves and the ever present metal clanging.

"What is your plan, scholar?"

"First I wish you to tell me why the serpent hunts you."

She stopped in the very midst of taking a breath. Her delicate nostrils flared. "How did you deduce that?"

"The only common feature of the ships the serpent harassed," Dabir said, "were high stern decks. Like your own. Then was the evident concern when we told you we'd encountered it. You know and fear it."

At that moment Dewei announced himself with a knock and

was granted permission to enter. He came to stand behind Lady Xin, reporting quietly in Chin to her ear.

"How are our men?" Dabir asked. "Do you have a doctor aboard to look at our cook?"

"We have bandaged him," Dewei said, looking self-satisfied.

Lady Xin shot him a disapproving look. "They have, of course, been well tended. Scholar, you are astute. The monster does hunt me. I have been cursed by a sorceress who desires my secrets. If she cannot have them, she would sink my ship. Thus must I remain upon the move."

"Why haven't you simply left the ocean?" Dabir asked.

She spread her hands. "The *Black Lotus* is my life's work!" Her voice rose indignantly. "Now tell me. What is your plan? Is there some way to defeat the serpent?"

"Its efficacy depends in part upon your stores. Lovely as your skin is," he said, "there is no missing the stains upon your fingertips. You speak of your life's work, I assume there is alchemy involved?"

"You are entirely too clever," she told him coolly. There was admiration in her voice, yes, but there was no missing the threat there besides.

"I've spent much time around alchemists," Dabir said easily, then offered a slight smile. It might have disarmed some other woman.

"As to your plan," she pressed.

"As to our fate," Dabir countered. "If I share this plan with you, I want food and water set within our boat, and to be set free upon it with my comrades."

"Done," she said easily. "You do not want transport to Basra itself?"

Dabir shook his head, and I knew not why, lest he wanted away from the ship as soon as possible. He looked over to me, but I could offer no reassurance. I did not trust her, yet perhaps she was eager enough for the information that she would honor her word. What other hope did we have?

He must have decided the same. "The matter is simple. The monster eats." Dabir's voice grew grim, for he had seen it chase down sailors from our crew. "We entice it to eat something that will kill it."

The woman leaned forward intently. "You mean to poison it."

"Aye. I do not know your stores, but I see you have apricots and peaches. Their pits, if ground, will produce a fine poison. So too is cinnabar poison, and likely you have arsenic and other potent powders known only to Chinese alchemists."

She touched her necklace with one long nail. "I would be loath to part with my cinnabar. I have a priceless collection."

"How much do you value your life?" Dabir asked her.

The Lady ignored this question. "How do you judge how much of any of these substances to give the creature? We had many pits, I'm certain, when first we took on stores—" here her eyes flickered to the dried fruit "—but the cooks may have been pitching them overboard since."

"Hazard all your poisons at once," Dabir advised. "I am certain I smelled sulfur mixed in with the steam when we boarded. Such would not kill the creature, but it certainly wouldn't aid its health. "

Dewei broke in, scoffing, "How do you propose to entice the serpent to consume foul smelling substances? Ask it to hold still while we pour them down its throat?"

Dabir answered him as though his question had been phrased politely. "Fill a watertight barrel with all the most potent poisons in the ship. Smear it with the flesh and blood of some of your fowl."

"And suppose something else eats the lure?" Dewei demanded. "There are sharks in these waters."

"That's the most dangerous part," Dabir agreed. "Are you willing to risk much for your freedom?" He looked down the table at Lady Xin. "If the monster tracks you, all you need do is slow, and wait for its arrival."

Dewei made a rude noise.

"Silence," the woman told him, then studied Dabir. "Your plan has greater merit than any I've yet heard. It will be expensive... but having the thing dead will be worth any price. Very well. Dewei," She spoke to him in Chinese and he listened, nodding. He considered us with a frown, then a smile, then his expression cleared.

"I am giving you and your man access to my chemical stores, scholar," Lady Xin told us. "Dewei will accompany you. A barrel will be provided. It should not take long to prepare this little trap," she went on, "so I will order the ship to slow now. Dewei?"

Her man opened the door and gestured for us to precede him.

The woman did not rise to bid us farewell, nor offer any word of parting.

The sky was shot with stars, obscured by strands of cloud hung upon the sky like tattered banners. Truly, only in the deep desert and upon the sea can one gaze upon the heavens in their greatest majesty. Staring into that immensity I held the brief fancy that I was in danger of falling up into the darkness.

Dewei guided us through a forest of those strange sliding pipes and then we descended after him into a long cramped narrow underdeck, small enough that I was forced to duck my head. The clanking was most loud, though I could likewise imagine I heard the pounding of my own heart. No matter the woman's assurances, I did not trust her.

Finally Dewei opened a door to starboard and, still smirking, gestured within.

I stepped through into a chamber of horrors.

The scent of blood permeated the place. Dozens of men lay on pallets thrown over low tables, still as death, dim light shining down on glazed eyes in slackened faces. A sickly green object was fastened about the chest of each man, and attached to each was a snaking, jerking tendril that led off towards a clanking metal contraption alive with spinning wheels.

Those upon the pallets came from many lands: Chin, India, Arabia, Ethiopia, and others I could not name. Most were dressed as sailors. All but the nearest, our comrades, were emaciated, and even Ghassan, the cook, and the helmsman were paling. Three burly crewman were advancing around the tables toward me, bludgeons in hand.

"You shared your plan," Dewei crowed. "Now all the captain needs is your blood!"

He stood still in the hallway, with Dabir, at whom he had pointed a sword.

You may wonder how it was I survived such a moment, but it was simpler than you think. If Dewei wished to assault us and win he should not have stopped to gloat.

I'd grown used to carrying a curved sword in part because it was one of the few things left to me from my father, may peace be his. But I prized them also because a skilled wielder may draw and strike at once.

The men with bludgeons were close, and my sword was but half drawn when the first rushed me. He took an elbow to the mouth as my sword came clear. He staggered into a table and both he and the insensate man upon it tumbled to the deck.

My next assailant, a man of Indian extraction instinctively warded my strike by throwing up his hands and discovered too late how finely I hone my sword, for I sheared both limbs off below the wrists. He sank screaming to his knees as blood fountained from the stumps.

Behind, Dewei cursed and shouted to his followers, who seemed reluctant to close upon me. Thus he ignored Dabir and ducked through the doorway, stabbing at my flank.

I sidestepped, slipping a little on the bloody deck, so that my return strike crossed not through his chest but his lantern, which splintered, spraying hot oil across his shirt, which flared up an instant later.

Dewei dropped the flaming remnant of his lantern to the floor, along with his sword, to beat at his shirt. Dewei did not end his life on fire, for Dabir's push set the man into my sword edge.

This was enough for the third sailor, for he ran toward the darkness forward, screaming alarm. Tongues of flame, meanwhile, licked eagerly across the deck.

I called out to Ghassan, our first mate, and his eyes flickered feebly.

"What is this?" I asked Dabir.

He answered in disgust. "Sorcery."

"Why does it always have to be sorcery?" I asked as I stepped to Ghassan. "Isn't a giant sea serpent enough of a problem?" I cut the line that led to Ghassan's chest. Blood flowed briefly from the connection and then the line fell away, like a withered vine.

I helped Ghassan to stand.

Dabir, meanwhile, roused the helmsman, though he was even more groggy than the first mate. The cook couldn't be wakened at all, which meant I had to carry the fat man over one shoulder.

Fast as we moved, the fire moved faster, and that space quickly filled with smoke and crackling red flames. We heard the patter of feet on the decks overhead, and some out in the corridor beyond, and we knew we had no more time, even had it seemed possible to save the wretched souls stretched on tables all around us.

Dabir had stolen glances toward that clanking bronze machine. "Dabir!" I cried. "We've got to get to the deck, and our boat!"

"We'll need water," he said distractedly, but led us toward a door in the stern.

It was wedged tight until I kicked it thrice. When it yielded before me we saw that we'd arrived at another cabin with yet another clanking machine, fed by a larger glowing sorcerous line, likely funneled from the one attached to the bleeding men. Further, this machine stretched from deck to rafter.

Had we been upon an exploratory outing I'm sure this cabin

would have been of great interest, but we were desperate for an exit. Apart from the door I'd just kicked open there was but one egress, a gangway leading up.

I left Ghassan holding the dead weight of the cook, snatched a lantern from Dabir, and ran up the passageway to the hatch.

Praise Allah, the portal was unlocked. I threw it open and found myself in an immense stern cabin. Great windows looked out upon the ocean behind us, where the moonlight cast a wavering silver pillar.

In most ships the stern galley is given over to the captain's quarters, and here was no exception, for I'd emerged within a nest of feminine luxury, replete with cushions and shelves filled with carven statues and scrolls. Also there were more of those painted silk images hung against the bulkheads.

But none of this held my attention for any time, for my eyes fell full upon the large glass pyramid anchored to the deck in the cabin's center. Its frame was fashioned with delicately intertwining creatures of the sea, masterwork that would have astonished me had I not been revolted by the contents of the pyramid itself.

It held strange green fluid that only partially managed to obscure an immense pulsating, bulbous, black organ of some kind.

I stared a moment longer than I should have, until I heard footfalls without the cabin. I shouted for Dabir and the others to hurry, then raced to the cabin door and barred it with a wooden crossbeam. Just in time, too, for someone was soon hammering upon the thing with a fist and shouting in Chinese.

Ghassan staggered up from the hatch on his own. Dabir had to push the helmsman, then called up that he could not move the cook even as there were shouts directly behind him.

I still regret that we'd made no better accommodation for that poor fellow. As it was, so swift was the pursuit after Dabir that I had to grab his wrists and pull him to safety as an enraged sailor cut at his leg. I shoved my friend roughly away then flung a handy blue pot upon the snarling face below.

There came a satisfying crash and thump and shouts, but I did not see the extent of the damage for Ghassan wisely slammed down the hatch, securing it with his own weight.

I found Dabir examining the pyramid, his face alight with both interest and horror. The helmsman bent his ear near the cabin door, where Lady Xin was addressing us.

"Harm my work," she cried, "and I shall flay you all alive! "

"Release us," Dabir called, "or we will destroy this heart."

Some determined fellow was banging upon the hatch. An ax blade driven part of the way through the wood a handspan off Ghasson's foot made him doubt the wisdom of his plan to prevent entry there. He looked to me for guidance.

"Call off your men!" I shouted to the captain. "Or I will break the glass and the heart in a single stroke!"

She called then in Chinese, and the activity below ceased, although I heard them shuffling around down there and wondered if she'd ordered some other mischief.

"The fire will be out shortly," Laid Xin told us confidently. "We have pumps, and hoses, and while you have caused some damage, you have been merely… inconvenient. I am willing to forgive, so long as you depart my ship immediately."

"Do you believe her?" Ghassan asked quietly.

Dabir answered him only with a shake of his head. "You underestimated us," Dabir called to her. "A true sage would act with greater care."

I shot him a look. Why was he baiting her?

He made a slow winding motion with his right hand, by which I inferred he hoped to stall her.

Her conversational tone sounded forced. "I rarely meet any intellect that approaches my own. Now what is it that you want? I shall give it to you. If you want gold and jewels, these, too, I can set aboard your boat."

"That sounds most fine," said Dabir. "How much gold will you give us?"

As I have elsewhere said, Dabir had no head for money, and we were well supported from the caliph's coffers in any case. Likely he neither knew nor cared about her riches.

"I can fill buckets with jade and rubies," she said, beginning to sound desperate.

"Do you have any emeralds?" Dabir briefly considered the small emerald ring upon his left hand, a gift from his great love, Sabirah. "I am especially fond of emeralds."

"I will give you as many emeralds as I possess!"

"Also," Dabir said slowly, "you must pledge that you shall leave our waters forever."

"Done!"

"She agrees," the helmsman said tiredly, "too fast."

"What is this all for?" I asked Dabir.

"The monster sank no ships but ours," he spoke out, loud enough for her to hear, "because we attacked it. Lady Xin has been the one sinking the ships, to find blood to keep this... travesty beating. Those poor men below were captured in her raids."

"It is no travesty," the sorceress shot back. "It is a work of genius! Can you even fathom the cocktail of chemicals I must use to make the heart beat? The sorcerous secrets I have unlocked?"

"At what price?" Dabir asked her.

She laughed at him. "What matter the price? The serpent's heart powers the ship, and me, and all who drink of its essence! That is no ordinary heart, but an engine of immortality!" More quietly, almost conspirationally, she said, "If you wish, "I will permit you and your man a single sip of the elixir I brew from the heart's fluids."

"What will that do?" Dabir asked. He thumbed me over towards the galley window. I wasn't sure what he meant me to observe, but I stepped over.

The ship had slowed, recall. The waters were too deep for an anchor to reach the sea bed, but the sails had been taken up, and the ship but drifted. And now, in the moonlight, I saw a disturbance in the waves closing upon the vessel. I knew then why Dabir had lingered, but it was truly a dangerous game he played.

"It shall lengthen your lifespan twofold!" she cried. "Do you not see?"

"The serpent wasn't sent after you by another sorceress at all, was it," Dabir said. "It hunts you because you slew its mate... nay, its child."

It was my turn to be struck still in surprise.

"It is just a beast!" the woman snarled. "It should never—"

Finally someone on the decks above spotted the serpent nearing, or so I inferred from the panicked Chinese shouting.

"I hope you've readied your poison barrel," Dabir said drolly. "There's no way you'll outrun it now."

And only a few dozen spear lengths out a great serpentine neck soared suddenly from the sea. It was wide around as a pair of teamed horses, and bore a head the size of a whole elephant. I heard the twang of bowstrings. The beast's roar of defiance rattled our cabin windows.

"Oh, Allah," the helmsman breathed.

Outside the cabin door was a chaos of voices, and Lady Xin shouting orders. Below the hatch I heard sailors fleeing.

"Should I skewer the heart?" I asked Dabir.

"It comes for the heart," he said, savagely. "So long as it beats, it will attack."

"But where are we to go?" Ghassan asked.

Dabir pointed at the sealed cabin door. "Take up any weapon you can find. We've little choice but to flee." He himself carried Dewei's sword. Both Ghassan and the helmsman lifted elaborate jade dragons that might be used as clubs.

I looked at the three of them, gauging their readiness. Our chances were slim, aye, but it was far better to go down fighting.

I threw open the crossbar and flung wide the door. "God is great!" I shouted, and charged forth.

Lady Xin was no longer directly before the cabin, and the fellow who was saw my onrush and parried. Mine was a strike to numb an arm. I did not break his guard, but I forced him back as the others hurried on across the weather deck for a ship's boat that Dabir pointed out, stowed along the rail.

Something heavy struck the ship behind us and set everyone sliding. The monster's roar was so loud I felt it through the deck and suppressed the urge to cover my ears.

The captain screamed commands amid the chaos and was frantically waving two men carrying a barrel after her. They raced up behind her towards the high stern galley.

Other sailors were pulling desperately at ropes to raise the ship's sails, and the clanking had increased in frequency, almost as thought the ship itself were panicked.

I locked swords at the hilt with my opponent, then gut punched him and slammed him in the temple as he sagged. Dabir called for me, for they had reached the boat and were throwing off its tarp.

"Cast it free!" I shouted and dashed up the stairs after Lady Xin.

By Allah, but the beast was angry. Its huge armored head was more lizard than serpent-like, and the spear I'd cast still stood out from beneath one of the heavy ridged eye sockets. Its scales were silvered in the moonlight as it brought its huge skull down upon the rear rail and tore most of it away with a terrific crunch.

The ship rocked, but the two men with the barrel righted themselves very near the top of the flight. Lady Xin, meanwhile, pointed them at the monster. She was fearless, that one.

I remember still how the beast threw back its head and cast away the rail and deck. I wondered if it could see through the gap in the decks to the weirdly beating heart of its dead child.

I thought of my own daughter then, and the anger that had kindled within me raged to a great flame.

I am loath to strike an unarmed man, so I kicked the leg out from under the rear barrel carrier, and he collapsed upon the stairs. I trod over him even as Lady Xin screeched at me, her eyes aglow with hate.

"Madman!" She cried. "What are you doing?!"

I have said before my sword was keen, and if I possessed it still I would beg you to study its length, for it was made of metals men never mastered. The sailor who yet gripped the barrel's other end gaped as I swung my blade. The wood parted like paper, and the foul smelling powders sprayed forth, along with a flutter of loose feathers from the parts of dead chickens tacked to its surface.

"Asim!" Dabir called to me.

The serpent's great head loomed even higher and it let out a mournful, angry cry before it swung down, clipping three sailors in half.

I threw myself down the shuddering gangway.

Dabir and Ghassan had pushed the helmsman into the boat and were now using a complicated rig of winches and pulleys to swing it over side. As I ran up, a trio of sailors charged them with swords. That might have been Dabir's end had not the beast struck the port side with its tail. Two of their attackers tumbled right past them and into the water and the third smashed his head on the side of the boat and fell, stunned. Ghassan was somersaulted onto the boat's rowing benches, and Dabir somehow held to the boat's side, though with it slung out from the ship this left him nearly horizontal.

Screams filled the air, though all sounds, even the measured clanks, were drowned by the roar of the angry serpent. I steadied Dabir as the small boat rocked back to port. He moved to fiddle with one of the winches, but we had no time. "Strike the line on three," I shouted, and on that count he used his sword against the aft rope, and I used mine on the fore.

Ghassan and the helmsman fell within the boat and cursed as it struck the waves far below. Dabir leapt after them to the sea. I sheathed my sword, then vaulted over as well.

In a brief moment I saw I'd jumped too far. There was the boat below, and a spluttering Dabir pulling himself aboard as Ghassan leaned for him. I bethought I would surely crack my bones upon the prow.

Yet the beast lashed the water, and through some erratic motion the boat slid away so that when I struck the water I missed the prow by the length of my nose. In a moment more I was blinking salt water from my eyes. Dabir yelled at Ghassan to row even as he thrust a dripping sleeve into my face and helped drag me aboard.

The sounds of screaming, and the rending of the ship, and the roar of the great beast echoed after us. I wasted no time finding my own way to oars, then set lustily to work.

Lady Xin's sailors dropped into the water after us, but it is a strange truth that many sailors cannot swim. They made no good speed after us, no matter our waning strength, and we soon out distanced them.

A quarter league out we ceased rowing and watched as the black vessel listed to starboard, then dropped deeper into the waves, prow pointed toward the moon. The clanking continued unabated even as it took on water. Here and there sailors clung to flotsam, but the great serpent snapped all of them up as it circled.

"It will come for us," the helmsman said.

"It might," I said. "And with just reason. The wound I gave it may yet slay the beast, and that shames me."

"Is that why you risked your life to spoil the poison barrel?" Dabir asked.

"Aye."

He clapped my shoulder. "Allah is merciful," he reminded me. After a moment he pointed further out to sea, in the direction of the moon. Beyond the sinking prow we perceived a second boat, and a bevy of sailors frantically rowing it. Silhouetted upon its stern was a proud, scarlet figure.

The monster spotted the boat at the same moment, and its sinuous course toward Lady Xin's vessel set little whitecaps rolling towards us.

I had not yet seen so much of the thing upon the surface of the water, and I swear to you that it must have stretched on for the length of five of the caliph's finest warships. In only a dozen heartbeats it had reached the Lady's boat.

I shall say one thing for Lady Xin. She did not lack courage. When the serpent reached them and rose with gaping mouth, the men cried out in fear. Yet I heard no woman's scream.

The monster circled the wreck for perhaps a half hour more, but never did it seek us out, and eventually it submerged. I never looked upon it again, nor heard of its presence south of Basra.

As for us, we four drifted until a few hours after dawn, when we were discovered by a spice merchant bound for the caliphate. He paid both Ghassan and the helmsman a tidy sum for their jade dragons, and plied us with fine foods and luxuries, so much did he love our tale

He did not believe a word of it, naturally, and I do not blame him.

THE BEHEMOTH

Jonathan Wood

:: Now

ANKLE DEEP IN WATER, MY Mech stumbles. I try to correct, overcook it. Massive, clumsy, the machine goes down on one knee. Around me, flat-bottomed fishing boats are swamped, sink with viscous gurgles. Gulls shriek angrily, billow around the Mech's knees.

I try to stand. Try to get my Mech to stand. In the cockpit it's hard to discern where my body ends and the Mech's begins. Overwhelming reams of data push into my consciousnesses, try to push me out.

Around me, water stretches off in every direction. The Shallow Sea. I search for reference points, for reasons to be here.

Get up. Get moving. You can do this.

Do what again?

:: Before: A memory, already fading

THE DAY LILA WON THE lottery, I vomited for almost half an hour.

I was in our bathroom, hunkered over white porcelain. She stood outside the door, tried to talk me down. That she was comforting me just made everything worse.

Illustration by **ROBERT ELROD**

The lottery has been a fact of life since before I was born. It's just the way things are. The lottery is needed to select the Proxies. The Proxies are needed to keep pilots safe from their Mech's operating systems. And the Mechs are needed by everyone. They keep us all safe. The loss of every memory in the Proxy's head is just the price we pay. That's the undeniable truth. That got me through rehab: I am a pilot; I am needed; I save people.

My stomach was empty. I stared at its contents swirling in the bowl before me. Like my whole life floating, excised and ugly. Where there had been food, now there was just rage. I stormed out of the bathroom, snatched the lottery ticket from Lila's hand.

"It'll be OK." She looked small and delicate. After all the strength she'd shown, that little piece of paper had stolen it from her.

I screwed the ticket up, flung it away. She put her hand on my arm. "Don't, Tyler. Just… Maybe one won't come this year."

The Leviathans. The goddamn Leviathans.

I could still taste the bile and acid on my tongue. My teeth felt loose in my gums.

"It's bullshit." I couldn't acquiesce. Couldn't just give up. Because screw undeniable facts. Screw everything else. It was her who had got me through, who had stood by me.

"I'm a goddamn pilot," I said. "This doesn't happen to us. I will stop this."

"Tyler…"

I shook my head. "I'm a pilot," I told her. "If I go into a fight, I win."

:: Back further: a memory almost lost

I REMEMBER THE FIRST TIME I saw a Leviathan. I was standing on Chicago's seawall. They built it back in 2050 once they realized Lake Michigan wasn't going to go back to its old shoreline. That was just before all the great lakes, joined up, became the Shallow Sea, swallowed everything north of the Carolinas. It had been standing thirty years or so by the time I stood upon it. I was eight. I remember that clearly enough.

The Leviathans had been coming from the north for about ten years at that point, but this was the furthest south anyone had ever reported one.

When the poles melted the Leviathans had been... What? Waiting? Sleeping? I dream about that sometimes. Vast and subterranean, waiting for their cages of ice to melt away, for us to screw up enough so that they could come forth once more.

They'd ripped the shit out of Canada. A flotilla of refugee boats was tied beneath where I stood. Families hunkered on decks, watching, working out if they should run.

The Mechs we had back then were for shit. The Leviathan had already ripped through three of them, jaws slicing armor, body crushing engines. I doubt it even noticed the pilots it consumed.

Chicago had its own Mech. The Behemoth. Its pilot, William Connor, had been doing the talk show rounds. He'd been going on about how he was going to be the one to stop it. No one believed him. The camera had done a close up of Connor's eyes. Connor didn't believe it either.

That was why I was there. I wasn't meant to be. My parents had strictly forbidden it. They were busy prepping an emergency shelter for when the Leviathan ripped through Chicago and killed everyone dumb enough to stand on the wall, but I had to see. I had to see Connor fight. So did half of Chicago. We all went to the seawall to see if he would save us or let us die.

Standing there, I was amazed at how small six hundred feet of steel built around a nuclear core could look.

It was the crowd's murmur that revealed the Leviathan to me. The fins of the beast slicing towards the Mech. Connor took a step. The spray was a white corona around the Behemoth's foot.

Then it began. If I had held my hand out in front of my face it would have seemed they were dancing in my palm. I remember it now as if I was standing on the Mech's shoulder.

The Leviathan reared up, eel-slick body whipping around and around its mechanical foe. A casual flexing of muscle that cracked foot-thick steel sheets and sent weapons spilling in explosive rain. Its massive head looked too big for its body. A heavy, under-slung jaw, a bony crest behind the eyes. Small, half-formed legs scrabbled at the Mech, claws carving through hydraulics.

The Behemoth's arms were pinned at its side. Missiles detonated at point blank range, did more damage to machine than monster.

But then, and the how of it is lost to me now, Connor got an arm free. He swung it like a piledriver into Leviathan's right eye. The force of the creature's scream almost knocked me off the wall.

Connor swung again. The Leviathan's jaw hung loose, and for a moment, we actually had hope.

Then the Leviathan's tail whipped out of the water, a hideous tumor of spikes and claws. It smashed into the Mech's arm, tore it free of its mooring. The Mech tottered, maimed, lopsided. The whole weight of the Leviathan was on it now.

It staggered, fell. The Leviathan wrapped sinuous coils around the Behemoth's chest. Metal folded like paper.

And then the explosion. A spot of bleach dropped onto the horizon, spreading, obliterating. The force of it driving the water in a wall towards us, exposing the seabed in the moment before the shockwave hit and bowled me over.

I lay on my back as a mushroom cloud rose into the sky.

:: Later

THEY FIGURED OUT WHAT HAD happened by the time they held the state funeral. Connor had sabotaged the failsafe mechanisms on his Mech's nuclear core. Transformed the machine into a walking tactical nuke. Then the fight started, and the core had no cooling, no gyrostabilization. It was only a matter of time before it went critical. When it had blown, fifty percent of the Leviathan's midriff had turned to meat paste.

Connor had even survived the initial blast. The Mech's auto-eject system. Radiation sickness did it for him two days later, though.

Even though he was a corpse, even though they had to close the coffin because the sight of him was so awful, from that moment on I knew I was going to be exactly like William Connor.

:: More recently, but mistier, barely grasped

I PUSHED THROUGH SHOUTING CROWD around the city council halls. They weren't calling Lila's name so I didn't care. I crashed through doors, stormed down corridors, the crumpled lottery ticket in my balled fist. A skinny secretary with a skinnier mustache was the only one who had the nerve to tell me, "It's a closed-door meeting." He flinched out the way before I could shoulder check him.

Marburg, the spineless shit of a mayor I voted for, stood at the middle of a long conference table. He looked up at me. His cheeks went white.

"The hell is this?" My flung lottery ticket bounced off his starched shirt.

He licked his lips, flicked his eyes around the crowd. He knew exactly what it was. Still, he took the time to unfold it.

"I…" he started, pretending to read. "I am so sorry, Tyler." Another eye flick. Scared, I'd have bought, but he'd have to have to try a hell of a lot harder to sell sorry.

"Look," said a large, puffy man, "this is a closed-door-"

I am not a big man. You do not need to be a big man when you fight in a two hundred ton suit of armor fueled by a nuclear reactor. You also do not need to be a big man to know the part of the neck to strike so that the ligaments in the first vertebrae snap, the hindbrain is crushed, and a man dies before he hits the floor. My gaze fell on the councilman and reminded him of this. His voice dried up.

"You," I pointed at Marburg. "Your piece of shit nephew." No one knows this story is true for sure. Except everyone knows. "You got him out of the lottery."

I scanned the room, spotted familiar faces. My finger picked them out.

"Your son-in-law's cousin."

"Your grandkid's best friend."

"The daughter of that janitor you were screwing."

I went round the room. I indicted them for their sins because everyone knows the lottery is a fact of life except these people. And I thought I was one of these people. The fights I'd won for them. I was their goddamn champion.

"It's Lila," I implored them. "It's my wife."

Adam Grant stood up. The one man in the room I respected. My old commanding officer. One of Connor's compatriots. A man I wanted to emulate. Right up until that moment.

"Tyler," he said. He pulled the ticket from the mayor's sweaty hand. "This…" He examined the paper, looked back at me. "…is unfortunate."

His voice galvanized the room. Postures shifted. And that was it. That was my reply. I could beat them all to a pulp but there was no bend in Grant's voice. Behind the fear there was steel. I've see fights like that. The ones where the clear favorite lies beaten and bloody because the little guy refused to just lie down and take his beating. Behind the bluster and the fear, that was this room. My fists would mean nothing, in the end. I needed words and connections. And I'd cast those aside years ago.

:: *A memory within a memory. Some distant nested thing.*

MY FIST SMASHED INTO THE Leviathan's mouth. It mewled, twisted away but my other fist grabbed it by the scruff of the neck. Snug in the Mech's cockpit the proxies filtered the raw data from the pressure sensors, translated it into something thick and satisfying in my fingertips.

Skin gave way. Blood gushed. The Leviathan tried to wrap its tail around my Mech's leg. I sent a knee into its midriff, brought it to the floor. Monstrous ribs cracked. The Leviathan smashed its tail uselessly in the water. My fist broke its teeth.

"You come to my town? My city? You think you can devour my friends?" I worked the Mech's fingers into the flesh beneath the base of the Leviathan's cracked skull. I thought of William Connor. Of the adoration of the people.

The Leviathan's head ripped free. I stood, waved my trophy and hollered.

The shout echoed emptily around the cockpit. The proxies, my only companions—their consciousnesses as battered by the Mech's sensory inputs as the Leviathan was by my fists—didn't say a word.

:: A short while later, one memory running into another

THE TECHNICIANS UNSTRAPPED ME FROM the seat, unplugged the electrodes. The Mech left me sensation by sensation. My body became my own.

I couldn't stop shaking. My first Leviathan. I annihilated it. People were patting me on the back, telling me how goddamn good I was. But I already knew. I *knew*. It was how deities felt. I didn't need the Mech to have my head scrape the clouds.

I didn't pay attention to the proxies until I was in the elevator going down. Adam Grant was there, unwrapping a cigar for me. I glanced back at the technicians manning the gurneys.

The proxies lay there, all sharing the same expression: bewilderment, mild horror, as if trying to remember what exactly they'd given up.

They wouldn't remember. Everything from before their

unplugging was gone. The human mind can't take the raw input of the Mech's sensors. It's too much to process. Once someone has been a proxy, who they were before is expunged. Their memories wiped. The propaganda fliers call it a rebirth.

A technician dabbed blood from a proxy's dripping nose.

Adam Grant saw my brow crease. "Don't worry about them," he said. "They'll be taken care of."

And proxies *are* necessary. If a pilot was exposed to the live feed from a Mech he would forget how to fight, why he was fighting. The Leviathans would tear him apart. And then they'd do the same to the city.

The proxies are necessary.

They're taken care of.

:: That night. I'm sure it was that night. The memories run into each other
LILA STROKED MY ARM. "I still can't believe it." She was wide-eyed, city lights reflecting in her pupils. "You did it."

I half-laughed. "You didn't think I could do it?"

She half-grimaces, half-smiles. "That's not what I meant. Of course I believed. But then… There's a difference between believing and actually seeing."

"So it was a religious experience?" I was cocksure, still too full of myself.

She kissed me. Her lips warm against mine. Her arms slipping around me. When it was over she pulled away. "I've honestly never been more scared in my life." In her eyes I saw her own brand of fearless honesty.

I pulled her to me. Kissed the top of her head. The scent of her filled my nostrils.

"Adam Grant wants me to go out and celebrate tonight," I said. "You deserve it."

I shook my head, kissed her again. "I want to stay with you."

She smiled. Big and broad, and it felt good to have put that smile on her face. Almost as good as tearing the Leviathan apart.

Almost.

We nestled into each other, talked. I wish I could remember the words, that the sweetness could linger.

But then… We were lying down, her head snug against me. She lifted it, a look of sudden sadness on her face.

"What about the proxies with you? They were okay, weren't they? I heard something on the news about some protest groups, and… God, it was awful some of the things they were saying."

That was it, I think. Maybe. The first bit of grit.

"They take care of them." I shrugged, wanting to move on.

"What did they do to them?"

Another shrug. "I don't know. They were on gurneys. They wheeled them away."

"Gurneys?"

The moment was shattering around me. It made me unfairly angry. It was my moment. Not the proxies. I sat up. She half fell off my chest, sat up beside me. "I don't know. One had a nosebleed. I guess they were taking them to the hospital."

"A nosebleed? What was wrong with him?"

"How the hell should I know? It was a nosebleed. Everyone has nosebleeds."

"So why do you think they were going to the hospital?" She looked like she was on the verge of tears.

That angered me more. That she cared so much when I had cared so little.

"I don't know. I just said it. They're just proxies."

She looked at me, blinked, as if trying to see clearly. "Just proxies?"

Dammit.

"That's not what I meant."

We stood there looking at each other. Both angry now. Both wishing we weren't.

"It's been a difficult day," she said. "Maybe we should… bed… rest." She shrugged.

But I still remembered the thunder of adrenaline—of being a *champion*—in my blood. "Actually, I think I might take Adam up on his offer."

I turned away from her.

:: The memory fades. Another comes up. Was it still that night? Or another? A memory so familiar it's worn a groove in my mind. Something repeated over, over, over so all that's left is one homogenous whole

YOU THINK, BY NOW, WE'D have invented something more glamorous.

In the nightclub bathroom, I bent over the white porcelain of the sink. I pinched off one nostril, inhaled the line of white powder.

:: And then… just once? Just many times? Was this even me?
"JESUS, LOOK AT THE STATE of him."

I don't remember who said it. It was hard to concentrate on things like that. My attention jumping from shining object to shining object. The straps on the pilot's seat. A pretty technician's face. The beeping of a cockpit dial. The desire to punch that man right in his eye.

"Screw you, you pen-pushing prick. I'll kick its ass." No idea who I was yelling at.

"He'll be fine." Was it Adam Grant who said that? Lila? Did I know who was there propping me up even back then?

"Jesus. Just strap him in."

I don't even remember the proxies I had fighting those Leviathans. They were there to stop the Mech from pushing me out of my own skull, and I'd already done the job. Some chemical substitute of me that ripped and kicked and split skulls.

I remember reaching my fist down one Leviathan's throat, turning its head inside out. I remember stomping, stomping,

stomping one into paste on the seabed. I remember them quoting how much damage the waves I made did to the seawall. I don't remember caring. The crowd still cheered. For every crash there was another high.

I loved fighting monsters while I was high. Truth be told, I miss it now, even after all the rehab and the therapy. I don't do it anymore. But I miss it.

:: More recently again. This is important. I want to get this right.

ADAM GRANT CAUGHT UP WITH me in the council hall lobby.

"Jesus, Tyler." He shook his head. "That was not the smart play. You have to understand the situation."

I cocked my head. "Really?" I asked him. "What the hell do you think I don't understand about them scrubbing my wife's memory clean? About her not knowing who I am? What part am I missing, Adam?"

"Jesus." He shook his head again. Looked out at the crowd surrounding the building. I thought I could see the word "Lottery" on a placard. "Not here," Grant said. He dragged me to a bar.

"It's over." He was intense over a tumbler of whiskey. "The party is done. No more free drinks. No more getting people out of the lottery."

I felt the urge to punch him again. Add to his scars. "You're telling me that Marburg's daughter gets a ticket, he won't get her out of it?"

"I'm telling you that if he does there will be riots. There'll be a damn revolution. The lottery… the proxies…it's a damn mess. There's too many people who don't remember the world we're fighting for any more." The creases in his brow deepened. He glanced at the back of the crowd, still visible through the glass in the bar's door. I looked too. They did not seem like happy people.

"The council has to appease the mob, Tyler. They've drunk too deep from the well, and now they need to make a sacrifice to fill it back up again."

And then I saw. There in that shitty little bar. It wasn't random chance. That ticket had been signed and sealed and addressed to Lila. They'd decided to do this to me.

I realized then the fight I was in.

"You have to help me. You have to remind them of everything I've done for them."

"Remind them?" Incredulity broke his stony façade. "Your show just now reminded them all of why they picked you. You've pissed off too many people. And you know as well as I do that you fight for shit now you're clean."

A dirty truth. An ugly truth. But a truth. It left me with nothing else to say.

"Hey," he offered the thinnest of smiles. "If you're lucky one won't come this year. She'll be clear of it."

"They come every year."

He nodded. "Go home, Tyler," he said. "Enjoy the time you have left together."

:: Drifting back in time again. To one memory that still shines bright.

I'M A TEENAGER. FOURTEEN YEARS old. Sitting in the bleachers while the football team runs its drills. Watching old Bruce Lee flats and trying to memorize the moves.

"Hey."

She startled me. I almost dropped the screen. I spun around.

"Sorry," she was half-laughing, half-nervous. Embarrassed maybe.

The new girl. Transferred in. I didn't know from where. Kind of pretty. Dark hair that she wore long, and a red shirt she wore loose.

"Studying?" she asked.

"Erm," I wasn't sure why she was talking to me, not sure what angle to take, "kind of."

She shrugged, sat down on the row of chairs behind me. "I feel so behind. You guys are all so far ahead of my old school. It's all so different here."

She looked more frustrated than anything else. Her honesty disarmed me. I ventured some of my own.

"I wasn't studying, like, school stuff," I say. I show her the screen.

"Who's that?"

"His name's Bruce Lee. He was, like, this actor back a hundred years ago or so. That's why it's a flat. But he was amazing. It's all wires and special effects now, but back then it was real. He did all this stuff." I let the flat play for a minute. She watched without comment, without judgment.

"You like fighting?" she asked when I paused it.

"Erm…" I hesitated. This was where conversations usually went wrong. "Kind of," I said.

She nodded. "My dad does thai-jitsu, or something."

"Tae Kwon Do?"

She smiled. "Yeah, that's it."

She was prettier when she smiled. "I do that, too," I said. "That and a bunch of others."

"What others?"

I listed them. After the third, she counted off on her fingers. "So," she said from behind eight raised digits. "Kind of?"

I was sheepish, felt some explanation was required. "I want…" I almost balked, it was like saying I want to be a movie star, but her eyes didn't let me go. "I want to be a pilot. Of, you know, a Mech and stuff. I want to fight the Leviathans."

I regretted it as soon as I said it. I tried to read the emotions on her face, to work out if she'd laugh at me or walk away.

I didn't expect what she actually did. She asked, "What about the proxies?"

"What about them?" I was off guard, still not seeing the angle.

"It seems sad." She kicked at a pebble perched on the metal seats. "What happens to them? They don't even know what they did to make themselves forget."

That seemed like an irrelevant fact. "We have to fight the Leviathans," I said, "or they'll kill us. We have to have the proxies. It's four memories for everyone's lives." I shrug. It was the simplest of math.

She shrugged. "I guess. It just seems sad."

I didn't know what to say to that. She just sat there next to me. And it was nice actually.

"Hey," I said after a while. "I'm Tyler."

She smiled that pretty smile of hers. "I'm Lila."

:: Closer. Approaching the now. Trying to hold the pieces together.
LILA WAS WATCHING TV WHEN I got home from the bar and my talk with Adam Grant, holding her knees to her chest.

"I was worried you weren't coming home."

The drugs. It seemed almost laughable that she was worried about that.

"I'm clean." I sat beside her, leaned in. "You know that."

"This is a lot of stress."

"I'm clean," I promised.

She put a hand on my cheek. "I need you to survive this fight, Tyler. I need you to be there to talk me back to myself."

I ran a hand over her cheek, through her hair, round to rest on the back of her neck. I pressed my forehead to hers. "Don't think like that," I told her. "One might not even come this year."

She let out the smallest, saddest laugh in the world as she pulled away. She pointed to the TV. "One already is."

:: And after that
I SLIPPED OUT OF BED when Lila's breathing grew deep and regular. There was one other solution perhaps. Adam's talk about riots and revolution had made me think. I've seen the downtown slums on the news. I've seen the refugees.

I took the car north, close to the seawall. A foot of water swilled around my tires. Everything smelled rotten or worse. Fractured light from neon signs painted the water-logged streets—logos become abstract and obscure. Street vendors marched around in thigh-high waders. Ragged men stood on floating platforms screaming about the lottery, about the man keeping them all down. Small crowds cheered them on. Deeper in, I watched a man reel out of a bar, drunk, fall into the swill. He emerged with an enormous leech clinging to his cheek. He ripped it away in spray of blood, staggered off.

I couldn't understand how people could live like that. Then I remembered they didn't really have a choice.

:: I try to keep the thread, keep ahold of my reasons, my history, but it's gone again, and I'm falling back into older times

"TYLER?" IT WAS SOME TALK show host whose name I couldn't remember. "Are you okay?" she asked. She's didn't look concerned.

An audience stared at me. Grinning idiots. Screw them. My high was burning out. I felt like shit.

"I'm fine." Even I could hear that I was slurring. "Can you repeat the question?"

There was a time when I loved this, the attention, the presenter's bated breath. I would talk and talk, and they would love it. Stories of violence. Stories of me saving them all.

This time I just wanted painkillers and a warm bed.

"I was asking about the proxies in your Mech," the presenter asked. "Do you ever talk to them? Or their families?"

There was something in the way she asked it. Accusatory.

"Look," I said. "I didn't come up with the system. I just fight. If you want to have some Leviathan come take a shit on this city, just so everyone can remember it clearly, then that's your priority."

A mass inhalation of breath. The presenter's elegantly plucked eyebrow rose.

"Not a popular opinion," she ventured.

"Oh screw you," I spat. "We all know how this works. We messed up the earth, now we pay the toll. Four memories at a time. You don't want to be a proxy, get on the council and dodge the lottery. You want to be able to sleep at night, too, become a pilot. It's worked out for me just fine."

Not an inhalation this time. A hesitation.

There was a time when I loved these things. When audiences cheered me. It was as big a high as the drugs.

Even the drugs didn't do much for me by then.

:: Then darkness descending, a gaping hole of memory. And then, on the far side:

LILA WOKE ME. I DIDN'T recognize her at first. Later, when I saw myself in a mirror, I was surprised she recognized me.

"Three days this time," she told me once I'd washed the vomit, and blood, and shit off myself. She didn't cry. She never cried. Just that same frustrated look she'd given me in the bleachers all those years ago.

"It was those assholes on that TV show," I said. I was full of excuses back then.

"You missed a fight, Tyler."

I was at the closet door, hand on a shirt. Something I could wear to my dealers. And that stopped me. The whole system shut down around those words. I tried to form a response. A question. A denial. An excuse.

I had nothing.

"They sent Lowry," she said. I pictured him. Young kid. Scrappy. He was good. He would have fought and won. The city wasn't in ruins. Of course he'd won.

But no thanks to me.

I still wanted to be a pilot. Beneath everything, beneath even the want for the drugs, there has always been that. Ever since I saw

Connor's Mech go critical and wipe out the horizon that has been the underlying, undeniable truth of my existence.

"It's time to get clean, Tyler," Lila said. "No more bullshit. No more excuses or you'll never pilot again. You get that right?"

I did. I got clean.

:: Swimming back to the present. Back to the slums, car parked, water swirling, a lottery ticket in my hand:

I PICKED A BAR AT random. The place was crowded, the music loud. People partied with a sense of desperation. Drinking until they could forget that tomorrow was coming—implacable as any sea monster.

I stood in the center of the room. It took a minute before someone recognized me. He stared, pointed. The woman he was with turned and looked. Soon they were all looking.

Apparently I wasn't popular at that bar. Not in many bars, I suspected. I couldn't even blame them.

But I didn't need to be popular. I just needed to be rich.

I held up the ticket.

"How much?" I asked, clear and loud, finally putting all the media training crap they'd sat me through to some use. "How much do I have to pay one of you to take my wife's place on the lottery?"

From the look I got, my popularity wasn't going up.

"Five million," I said. "I'm good for it. Five million and get you and your family out of this life." I nodded at the water currently ruining my socks and shoes.

The room was very quiet. The music had died. Grim faces all around me. Folded arms. The smell of the wooden bar slowly rotting away.

One man, shorter than me, wider though, tattoos up his arms and neck, maybe in his fifties—he walked towards me. A few rumbling paces. "I think you want to get out of here."

"Ten million." Just one greedy soul. Just one. That's all I needed.

"You ain't listening."

"Twenty million." It would leave me with a pittance, I would have to move, but it'd be worth it. "You won't care what you forget with twenty million."

It was the wrong thing to say. Adam Grant had been right. The lottery was a tipping point.

I didn't recognize the signal, but suddenly eight of them rushed me. More than one held a beer bottle in his hand.

I remembered Adam saying I don't fight as well now I'm sober. He was right. Still, I can hold my own.

I ducked the first blow, jabbed a fist up under the guy's jaw, into the soft part of the palette. I spun as I did it, slammed my foot into another man's groin, sent him crashing to the floor. I came out of the spin, put my fist into another man's nose, dodged a bottle, clotheslined his friend, then slammed my elbow back into the neck of the idiot trying to sneak up behind me.

Three left. One got in a good blow to my kidney, sent me to my knees, spitting a curse. Another lined up a blow to my jaw. I snatched his arm, slammed a palm into his elbow and watched the joint snap.

The kidney puncher, grabbed me behind the arms. I swung my head back, shattered his nose. Then I crushed his kneecap for good measure.

One left.

But the crowd was not cowed. I was breathing hard, and my hands hurt. The pain in my kidney was like a lance of fire. And then they went from one to forty-one.

I got lost in the violence. I took men down with short efficient blows, but for every six or seven I landed, they landed one of their own. A bottle shattered over my skull, blood ran into my eyes. An elbow crashed into my ribs.

I needed to get out. I recognized my actions as a mistake too late. I stopped fighting to win. Started fighting to escape.

It cost me. Two ribs. And I couldn't lift my left arm above my shoulder any more. But I made it out. It took me two blocks before

I realized no one was chasing me.

:: I remember that fight. For a moment the pain in my side makes sense. And then it drifts away again. Just is. Then something else swims up. After the fight.

LILA FETCHED A FRESH ICE pack for my ribs.

"You're an idiot." The way she said it made it sound like a compliment.

"I have to fight," I told her. "It's who I am."

She smiled. "There's no winning this, Tyler. It is what it is. You fight that Leviathan. You bring me home. And I get to meet you again. Fall in love with you again."

I swallowed. "What if you don't?"

She shook her head. "All the shit you've done, I've stuck with you. You really doubt me now?"

She almost managed to make me laugh. The moment passed. "Maybe afterward you'll be smarter," I said.

She kissed me on the forehead. Snuggled in beside me.

They showed the Leviathan on the news that night. It had destroyed three townsteads on its way south. Casualties in the thousands. They said it would be visible from the seawall in two days. They said it might be the biggest in a decade.

They questioned whether I could stop it. For the first time in a long time, I did too.

:: Almost here. Almost at this moment.

IN A VAST HANGAR NEAR the seawall, I stood before my Mech. The Behemoth II—named after Connor's machine. But I had always been safe in the knowledge it outranked its predecessor in every regard. It could tear a Leviathan apart. The original could only explode.

It still demanded the proxies to operate, though. Connor, who thought up a way to win an unfair fight, couldn't think his way out of that. They all died when his Mech blew.

If I went out there without proxies the sensory overload would wipe out my memory. I would forget to fight. The Leviathan would tear me apart first, then the city.

Then, staring up, up, up at the distant cockpit, almost hidden beyond the curve of the reactor in the machine's chest…the faintest stirrings of an idea.

The Behemoth II. The clue was in the name.

All Connor could do was explode.

The Leviathans always initiate the fights. A walking bomb doesn't need to know how to fight. It just needs to go off.

But would I remember what I was doing for long enough to get clear of the city?

Maybe…

I would die. There was that.

But the auto-eject… No, Connor died.

Hadn't they improved the radiation seals? Some distant memory of joking with Adam Grant after some tech demo where they talked about it. Not really believing it because when would that ever be an issue?

When would any other pilot be that desperate again?

When…

Now. Now is exactly when a pilot would be that desperate.

:: An elevator ride up to a door in the Mech's midriff marked with a radiation warning. I remember that sign clearly.

THE FAILSAFE MECHANISMS ARE WELL designed. There are backup systems of backup systems. All are carefully programmed.

They are beyond my understanding. I was not a careful student at school. I was never a jock, never quite a geek, but that awkward middle position of being nobody in particular.

But then Lila.

It wasn't a revolution. There was no astonishing makeover. It was simply that being nobody to everybody else didn't matter if I was somebody to her.

Love is a slow creature. It isn't like a Leviathan. There is no sudden violence. Rather it wraps its tendrils around you slowly. By the time you are aware of it, it has already won.

Or maybe I was as slow at grasping the concept of love as I was at understanding the complexities of a programming language.

In the end, I reprogramed the machine with a ballpoint hammer. That seemed to suffice.

:: The cockpit. Closer to the now.

MECH'S AREN'T MEANT TO WORK without proxies. Some inputs require needles pressing deep into muscle. They sample DNA. They demand diversity.

But I remember once: a proxy, an older woman, she had a heart attack on the elevator ride up to cockpit. The Leviathan was already visible. There was no time to call in a backup.

Adam Grant showed me the trick.

"Give me that damn thing." He'd grabbed the needle from a panicked technician. "DNA is everywhere." He wiped the needle along the crevices of the seat. Dirt, lint, and hair clinging to it. They never really cleaned the cockpits.

Grant rammed the filthy needle into the arm of a proxy already getting input from other sensors. The technician looked appalled

Grant shrugged. "He's a proxy. He won't remember."

It worked. That proxy took input from two sensors. I don't know what happened to him. Maybe nothing. Maybe he was fine. Maybe the poor bastard died of septic shock.

It was harder jamming the dirty needles into my own flesh. But, I reasoned, it wasn't like I'd remember.

:: Closer

THEY TRIED TO STOP ME leaving. They sealed the city gates against me. I could hear someone raging through my headset but her voice was overwhelmed by the data pouring into me. Heat readings, pressure sensors, gyrostabilizations, revolutions per minute.

I fired missiles. I felt them leaving my body. I felt the heat of their burning fuel burn inside of me. And worse. I could feel pieces of me leaking out with each projectile. The taste of strawberries carried away in a burst of flame. My father's name. What I'd eaten last night. All the inconsequential minutia that we're made of.

But I had sabotaged a nuclear reactor. I had re-engineered hardwired failsafes. Mere doors and words couldn't stop me. I blew my way out of the city. I marched on, marched out. I went to face my Leviathan.

:: One final memory

"WHAT DO YOU THINK?"

Lila on the doorstep of our apartment. She had redecorated. Repainted. New furniture. New art on the walls.

They'd not allowed her to go to the rehab facility to pick me up. A driver had dropped me off at the curb. She'd been waiting when the penthouse elevator doors opened. She looked perfect and anxious in equal measures.

I hesitated, trying to work why she was worried. I was the one who should be worried.

But she misread my hesitation, thought I didn't like her work. And I could see how much she had wanted me to like it. But she just nodded and bore it. She didn't bend, didn't break.

All I had done to her. And she thought I was doing it again, but she remained undefeated. All the monsters I had beaten, but she was the one thing I could never conquer. I loved her for that. So deep and so strong.

"You made it beautiful," I said.

She smiled. The sun banishing clouds. "Good."

:: Now

ANKLE DEEP IN WATER, MY Mech stumbles. I try to correct, overcook it. Massive, clumsy, the machine goes down on one knee. Around me, flat-bottomed fishing boats are swamped, sink with viscous gurgles. Gulls shriek angrily, billow around the Mech's knees.

Get up. Get moving. You can do this.

Do what again?

I make it to my feet. And for a moment memory bubbles up, surrounds me. For a moment I remember everything. Lila. Grant. The people down in the slums of Chicago. The broken ribs. The sabotaged core at my Mech's heart. I know exactly who I am and exactly why I am here.

Then it's all gone.

:: Later?

I STAND. I WAIT. I marvel at the world. The water is so beautiful. I wonder how it got there.

Movement on the horizon catches my eye. Something cutting through the water. I stare at it. Red signs flash in the corner of my vision but they are just one more confusing detail in the mass of data piling into my head. I want to ignore them. There is peace in that line of water as it races towards me.

I watch it. The efficient beauty of it. It distracts me from the wrongness in my limbs. From the foreignness of my body.

It is almost on me. I want to see what it is. I am curious.

And then—rearing out of the water—a vast unspooling nightmare of flesh. And God. Oh God.

Peace is gone. I scream, flail. And the wrongness of my limbs can't be ignored now.

Why am I made of metal? Why are my thoughts numbers?

The monstrosity's jaws smash into me, tear pieces from me. I can feel teeth in skin that is not my skin. Coils ensnaring me. Sensors scream in my head. A strangely remote disemboweling of my electronic innards. Reams of my coolant system spilling out onto the ground.

Why am I made of wires and metal? Why am I dying?

Warning sirens split my skull. And heat. A jagged spike of heat in my chest. Building unbearably.

What is wrong with me? Why am I wrong?

Jaws, and claws, and teeth, and scales, and death and crushing and heat and everything caving in caving in and heat *ohgodtheheat Iamgoingto-*

And then the heat in my chest crescendos, swells, consumes. Everything is eclipsed. Pain, and heat, and light, and the world, and memory. All reduced to single point and blown away.

:: Afterward

A VOICE. A VOICE BRINGS me out of the darkness. It repeats the same word over and over. There is something familiar about the word. I grasp at it for a moment, but cannot place it.

Where am I?

Somewhere dark. I am strapped in. Wires cover my body. I work one hand free, pull at them. They come away with small wet sucking noises.

The voice is getting nearer.

How did I get here?

Light bursts into the room. I blink, try to shield my eyes with my free hand.

When I can see again, an open door floods the room with light. It is small, full of smashed screens, cracked dials, and trailing wires. I am strapped into a chair in the middle of it all.

A woman stands in the doorway. Tall. Dark hair worn long. A muddy red shirt worn loose. She stares at me.

"Hello," I say when the silence becomes as strange as everything else about this situation. "Could you please help me?"

The woman starts as if breathed to life that very moment. She crosses the small room, pulls at the straps holding me in place. Halfway through she stops. I look at her face, and I almost believe she is going to cry.

"Are you alright?" I ask.

She closes her eyes. When she opens them they are clear. She nods, resumes her work. While she frees my legs I massage life into my arms.

"I'm sorry," I tell her, "but I think I took a bump on the head. I really don't remember where I am."

She nods, frees my legs. She lets me lean on her shoulders as we cross the room's sloping floor.

Then, as we reach the doorway, I stop, stare, gasp. In the distance there is the wreckage of a massive robot lying half drowned in a shallow sea.

The woman grabs my head, pulls it around, studies me carefully.

"Are you alright?" They are the first words she's spoken to me. They are full of concern.

I turn to stare again at the fallen machine. I point. "What is that?"

Her eyes cloud again. She hesitates before she answers. "It was called the Behemoth," she says.

The name rings some deep drowned bell. I try to put a finger on the swirl of emotions. Something is wrong with my memory. Is that what's upsetting me?

The Behemoth. I shudder. "That sounds like the name of a monster."

She nods. "It could be." Then, after a hesitation. "But it was a savior, too." She smiles suddenly, and it strikes me that it is a very pretty smile. "It could do terrible things, but it was beautiful when it did them." A second smile. "When it fought, it always reminded me of Bruce Lee."

I don't recognize the name. "Who's that?"

Another smile. *Like the sun through clouds*, I think. She lets go of my head, takes my hand instead. "Why don't you come with me," she says, "and let me show you?"

THE GREATEST HUNGER

Jaym Gates

DERECHO BACKS INTO HER CORNER and huffs, watching her opponent. I can feel her assessing its weaknesses, the deep gashes on its pale, dripping belly, the broken antler. Its other antler is still proud, and streaked with Derecho's red blood, but its intestines must be barely held in. A little green blood trickles down a tusk, into her mouth, and her deep-set eyes gleam ruby under the bright lights, vivid against her black hide.

I set my jaw against a rash move—Derecho is too expensive to risk in a kamikaze, blood and glory run—and gather her focus. Time to kill.

I STILL REMEMBER THE NIGHT this mess started. Las Vegas. New Year's Eve. 1946. The night was desert-cold, a thin dusting of snow on the ground. The city was on watch, waiting to see if the monster that had wrecked Reno was on its way north. I was huddled in a doorway in a bad section of town, trying to keep warm and out of sight.

It was a strange new world we entered when the war finally ended.

Hiroshima and Nagasaki had been the first salvos, a few months before, the beginning of the end. For a while, everyone thought it was over. But that was just the beginning. Project Manhattan

Illustration by **ROBERT ELROD**

had been compromised so quietly that no one even knew it…until London, Washington D.C, Berlin, and Rome exploded in great gouts of cancerous fire.

We never figured out who was behind it, but it put an end to the aggression. Stunned, horrified, desperate, we turned our eyes inward to repair our ruined world. We found a fragile peace, dependent on depleted resources as much as brotherly love. We were still living under the terror of nuclear fallout, waiting for winds to shift or another mysterious strike. An air of hysterical hedonism clung to everyone, from New York to Tokyo to Johannesburg. The Roaring 20s looked like a pale omen of the Raging 50s, silky and gilded compared to the macabre glory of now.

And then, in a final, crushing twist of fate, the monsters came. Drawn by the blood and death and war, birthed by unholy science, they fell from the skies and rose from the seas, unearthed themselves from ancient caverns and crept out of dark forests. We lost almost as many souls to them as to the war, and we quickly learned the fear and respect our ancestors accorded the unknown.

The first ones were small and warped, more a danger to individuals than cities. These, we could blame on the bombs. But they got bigger, and science was suddenly at a loss. We knew we had a problem when something huge and tentacled rose from the sea and stormed through Boston. (Maybe Lovecraft was prophetic, if a little geographically-challenged.)

Our communications were rebuilding slowly, so it took us a little while to find out we weren't the only ones. A monstrous reptile had rampaged through Tokyo. A hundred-foot anaconda was killed in Rio. A six-legged water buffalo…thing…was being butchered for its meat after taking out nearly half of Johannesburg's business district. Japan called them *Kaiju*. We called them monsters.

Being American, we also called them profit. Even nuclear winter couldn't take that away from us. The warlords, coal kings, industrial princes, and oil barons had more money than they could burn. They paid big game hunters to lead expeditions to bag the biggest trophies in the world, but a house could only hold so many of those.

John Goodnight, heir to a vast silver fortune, financed the first Blood Pits. Four millionaires paid hunters to live-capture the biggest Kaiju they could get their hands on, and pitted the four against each other. The event raised millions of dollars, and Goodnight more than recovered his investment. The next year, Japan had its own Kaiju Wars, supposedly also financed by Goodnight, who had bought heavily into the decimated nation.

That night in Las Vegas, I proved that some of us had been ruptured in ways you couldn't see.

A horn wailed from the police department. It used to be there to warn us about incoming bombers—not that any ever came near Vegas, but you couldn't be careful enough. This time, it was warning of a bigger threat. Take cover. Bombs don't hunt. Bombers screamed overhead, the regional guard heading to intercept the beast.

When the dying Hellcat clawed its way into Las Vegas, her body riddled with bullets and missiles, I didn't have anywhere, or any will, to run. Her yellow eyes, mad with pain and fury, glared down at me, ready to inflict some of her suffering on the creatures who had caused it. I thought she was the most beautiful creature I'd ever seen, and I cried for her pain.

I don't know how, but I talked to her, and she understood. Laid down right beside me, her dying breaths blowing my dirty hair aside, and passed away next to me. They found me with my face buried in her blood-matted fur, sobbing.

The hospital patched me up, but within twenty-four hours, I was back on the street, hiding from the newfound celebrity. The bounty hunters found me less than a week later, and only chance threw me into gentler arms, saved me from government interest. Nikolai Kuznetsov paid over two hundred thousand dollars for me, and put me in the arena with his beast, the Drakon, and won the

Blood Pits. Charles Goodnight's agent, Mason Kincaid, bought me for two million, two years ago, to handle Derecho. We're undefeated.

The Blue Hurricane was the first celebrity Kaiju. Derecho, eight Blood Pits removed from her predecessor, is the latest.

Derecho's hooves shred the hard-packed earth as she charges her victim. The crowd is deathly silent as the slime-thing spits poisonous goo, but it doesn't slow Derecho a bit, and her gleaming tusks bite deep into the thing's belly, ripping it open. Steaming green guts gush to the arena floor, and Derecho roars her victory.

BACK IN THE CATACOMBS—THE Goodnight Arena's monster-holding area—Derecho slumps to the straw with a weary sigh. Whatever her opponent spat was caustic, and she has burns all over her back and haunches. I can feel her pain like a vague burning at the back of my mind, and it annoys me. The monsters are dangerous, but there is no need to make them suffer for our enjoyment.

I have two boys helping me, scarred young street rats who will risk their lives for a warm meal and a roof over their heads. They already have the tub of ointment waiting, painter's poles for the hard-to-reach areas, and softer brushes to clean the wounds. I put my hand on Derecho's snout and lull her into complacence while the boys start cleaning and mending.

I am exhausted when I leave her, wracked with pain and the ashy collapse of adrenaline. I don't know how many more of these fights I have in me. She may be a beast, slow and dull, clouded with the fumes of rage, but how much of that is her captivity, her fear? And, too, there is the darker bitterness against those who sit in their boxes and feed on the misery below, the slow wearing of their bloodthirsty glee.

I am not so far removed from the creatures I shepherd. I didn't come from wealth, didn't learn fine manners. I taught myself to read, to write. I have no grace, no charm, no beauty worth a man's money. No gifts to buy myself out of their pits. Would they revel in my pain, too, if my mutations were visible? Treat me like the gladiators of Rome, goading me with cattle prods and whips, feeding me the barely-dead meat of my horrible cousins?

Why do I ask myself these questions? I am certainly too tired.

"What do monsters fear?" my captor asked me, the night before he sold me to Kusnetsov. We were sitting in a seedy motel room, eating cheap take-out food with lukewarm beer. He had been one of Hellcat's hunters, the first to see me, and he'd saved me from the bounty hunters. My gifts didn't work on him, and I was tired of running. It was a relief to be sitting there, eating my first real meal since the hospital. "How do you make them obey you?"

I didn't know. I still don't, but maybe I am starting to understand.

The door to my hotel room is locked, but I can smell him, waiting. A monster waits for me, a monster I have called, wished for, lusted after, invited through my door. He knows what I am, and does not fear me. There is comfort in that.

I am still locking the door behind me when his breath touches my neck.

THE NEXT DAY, HER BURNS freshly crusted with scabs and healing skin, Derecho paces restlessly in her huge pen. She stops, occasionally, to root through the dirt with her tusks, some dim, racial memory maybe of when her kind ate roots and leaves. Dust clings to the drying blood along her mouth. I hope they did not feed her yesterday's kill, it was poisoned beyond use, but they do not always have sense. If she falls ill, I will flay their minds myself. Derecho has become precious to me.

I let myself into her cage, and she comes to me, snuffling concern. The top of my head comes barely to her knee, yet she comes to me and lowers her giant's head to look me in the eye. I hope no one is watching, it should not be known that the animals love, not fear, me.

She thinks she is protecting me, a mother sow defending her child.

A few minutes to calm her, then it is time to gild myself in my garish costume—the purple and gold of Goodnight Industrial, low-cut and tasteless—to take my place beside the other Shepherd. I don't even know who we're fighting. I had more important things to think about last night.

My assistant kneels in front of me to begin buttoning my dress and, for a moment, I am overcome with a memory of the night before. The bruises on my neck ache, although they don't show, and my back aches with the weight of the monster I called.

He is like me, invisible in his mutations. If the people around us knew, would they pick up torches and pitchforks?

I was the first of many, but we are sheep in wolves' clothing, as unlike the others as they are unlike the Silent. (We call them that, because they have no voice except the crude one in their throats, ungainly and unlovely, unlike the smooth-flowing stream of our own communication.)

The assistant finishes the last button and crisply adjusts the gold lace over my breasts, lays the heavy gold-and-amethyst chain of Bond around my neck. It is a circus, and I am the invisible ringmaster, dressed the part of the clown.

The contempt in the girl's eyes is palpable, and I nearly reach into her to squeeze that smug superiority out of her, but the crowd roars, and I can feel Derecho's fear seeping into me.

Of course they would pick up pitchforks and torches if they knew about me. After all, they burned my kind in the Middle Ages, didn't they?

And those unfortunates couldn't do half of what I can barely refrain from doing with every breath.

ANOTHER BATTLE, NEARLY OVER.

This Shepherd was too weak to repel me, and as Derecho savaged the hurtful thing, I toyed with him. He is a Balm, meant to keep his charge passive. He doesn't understand the sharp, bitter joy of killing, but he watched his beast's desperate battle with a half-smile, enjoying the pain it suffered, and so I took his limp little mind in hand and chained him to his beast while Derecho broke its legs, bringing it to the ground.

His scream should not have pleased me so much. I was not wounded enough last night, not brought to heel. I hope it is that, rather than my greater fear that my bloodlust is growing, that I will lose myself in the need for death. There is too much to do still, too many things to protect, too many delicate manipulations necessary.

And Shepherds die all the time. They are weak. The weak do not deserve to live.

Derecho crushes the other beast's chest, and the joy of the Shepherd's death tears through me like an orgasm.

AGAIN, I HAVE BARELY CLOSED the door before rough hands have locked my wrists in front of me.

"You killed him." His breath is hot and dry. He is not as huge as my young memories painted him, but his compact power easily dwarfs my wiry strength. Struggle is pointless. "You killed the Shepherd for pleasure. You are losing control."

Reflexively, I poke at his mind, try to prod him into the actions I want, but I fail, as always. Somehow, I cannot get into his soul to twist and tear and destroy. I have never met another—man, beast, or monster—capable of withstanding me. He is my refuge, the one who knows what I am, who can stop me if I can't stop myself. He kept me safe from the bounty hunters that night in Vegas, delivered me safe to a place that would protect me for my monetary value, if nothing else, and I still sometimes indulge myself in his protection.

I cannot touch his mind, but he can pull my soul out and sate it with violence and the knife-edged pleasure of being helpless again, of not worrying over the powerless, deadly beasts who speak in my dreams every time I sleep.

IT IS THE SEMI-FINALS. MY costume is more transparent than before, the thin silks clinging to my legs, heavy with golden beads that provide more concealment than the cloth. I am maskless, a brag by the barons that they have the money to filter the air sufficiently, even with all these people. I loathe these costumes, flimsy and fragile, and expensive.

I am a free woman in name, but I would never have achieved that if I hadn't struck a deal with Goodnight Industrial: freedom in name, so long as I signed away my life in service to their sport. They couldn't breed or sell me, but neither could I leave, and I could never work for anyone else even if the Goodnights retired me.

It isn't much but it is better than many people have, these days, regardless of skin color or gender.

I should have specified the right to choose my own costumes.

Derecho is wearying. She will have a full day between this bout and the next—there is no question that we will win and move on to the finals, Goodnight Industrial doesn't keep me for nothing—but she must have some rest.

Derecho's tusks will be gilded on Saturday, for the finals, but today, they gleam a soft, waxen cream under the harsh lights. We groomed her well, and showed her affection, bolstered her flagging spirits. She does not understand, but she will fight.

Her opponent is alien, I'm sure of it. I haven't seen her, but in my head, she's sleek and sharp as a razorblade. Doesn't need a Shepherd, probably can't actually be held by one but restrains herself so she can torment him. Poor kid. He is real proud of himself, how easily he tamed her when she was found. Sociopathic fuck. Just waiting for him to get boring. The doctors probably can't explain what is eating his body and mind, turning him into a puppet. Not all monsters are worthy of my pity, but I do appreciate the irony. I will not abide competition though, and this one…

…this one's angular white head flies across the arena, torn whole from her neck. Derecho is wounded, badly, raining blood and panting in exhaustion, but I am glad of her victory. The alien beast is not something I want in my head anymore.

I finger the chain around my neck, disguising my disgust as nerves. Two more days. One more fight.

"YOU SHOULD BE COMMITTED."

My punished body is limp and quieted, but he has not, for some reason, left. We have played this deadly game for four years, since I was old enough to want a man in my bed, and he has always left as soon as possible.

"Whatever are you talking about, Hunter?" I stretch languidly, but he growls and grabs my jaw, dragging me up face him.

"I hate this world as much as you do, but you are mad to think you can change it."

Ahh. That. The playfulness flees, bloodlust nibbling the corners of my mind again.

In the aftermath of the apocalypse, those few fortunates who maintained control of the most necessary resources—oil, steel, guns, copper, food—leveraged their power to turn themselves into fat parasites on the broken backs of humanity. I'd lost count of how many soldiers I saw wandering the streets those few times I was allowed out, missing arms, legs, souls. How many broken hovels housed how many families, how many slaves powered the dawning age.

"It is a madness worth indulging, if it changes."

"You would alert them that our kind exists."

"Maybe that's the plan. We've hidden behind our cousins long enough, made them suffer while we stayed safe. We're not much better than the barons."

His powerful hand tightens even more. He is making speech difficult. "It wouldn't end for them, just because you put us in harm's way. You think you'd be a free woman if they knew? Think you'd have those beautiful gowns and the luxury of choosing your bedmate?"

I envy my bestial cousins. Some of them can spit fire, and I would dearly love to melt him right now. "Maybe they won't be around to threaten us."

I beat my fist into the bed and sit up, heat burning in my eyes. "I *hate* this life, hate making the beasts kill and die for someone's momentary pleasure."

He holds me for a minute longer, before pulling me into his lap and kissing me deeply. "What can I do?"

MY GOWN TODAY IS CLOTH-OF-GOLD in an outlandish style, the sheer bodice beaded with purple and pearl, my hair caught in a net of gold wire, a filigree of gold covering my face. The weather reports are good, the wind blowing any contamination away from us. Today only, the roof will be drawn back, the public will be welcomed into the cheap seats, and I will shine in the hot sun like the vengeful goddess I am. My hunter stands in the shadows, protecting me in case I miss a few dangers, ready to bolster me if I encounter unexpected resistance. He is no longer my escape, but my consort and right hand. He fears that I am not prepared for what I will unleash, but he will stand with me.

Derecho senses my turmoil. Her tusks gleam as brightly as my dress, her little eyes squinting, dazzled by the sun she hasn't seen since her capture. Perhaps she knows that she will not be the one on display today.

The band is lively, the crowds eager to see the monsters. Charlie Goodnight takes my hand and leads me onto the platform, facing the crowd, and introduces me. His smart cream suit and burgundy ascot do nothing for his doughy face, and I can only imagine how awful our costumes must look next to my fellow Shepherd, who wears the yellow and green of Hercules Oil.

I am briefly annoyed, as Melusine, the HO monster, is a beautiful, draconian beast, but devilishly hard to manage, as I recall. I would have preferred Emma Innismoth's privately-owned beast, a tentacled, horrific monstrosity who struck fear into human and monster alike, but was relatively stupid and tractable. Ah, well. Melusine's beauty next to Derecho's terrible, raw strength would play well on the news, when my plan was finished, and I had handled worse.

The brass band strikes up, the introductions must be done. I am already deep in the other Shepherd's head, although she doesn't seem to know it yet. I am similarly curled beneath the waking minds of every luminary in the crowd. The commoners may or may not survive, I really don't care. It is the bright and beautiful I will collect today. Peasants die all the time. I should know, I was one. I would be sorry for them, but they had chosen to be here, to revel in the sickness.

"What do monsters fear?" my hunter asked me that day, sitting next to me in Nikolai's office. My lip had been split a few days, and was oozing again, and he'd wiped it away, gently, and given me water. I realize now that he wasn't much older than I was, making a living, hiding as best he could in plain sight, the hunted masquerading as the Hunter, comforting the monstrous queen in the garb of the slave. Looking back, I can appreciate what brought us together.

"Monsters fear nothing," I'd said, but now I knew better.

The stage is set. I step away from Charlie, a strange, thrilling certainty stringing through me.

They fear the greater evil, and today, that evil is not tentacled horror from the depths, or blood-stained hell-pig, or beautiful, mythological monster.

In each mind, I stretch. This is the first time I have unfurled my full power. Even I do not know what I am capable of, or what other monsters are hiding in plain sight. I relish the possibilities.

Monsters fear waking to something worse leaning over their beds, reaching from between the stairs to grasp their ankles, pulling that one critical tile from their empire.

They struggle, no more to my power than wiggling worms on

a hook. One by one, they rise from their seats. Melusine's handler opens the cage door, as does Derecho's. Melusine will not hold for long, she is slippery and fractious. Derecho is curious, the fog of battle cleared from her mind. This is what I was made for.

Perhaps it is the most fearful who scrabble the most power to themselves, creating shells and buttressed walls of influence and wealth. Perhaps they forget that this armor is a thing outside themselves, but they never forget that empty space just a breath below their feet.

I puppet-march the kings and queens of the world to the killing floor for my kindred to feed on, and in their blood is painted retribution, and revolution.

Monsters fear what we all fear: that someday, they will find that they are not the sharpest teeth, the greatest hunger, the most dreadful nightmare.

DEVIL'S CAP BRAWL

EDWARD M. ERDELAC

:: A 'Dead West' short story

JOE BLAS WAS SO CALLED because his papist upbringing in Drom, County Tipperary, had given him a knack for devising the most ingenious blasphemies anyone on either side of the Sierras had ever heard.

He blew hot air into the cold red palms of his hands and turned that coarse and inventive tongue against Chow Lan, the agent for the forty coolies under his charge.

"Jesus Christ's holey hands an' feet! What d'you mean they're scared to blast? We've blown though every goddamned cliff and mountain since Dutch Flat with no issue. What's different about this one?"

Chow Lan's job was to act as liaison between the red-in-the-face Irish riding boss and his aforementioned forty countrymen, who made up the spearhead of the work gang Charles Crocker had hired on to get the Central Pacific Railroad into Utah by 1867. He divvied up their paychecks, keeping a customary cut of it for himself, placed orders with the *gwailo* agent for suitable foodstuffs for their cook, and voiced employee concerns when the situation arose.

Illustration by **CHUCK LUKACS**

"Hesutu say mountain home to devil. He say brasting powder free devil. Coolies scared. Say no brast."

Joe slapped his hat down on his knee.

"That goddamned Indian."

Hesutu was a halfbreed Shoshone and Miwok who had signed on with them six weeks ago along with a gaggle of Paiutes, specially hired to drive a ten-yoke team of oxen up to the camp. To avoid the troubles their Union Pacific cousins had been having with the Sioux and the Cheyenne, Strobridge, the superintendent of the CP, had signed treaties with the local Sierra tribes and offered them all jobs. Males *and* females had answered the call.

Though the Celestials were diligent, they were superstitious beasties, even requiring their own joss house in camp with a heathen priest on duty. Joe had found the Indians liked to sport with them from time to time. One joker of a Paiute had convinced the Celestials that a dragon lived in the high country, and they had lost a day convincing them there wasn't any such thing. Hesutu was a name that had come up again and again in the past few days.

"Look," said Joe, rubbing his patchy jaw in exasperation. "You tell them Hesutu talks with a forked tongue, that red serpent. Tell them they better get to work or I'll send the whole lot of 'em hoofin' like sorefooted Israelites back to Sacramento through the snow."

"I tell, but they no listen," Chow Lan said.

Joe sighed. He snatched his brass speaking trumpet off the table and slapped his hat back on his head. He shoved Chow Lan aside and went out into the cold air.

They were fifteen miles west of Cisco, high up in the Sierras. Last year they'd been delayed in blasting by an early snow. Word had come down to his lowly ear from Charles Crocker himself; no such setbacks this time around. The line was to be open from Sacramento to Cisco by December and to the far end of Devil's Cap summit by the same time next year. They had three and half months to get there, and neither mountain nor the buckskin hoodoo tales of any damned Indian was to retard their progress.

Joe saw the young Chinee priest, barefoot in the snow, doing the same weird, slow dance he did every morning outside the crude joss house. He looked like an only child play fighting, but underwater, turning and bending, throwing an occasional sluggish punch or a ridiculously high kick. Only his queue-less, shaven head distinguished him as a priest; he wore the same patchy blue loose clothes all the coolies wore. There was an air of ease and self-assurance about him that annoyed Joe, but he wasn't some fat, soft handed parson. He did his fair share of work. He brewed tea for the workers all day, kept the big forty gallon whiskey barrel the men drank from brimming, and was even known to fill in for a man struck sick on the gangs now and again, so he wouldn't lose his place. The heathens respected him, bowing to him when they saw him pass, and at night he directed their prayers up to Buddha or wherever with his droning chants. Mainly, he stayed quiet and out of the way, which Joe liked. He'd been at Wilson's Ranch when they'd arrived at the beginning of the year and had volunteered with them, solely to see to their spiritual wellbeing. He figured the priest had some angle on the side, fleecing the coolies out of their fantan money, or dealing opium, though he had never seen him pass the collection plate.

It was a two hundred foot walk through a tunnel of snow from the camp to the work gang. Walking that tunnel made Joe nervous. Due to the blasting, snowslides were not infrequent, and had carried off whole gangs of men. In most cases their bodies hadn't been found. The avalanche that claimed them also made their only graves.

The railway tunnel through the bare granite peak called Devil's Cap was being assaulted from four points. Two teams of thirty men each worked simultaneously from the east and west, and another pair from the center of the mountain itself. They'd sunk a shaft midway through and lowered the Celestials in, but the hand derrick used to hoist the rubble out had finally failed and they'd had to halt the center work for about five weeks while a twelve ton steam engine, the Old Judah, and its tender, were stripped of their wheels and hauled up the mountainside from the railhead at Gold Run by the Indians and oxen. They'd finally settled the engine down over the shaft last week, and built a sturdy wooden enclosure over it to hold back the snow.

Yet the 440 engine was not chugging along. There was no ringing of chisels and hammers, no intermittent, muffled explosions, no nothing.

Tom Tolliver and a couple of the Paiutes who ran the engine were standing expectantly outside the enclosure, smoking. All the west end tunnel coolies were milling around chattering like it was tea time.

"What'n the name of the Blessed Virgin's holy hymen are you yellow niggers doin' standin' around?" Joe roared through the speaking trumpet when he got in their midst, Chow Lan running alongside him. "Get to work!"

There was a lot of muttering and head shaking, a lot of heads turning towards where some of the Indians, too, were standing around.

"Where'n the hell's Hesutu?" Joe Blas demanded.

He came forward at the mention of his name, a lanky, long haired redskin with a wispy mustache, hide boots and a knife through his belt, a big black hat pulled low over his eyes.

"Here, boss."

"Alright now, boyo," Joe Blas said lowly. "'You the one been fillin' these heathens' ears with a lot of guff about the devil bein' in the center of that grand high rock?"

"I didn't say no such thing, boss," said Hesutu, smiling with his dark eyes.

Joe looked back at Chow Lan, who shrugged and adjusted his spectacles.

"That what *they* tell me!" he protested, encompassing the crowd of Chinamen with a sweep of his arm.

"I didn't say it was the devil," amended Hesutu. "What I said was, Dzoavits is in there."

"What?"

"Dzoavits," Hesutu said again. "It's like a giant. Eats babies. But don't make no mistake, you all keep breakin' up Dzoavits' mountain, he'll come out and eat you too. He ain't particular, what I hear."

"What are you on about?"

"Some say it was always there, some say it fell from the sky. It's big enough to blot out the sun. It went after Dove and her children in the old times, but Badger dug a hole, and tricked Dzoavits into it. Then Dove threw hot rocks down over the hole and trapped him inside. It was up there," he said, pointing to the rise on which sat the snow covered building housing Old Judah. That's why they call this place Devil's Cap. He's been in there since."

Joe Blas bunched and unbunched his fists at his sides. It was all he could do not to grab up this crazy Indian and drown him like a kitten in the Celestials' tea barrel.

"Boyo," he said through his teeth, "you're gonna stop talkin' this bollocks in front of my coolies, or so help me I'm going to boot your red arse into the happy huntin' ground."

"Can't you feel it, white man?" Hesutu asked, staring at the summit. "At night, when you're sleepin' in the shadow of that rock? Can't you feel it watchin' you?"

Joe Blas tucked himself in with a bottle of tarantula juice every night. His own mother's shade could stand waling at the foot of his bed until the break of dawn and he'd snore through it. But he was no believer in bugaboos. He had turned his back on all such nonsense when the English had taken his father's farm and the old man had died on a boat bound for New York City. There was no God but what the priests made up to fill their coffers.

"Skipper Noah's whiskey dick, man! The only eyes I feel at night are those of Boss Crocker in Sacramento, waitin' for us to bust through the other side of that damned rock. Now, will you tell these gullible sonsabitches the truth, or is it a walk over the rocks to Coburn Station you'll be wantin?"

Hesutu chewed his lips a minute before answering.

"If you aim to continue along your course, then I b'lieve I'll take my leave. Won't no place be far enough way from here once you let that thing loose. You take my advice, dig over t'the north instead, through Donner's summit."

"Oh so it's a surveyor you are now, eh?" He blew up at last, hollering through the megaphone in the Indian's face. "You get the fuck down off my mountain, chief, or I'll club you like Sebastian!"

Hesutu held up his hands and walked away, shaking his head.

"Alright, boss. But you stay here, you're gonna get swallered up like Jonah."

Joe turned to the gathered Chinese, all of them huddled together and whispering.

"Shut your gobs, you noodle suckin' yellow pagans!" he hollered through his speaking trumpet, stomping through their midst and clambering up on a boulder to shout down at them good and proper. "Chow Lan tells me you won't work because you're afraid. Don't fear any devil in that mountain, fear me. You want to bring your yellow wives and your little slant-eyed nippers over here from the old country? Well, you know that takes money. Each of you has a contract with the Central Pacific Railroad at twenty eight dollars a month. Twenty eight dollars! Can you make that washing dishes back in San Francisco, or sweeping up the Five Star Saloon down in Dutch Flat? How old will your children be by the time you save enough money shoveling shite? Will they remember your ugly faces? Will your wives? How long before they let some other opium smoker in to buck their sideways cocktroughs? You want to see your kith and kin, see the other side of that rock. If not, pack up your stinkin' cuttlefish and your bamboo shoots and your goddamned piss warm tea and point your squinty faces west, because that's all you'll be taking with you. I don't pay any man till the job's done."

One man, Lo Shu, stepped up, scowling.

"We work long time a'ready! We earn—"

"You've earned nothing, you little squint! Get back in line or I'll fetch your skull so grand a clout you'll forget your father's name, if you ever knew it to begin with. I'll say it again, and slowly so's it'll penetrate your muley heads. No work-ee no money. Savvy that?"

This set up a frenzy of protests from the men, but again Joe shouted them down.

"Read your contracts, you goddamned ignoramuses. Or get Chow Lan to read 'em if you can't or don't believe me."

Some grabbed Chow Lan by the shirt front and shouted questions at him, and after a bit he explained to them that yes, the *gwailo* was correct. They were contracted for the end of the job. The only way to leave early with a paycheck was to lose a limb.

"Now you know where you stand?" Joe yelled, when Chow Lan had finished his spiel. "Reform your gangs and get to work, and no more of this heathen tripe about monsters and devils."

The Chinamen grumbled and scowled, but after lingering, they grudgingly went off to their respective jobs.

Joe Blas stood on the rock with his hands on his belt until the last of them had climbed up to the summit and Tolliver signaled to him and went inside the engine house. A minute later Old Judah wheezed to life. The sharp whistle signaled the delayed start of the work day.

The sun peaked behind Devil's Cap and shone like a halo, causing Joe to look away, eyes watering. He reached into his coat pocket and took a pull of firewater, shivered and spat.

IN AN HOUR THE GANGS were in full swing, hammering at the rock, filling it with powder, and blowing holes as if Hesutu's talk had been a bad dream. Joe wasn't surprised. He knew money dispelled more demons than holy water and crucifixes.

The work was slow and tedious. They could expect to get about seven inches a day all in all if they kept it safe, eight if Joe booted their arses a bit. But the latter usually led to blown off fingers and worse. The Indians and the whites wouldn't dangle in a basket over a cliff face with a barrel of blasting powder, and he didn't like to waste Chinamen. If they fell behind, of course, they were a commodity to be spent. Blasting could be a dicey business, but he had never lost a white man yet, although admittedly the company didn't count how many Honest Johns had gone to China feet first.

There was a subterranean explosion, the summit gang blasting in the center shaft. The priest came out of the snow tunnel, a bamboo pole over one of his sturdy shoulders, a powder keg filled with fresh tea bouncing on either end.

Joe watched the priest set down his burden, lift the lid off the big communal tea barrel, and pour the steaming new stuff in.

"Hey, Priest!" Joe called, since he had never learned the man's name.

The priest replaced the lid of the barrel, picked up his pole and the empty kegs, and came over.

"You speak-ee English, yeah?"

The priest nodded.

Joe pursed his lips. He knew that one.

"That ain't no answer. Yes or no?"

"I speak English," the priest said, with only a faint accent.

Joe raised his eyebrows.

"I've known priests. Lots in my day. But you ain't like them. You don't ask for nothin.' You don't tithe, you do a fair bit of work around here, free of charge. So what the hell kinda man are you?"

The priest shrugged. "Just a man, like you."

Joe rankled. "Like me? Mary Magdalene's festerin' cunt, you are. What's your angle, Priest? I can't figure it."

"Angle?"

"What're you doin' here?"

The priest looked puzzled. "I am working. Serving, when I can."

"Servin' who?"

"Them," he said, glancing at the coolies lining up for fresh tea. He turned back to Joe. "You."

Joe snorted. "What the hell could you do for me? And why?"

"If we do not take care of each other, who will?"

"Who said that? Buddha?"

The priest nodded.

Joe spat in the snow. "And that's the shite you tell these coolies to keep 'em in line?"

"I don't understand."

"Religion. It ain't nothin' but a means of controllin' the poor and ignorant. And who's poorer or more ignorant than them pigtails, bustin' their scrawny arses for twenty eight dollars a month."

"How much do you bust your arse for a month, Boss Joe?" the priest asked.

Joe bristled. "That ain't none of your affair, boyo. I'm a free man with no ties. I can leave anytime I want to. I'm beholden to neither man nor God, no, nor Buddha neither. I walk me own road."

"One path is better than no path, but the right path is best of all," said the priest.

"And you figure what you preach is the right path. Aha! Now you're talkin' like a priest."

The priest smiled thinly and bowed. "Please excuse me. I have work to do," he said.

Joe grinned. "Sure, go ahead. I respect a man who knows when he's beat."

"To win a thousand battles is good, but to win one battle over ourselves is great," said the priest, bowing again before turning to go.

Joe frowned. What the hell did that mean? He didn't know just why had taken a sudden interest in the priest. Boredom maybe. All his minor curiosity fled his mind when the door to the engine house atop the summit flung open and Tolliver stumbled out, drenched in blood and black with powder, a plume of smoke billowing out behind him.

He nearly fell down the mountain, but one of the Paiutes rushed out and caught him.

"Hey boss!" the Indian yelled.

Joe cussed and trudged up the incline. He heard a crash behind him and all of a sudden the Chinese priest was climbing alongside him. Halfway up the top, the ground shook hard and rumbled. A pile of loose rocks tumbled free and one struck Joe bloody in the head. The priest grabbed his shirt and kept him from falling. For nearly a full minute they hugged the rock, watching the trees sway and shed snow down on them. It was like gripping a bull trying to shake them loose.

"Earthquake!" he managed to yell.

Below, the coolies working the west tunnel ran into the open shouting, dirt and rubble sliding from their shoulders.

Bushy bearded Jesus, he had never felt one *this* bad. It seemed like it would never end. He glanced up and saw the wood enclosure trembling atop the summit. His heart sank when he heard a crack and saw part of the roof shift. The Paiutes spilled out and fell to their bellies just as the roof collapsed inward, the whole structure crashing flat over the engine and the tender. Debris slid down the embankment, carrying a couple screaming Paiutes with it.

Joe put his head down and quietly willed the engine not to fall from the mountain. Christ's bloody breechclout, they would be here another year if they lost it. What would he tell Crocker? He had talked big to the priest about being footloose and fancy free. Damn if it didn't look like he really would be. Sure, he'd get the blame, even for an earthquake. And Crocker would put some other mick in his place. It'd be back to Fisherman's Wharf for him, bareknuckle fighting, spittin' teeth, and pissin' blood and whiskey till a good job came his way again, if it ever did.

He looked over at the priest, but he was gone. Fallen or carried off by a boulder or bit of rubble, no doubt. But no, Joe saw him above then, springing nimble as a goat from rock to rock, even in the midst of the shaking, making his way up to the summit.

Joe held on for dear life, and watched as the priest reached Tolliver where the Paiute had laid him when the shaking had started. He lifted the bloody man up in his arms and hurled himself over the edge like a madman. But instead of tumbling to his death, he skipped lightly till he reached the bottom of the hill, and then knelt there over Tolliver, shielding him from falling rocks with his own body.

No priest Joe had ever seen was like that.

The shaking stopped, and he looked up at the pile of wood and snow that once covered the engine, and saw Old Judah's smokestack poking through.

"Well thank Missus Lot's salt tits for that!" he exclaimed.

Just then something burst from the side of the rock to his immediate left. It looked like a huge, mossy mass of tendril roots.

Joe was so surprised he relaxed his grip on the stone and fell backwards.

Well, that's the end of me, he thought, as he plummeted into the open air. He supposed he would land on that rock he had been standing on before, and be broken in two. If he was lucky, he might squash a Chinaman and be saved.

But neither happened.

Instead, he felt a dull impact on his upper back and behind his knees, and found himself sagging in the surprisingly hard, strong arms of the priest like a suckling baby.

He looked at the priest in surprise, and noticed the inside of his forearms were tattooed…no, not tattooed. There were designs branded on his skin, puffy scars in the shape of a fanciful Oriental dragon on his right arm, and a tiger on his left.

He put down his feet.

"Ta, boyo," Joe muttered.

But the priest wasn't looking at him. No one was. The coolies and the Indians were uniformly staring wide eyed up at the top of Devil's Cap.

The mass of tangled roots that had surprised Joe were moving, waggling like great knotty, long nailed fingers.

Because that's what they were.

He didn't want to believe it, but when the splayed things shot further out causing the rock to crack and crumble, they were on the end of an immensely long, muscular arm, shaggy with string grey hair stained brown by the dirt.

The top of Devil's Cap *moved*. It rose and fell once, like something beneath were testing the weight, then it swelled again, enough to tip Old Judah and its tender off the slope at last. The noise of all that iron and steel rolling down was a terrible cacophony, and a few men were caught up in it and smashed flat.

Something burst through the snowy cap...no, not something. What had Hesutu called it?

Dzoavits.

It erupted from the stone, doing to Devil's Cap in seven seconds what it would have taken another eleven months for them to do with hand drills and blasting powder.

It was immense. At least a hundred and fifty feet tall. Another arm punched through the side of the rock and it extricated itself from the encasing rock like a fat man wriggling out of a barrel. It was moundish, with a huge hairy hump between its muscled shoulders, covered with spiky, quartz-like protuberances of a muddy hue that poked through its dirty grey-black hair. In the center of its chest was a hint of a head, framed by long, scraggly hair. There was an overlarge disapproving mouth that stretched almost from shoulder to shoulder, and was hung with fleshy lips and shot through with a row of yellow, serrated shark teeth. Above that maw, two bulging red eyes glowed. The thing opened its mouth, took its first cold breath of fresh air in God only knew how long, and let out a terrifying, protracted howl, which washed over them in a wave that drove them all physically back in horror.

Rocks cascading off its body, it pulled itself free of its prison, revealing a pair of strange, spindly, kangaroo-like legs that ended in long grasping black talons. It seemed to rest on its massive arms, and use them for locomotion, like a great gorilla, or a man with withered legs.

The horrible thing perched atop the ruins of Devil's Cap and surveyed the countryside, a newly emerged monarch. It sucked the air with its ponderous lungs and regarded the milling men below.

Joe tried to run, and tripped over Chow Lan, who had fallen sprawling in the snow and was groping for his spectacles. The Chinese and Indians were in full route, except for the priest, who knelt beside Tolliver, yelling in Chinese at the men who passed, apparently urging them to take him with them.

Joe heard gunshots, and looked over. Several of the Indians and white men in the camp had seen the thing and had emerged from the snow tunnel. They were firing at it with shotguns and muskets. Joe almost laughed as he scrabbled to his feet.

But before he could run, the priest grabbed a hold of his sleeve.

"You must take Boss Tom with you," said the priest.

"Let go of me, you bloody monkey!" Joe shrieked and swung at him.

It was an old prizefighter's instinctual blow, the kind that would have knocked an untrained man unconscious had it landed. But the priest did something peculiar with his free hand, and Joe's punch seemed to slide uselessly down his branded arm. Then the smaller man's two fingers pinched Joe's wrist and twisted. The pain was so intense Joe gasped and fell to his knees, all thought of struggle gone.

He found himself face to face with Tolliver, laying nearby. The man was a black and bloody mess. He must have been caught in the explosion Joe had heard earlier, the one that had awakened this thing. He had known Tolliver back when Irish muscle had done the backbreaking work, not Chinese. They had come up together. He felt ashamed at having tried to abandon him.

But they were all dead men anyhow, in the face of this thing from the pit of Hell.

"Chow Lan!" the priest yelled. "Help him!"

"Where can we go?" Chow Lan yelled, having fitted his glasses back on his nose. One lens looked like a spiderweb.

The priest looked about for a moment, then pointed to the shallow western tunnel in the base of Devil's Cap which the terrified coolies had abandoned.

He pointed.

Joe looked up as a massive shadow fell across the entire area. The air grew chill. The sky was dark.

Then were was a tremendous impact that knocked Chow Lan to the ground and sent the snow and the loose stones hovering for a surreal moment before everything crashed back down.

The thing had leapt from the summit and landed behind them.

Joe watched as it scooped up a fistful of the fleeing workmen. He saw dozens of men flailing between its huge ruddy fingers and heard their screams as it stuffed them hungrily into its mouth.

"Let me go!" Joe yelled.

"You will help Boss Tom?"

Joe nodded, exhaling as the pressure on his wrist disappeared.

"Go then," the priest ordered, and to Joe's surprise, he began to strip away his shirt and pants.

"Come on, Chow Lan," Joe urged, taking Tolliver under the armpits.

"Where he go?" Chow Lan wondered, taking Tolliver's feet and watching mystified as the priest discarded his pants.

"Never mind him! He's barmy. Let's go."

They bore Tolliver back to the shallow depression and huddled among the rubble and abandoned equipment.

The priest was bare-ass naked. He sat down on the spot and closed his eyes. He was muttering something, and his fingers were interlacing in weird passes.

Tolliver groaned.

Joe reached into his coat and pulled out his bottle.

"Here, Tom, here now," he said, pulling out the cork and tipping it to Tolliver's bruised lips. "Mother Mary's milk, it is. You drink. I'm sorry, Tom."

Beside him, Chow Lan gave a cry of surprise and fell to his knees, throwing his forehead to the ground.

Joe looked over and nearly dumped the rest of the firewater up Tolliver's right nostril.

The priest was getting to his feet.

But he had changed.

Somehow, in the few instants it had taken Joe to speak to Tolliver, the man had grown abnormally large. Taller than the tallest man Joe had ever seen in a freak show.

The priest took a step toward the thing massacring the fleeing workmen, and he shot up another ten feet, his legs and arms swelling and growing proportionately. In another step, he was thirty feet high. A third, he was forty.

"Saint Stephen dodgin' fuckin' rocks," Joe stammered, and fell back against the wall of the tunnel trembling.

By the time the priest was upon Dzoavits, they were the same size. A hundred and fifty foot tall Chinaman, naked as a jaybird, muscled and smooth as a yellow colossus dominating some pagan temple. His eyes shined with a strange sunlight golden light.

As Dzoavits raked one of its huge hands through the crowd of screaming Chinamen, the priest reached out and took hold of its wrist, spinning the creature around to face him.

It howled in rage as he gave its clawed hand a twist and a dozen men fell shrieking from its grip, crashed to the ground. They stumbled away, gaping at the two giants in horror.

The ogre wasn't brought down so easily as Joe had been, though. It kicked out with both its marsupial feet and sent the giant priest flying backwards.

But for all his newfound immensity, he had lost none of the agility Joe had seen him display in the rescue of Tolliver. He arched his back and flipped entirely backwards, landing on his feet and putting up his fists, feet set apart in a weird fighting stance.

Joe regained some of his reason and jerked Chow Lan to his feet by his queue.

"Chow Lan, boyo, tell me you see what I'm seein,'" he pleaded.

"I see! I see!"

"What *is* he? *How?*"

"He Shaolin, Boss," Chow Lan mumbled with a hint of reverence amid his own fear.

"What the bloody hell is show-linn?"

"Fighting monks, Boss. Strong. They know things. Secrets. Maybe magic. Make them strong, fast, fight like demons. I read about such stuff, but never think I see."

"But how? *How?*" Joe repeated.

There was no answer from Chow Lan.

Dzoavits let out an angry howl and came charging like a bull gorilla at the priest, knocking aside trees and crushing the tea barrel to splinters.

The priest intercepted its charge with his foot, lashing out and kicking it between the eyes.

The creature fell flat on its back with a staggering crash that shook the earth.

It somersaulted weirdly to its hands though, and began to sweep at the priest with its massive arms.

The priest leapt above these savage lunges, but the monster's wicked, clawed feet lashed out in deceptively short, one-two combinations. Though the priest dodged and slapped aside the slashing appendages with his forearms, it managed to rip a shallow furrow in his left side, and Joe gaped as a gout of blood splashed the rocks at the entrance to the tunnel in a red shower.

The priest countered, the monster slashed and snapped, each of them fighting alternately with their hands and feet. Every checked blow resounded in the mountains like a burst of artillery. They were sometimes so rapid and close together it gave Joe the impression of a thunderous fusillade. The creature's awful howling and roaring intermixed with the occasional martial shout or grunt of the priest.

One titanic combatant would go smashing to the ground only to leap or roll aright again and rejoin the fray. Great ropes of fur and tides of blood covered the snow.

Then the priest jabbed a knife hand into Dzoavit's left eye, putting out the red bulging orb and causing a steady stream of black blood to gush down its horrible face.

The monster howled and leapt back.

The priest, gasping, his olive skin now leaking bubbling creeks of blood from a half a dozen places, jumped back, too, and flicked the dark slime from his fist, splashing a stand of trees in the stuff.

The monster seemed to double over in agony, and shook its body. The dark, crystalline spines protruding from its back shined blue, each glowing with its own light.

The priest gripped the base of a tall, full grown fir tree, and striking it with the edge of his foot, uprooted it and whirled it one hand. He turned to face the creature, poised with the huge timber set in front of him like a partisan.

Dzoavits straightened and opened its wide, bloody maw. Like a toad, its black tongue sprang from its mouth, shooting across the distance. The priest was slow to block the thing, and it lashed around his corded neck like a bullwhip.

The blue phosphorescence, which had glowed on its back, traveled like St. Elmo's fire down the length of its tongue. When that visible, unknowable energy reached the monk's neck, he cried out and fell to his knees, dropped his makeshift weapon, and wrestled with the source of his pain constricting his neck like a ravenous anaconda.

Joe blanched, watching as the flesh around the giant monk's neck began to sizzle and smoke and he clenched his eyes and teeth in pain. His hands, trying to grip the tongue, recoiled again and again in pain.

"Cuckold Joseph!" he exclaimed. "It's murderin' him, sure!"

"What can we do?" Chow Lan pleaded.

Joe looked around the tunnel and felt a wavering in his knees when he realized they'd been taking cover among unused crates of blasting powder. Water walking Jesus, any stray bullet or flame could've blown them all to Moses.

Dzoavits was retracting its glowing tongue now, and the priest was dragged towards its toothy maw, knees plowing great trails in the earth as he gamely resisted.

"We must help him," Chow Lan cried.

"Help him? What can we do?" Joe mumbled, but even as he dropped the question mark his eyes lit on Old Judah, lying on its side between the two tugging giants, spewing water in little arcs like a garden fountain.

Then he looked at a crate of blasting powder barrels and the coil of fuse lying next to it. It had to weigh three hundred pounds. He considered Chow Lan's skinny arms dubiously.

"Awright, boyo. You think you can help me carry that box?"

"What we do with that?" Chow Lan asked, though he went to the other side of the box and tested the weight.

Joe looped the fuse coil over his arm and gripped the hemp

handle of the crate. "Just you follow my lead."

Chow Lan's end of the crate sagged sharply, but the little man was stronger than he looked, and made no complaint as they stiff-walked the heavy burden out of the tunnel and beneath the giant Chinaman's spread legs.

"Christ's Granny Anne, what a view," he muttered, trying not to look up as he guided Chow Lan toward Old Judah, slipping through the snow and splashing through ponds of blood.

At the midway point, the creature's glowing tongue over their heads, Chow Lan gasped and dropped his end with a jarring thud.

"Don't break the thing, you bloody leper, or we're lost."

Chow Lan nodded and gave it a second go.

It took some doing, but they finally reached the battered engine, which was piddling water from a dozen cracks in the tubes and billowing steam. They lifted the crate into the engineer's cab with a roaring effort.

Joe considered the state of the leaky old engine with dread, and checked the boiler level. Hell, they hardly needed to have brought the blasting powder. The engine would explode in a matter of minutes.

"Start fixin' this crate to blow, Chow Lan," Joe yelled, as he leapt out of the cab. He tossed the coil of fuse to the Chinaman.

As Chow Lan went into the cab, he looked up at the huge priest and the slavering monster. They were just massive, unreal, silhouettes against the bright sky from this angle, but the glow of the tongue between them lit the grimacing face of the golden-eyed priest. Joe noticed that of the spines on the back of Dzoavits, only a few were shining now, and one flickered and went out as he looked.

But the priest was losing his ground. In a few minutes, he would be dragged past the engine.

"Okey dokey, Boss," Chow Lan yelled, jumping down.

"Get to cover, Chow," Joe said, taking out his matches.

"Boss," Chow Lan said, wide-eyed. "What you do now?"

"I said get to cover, you damn fool!"

Chow Lan loped off for the trees, and Joe climbed into the hot, shuddering engine cab. Chow Lan had cracked open the crate and slipped the fuse inside one of the barrels.

The boiler gauge was quivering in the danger zone.

The giant Chinaman's great foot dug in a few dozen feet away.

How to get his attention?

But of course.

Joe reached up and blew the engine whistle, a shrill scream that pierced the air, audible even above the contention of the giants.

He jumped down and touched the match to the fuse.

He looked up.

The Chinaman's enormous glowing eyes focused on him.

Joe waved his hands, mimicked an explosion, and ran after Chow Lan, hoping the giant would get his meaning.

He did.

Joe looked back as he ran for the trees.

The priest seemed to relax, and let the glowing tongue pull him forward. As he was drawn towards Dzoavits, he reached down and scooped up Old Judah in his hand with a groan of metal and a great hissing. Surely he was scalded, but if the brands on his arms meant anything, he could take it.

Dzoavits' tongue ceased glowing as the priest came toe to toe with it, and it grabbed at him with its forelegs.

The priest brought up Old Judah and drove it into the thing's wide open mouth, cracking off a couple of its wicked teeth in the process. At precisely that moment, either the boiler or the blasting powder exploded. Joe didn't know which, but one definitely helped the other along.

The fiery explosion blew the priest back, severed Dzoavits' tongue, and left a gaping, drippy hole where its face had been. Shards of superheated iron and steel riddled its body. A few teeth hung like bits of broken glass in a window frame, twisted on strings of gummy tissue, before falling to the earth.

Then the enormous beast teetered and fell face forward with an enormous crash.

When Joe and Chow Lan dared to pick their way from the trees, the priest was nowhere to be seen. There was just an impression where he had fallen, and a great ragged, smoking coil of Dzoavit's severed tongue.

Without a word, Joe and Chow Lan went to this, and found the priest, normal sized again, lying half beneath the rubbery debris, naked and bloodied.

As Chow Lan laid a tentative hand on him, he opened his eyes. They weren't glowing anymore.

"Great God in Heaven," Joe said, unironically, taking his hat from his head as Chow Lan fell to his knees and bowed his head. "Boyo, can all you show-linn do that? Grow like that?"

"Not without sacrificing eight years of life," the priest muttered, closing his eyes again.

BY THE TIME CHOW LAN found the priest's clothes and Joe had salved his cuts with medicinal from the camp stores, the survivors were crowding the man in silent awe. The coolies uniformly prostrated themselves, yammering their thanks in their native tongue. He only answered them with a thin smile and a simple salute, fist in hand, and when he had dressed, he retired to his joss house.

When he emerged, he was dressed for travel, with a bindle and a saucer hat.

Joe had stood outside the whole time, waiting. What was that Shakespeare line, about more things in Heaven and earth? Well call him Horatio.

"What are you, mister?" he asked.

"I am like you. Like them," he added, nodding to the coolies.

"He who pulls the rickshaw is as much a man as those who ride."

Joe grinned and shook his head.

"Still preachin.'"

"Burn the carcass," the priest said to the gathered workers in a loud voice. "And seal the hole," he told Joe.

They all nodded as if he stood on a cloud.

"We will remember you with honor. All of us," said Chow Lan.

"Where you headed?" Joe asked.

"Over the mountains," the priest said, looking east.

Joe held out his hand.

"You're a hell of a man, for a heathen priest."

The priest smiled thinly and shook. "It is not the creed that makes the man. It is the man who justifies the creed."

"Boy, you're full of 'em. Well here's one you taught me. Don't judge a horse by the saddle he wears."

The priest bowed his chin and walked off.

They all watched him, holding their breath as he disappeared into the snow tunnel.

Joe sighed and took out his dented speaking tube, turning on the men.

"Well alright boyos, you heard the man. Let's burn that great monstrosity, blast the hole shut, and get on with our work. We'll be shiftin' course for Donner summit, so pack it up."

"Like Hesutu said?" Chow Lan ventured.

Joe only rumbled, keeping his tongue in check. He felt disinclined to cuss these heathens just now.

"What will Mr. Crocker say?"

"That's a good question," Joe sighed. "But there aint' no helpin' it."

He went off to his shanty as the men dispersed, looking forward to a pull of who-hit-john to put all these wonders into perspective.

"Boss Joe," Chow Lan said, rushing to keep up with him.

"What is it?"

"You asked the priest what he was. We have a name for it. *Yīngxióng.*"

"Ying-she-yong?" Joe repeated.

Chow Lan seemed to be swelling, smiling.

"It means hero."

Joe nodded.

"Sure, boyo. I guess that's a good fit."

THE FLIGHT OF THE RED MONSTERS

BONNIE JO STUFFLEBEAM

IT IS A PLEASURE TO crush. Under the slap weight of our tails, human vehicles crunch like breaking seashells. When walking, I try to avoid the ones that move, but like the microscopic snails that litter the pools at low tide, they are too difficult to avoid altogether. It is not pleasant to suck their slick guts from the points of our crusher walkers. They leave behind a red goo that reeks like the earth outside the sea. If it were up to us, they would not be here. It would be easier if they were not here.

Because of them we have been forced to make our way from the world below the sea, that place that we called home for longer than humans existed. It took a while for their stain to reach where we dwell, but we knew whose doing it was when we saw the ink so much like the squid but thicker, darker, invasive, coating the scales of our food fish, our food weeds, until they were inedible. Would they have us starve? We had heard from ones who have seen them in their habitat that they are a compassionate species, for their part, and so we hoped they would not have us starve but would allow us to cross their dirt to get at the other side, where maybe their oceans were not as saturated and where maybe we could find another world beneath the waves.

ELROD 13

Illustration by **ROBERT ELROD**

We did not know they would kill as many of us as they could. We did not know they would be able to kill any of us, the ones of hard shells, at all. We cannot let such a crime go unpunished. We will ruin the human cities as they ruined ours. I will ruin their home as they ruined mine.

It is a pleasure.

THE RED MONSTERS TOOK EVERYTHING. First they took my car, a brand new Honda Hybrid Civic, still in payments. Second they crushed my parents' condo in Marina del Rey, forcing Mom and Dad to pack up what was left of their belongings and move in with Simon and me in Venice, leaving behind a pile of rubble, that nostalgic salt water home smell wiped out forever. Then, the red monsters took Simon.

We were out with some friends when it happened, having a drink at a local bar in a desperate attempt to get away from my folks for a second. They'd been pestering us about when we were going to get married, been trying to convince us that one of us should sleep on the couch while they were there. They weren't normally so crazy; it was the red monsters. The red monsters made people freak the fuck out. Simon was handling it remarkably well, but I was starting to wonder, too, when we might get married, if we might get married, the thought leaving me with equal parts fear, revulsion, and a warm glee. Marriage was a weird, outdated thing, wasn't it?

I didn't have to figure it out. Because on the way back to our apartment that night, the ground shook like an earthquake. We were used to it. We knew the protocol. We ran away from their noise, which was like a broken pipe hissing water. As if they had water in their shells which squeezed itself out as they walked. Was this how they survived on land, then, this water storage? Not even the experts knew.

Two of them came at us, from both sides of Rose Avenue,

piercing car after car with those eight sharp feet, crushing shit with those snapping claws. Who the fuck thought they'd see lobsters with huge, buggy eyes searching out the metal glint of cars? Who the fuck thought they'd see giant fucking lobsters at all? Not me. Not Simon, who froze when he realized how blocked in we were, the two monsters walking toward each other as though they meant to greet an old friend, their antennae roaming the street like two oversized pieces of spaghetti. As if they didn't even notice us down there. The red monsters never noticed us, any of us.

"We have to spread out," Simon yelled. The red monsters' tails were wide as the street. They were both about ten human feet away from us. With every stride they left eight holes in the cracked concrete. Buildings trembled in their wake. Luckily, none of them fell. It was my only luck.

"What are you talking about?" I yelled. "Stay with me!"

But Simon was already running. "It's better," he said. "Better this way."

The red foot barely missed him. I'd seen those things pierce a body right through the stomach. I breathed, my hand at my throat, and chased after him. He looked back at me and smiled. *I'll marry you, Mr. Simon Monk,* I thought. Well, maybe I will. And then the red tail came down on him. He didn't have time to scream. I stood there gaping, stupid. I had been missed.

I ran home to find no home there. It was still standing, sure, but it felt like a place I had imagined. My parents tried to pry what happened from my choked words. They sat next to me on the couch and wrapped me in a blanket Simon bought me for Valentine's Day two years ago. It had stupid red hearts on it. It was all red, and I stared at the color for hours and wanted to kill. I wanted to see one of those monsters split open and seared over a giant fire. I wanted to pick him apart with a fork and dip his guts in butter.

My parents tell me it wouldn't help, to go out and get myself in trouble. My mom reads the news every day and tells me the good stories: two more of them dead. The authorities are having some success with flame throwers. They left Venice for a while. When she goes to sleep, I pore over the bad stories: more dead. More damaged. More buildings fallen and crushed. Then, yes, what I've been looking for: they're spotted again near L.A.

It's been three weeks. My home is not my home anymore. I have no home, not anywhere in the world.

Yes, I think as I read it over and over. *The red monsters are here again.*

I COME FROM A BLUE metropolis of beautiful giants. We are the biggest ones, but there are others like us: snake ones and sleek black ones with green lights that dangle in front of their mouths. There are white ones with many ropey tentacles and suckers which will never let you go if you let them touch you. There, too, were red ones similar to us but smaller and therefore ours to snap with our grabbers and suck the meat.

On land there is little food for us. This worries me. I know my kind. I know our ways when we are hungry. I will try to be civil, but there is no guarantee. All we can do to stave off the savage is to remind each other of our old world, of the world which we will make anew.

There was so much darkness in our world. There were beautiful clouds of food fish. Beautiful clouds of waving worm plants to look at when we were restless of wading through the cloud mud ocean bottom. There were hills and places to hide when we were too tired for our eyes to be open anymore. There was none of this choking air. There was none of this choking black smoke which billows like walked-across sand but looks and smells of death.

Our world now is rotting carcasses. The sea flowers do not live anymore. The worms wilt and die into the dirt. We die from eating our own food fish. When we molt, our inner skins soak too much poison into them, and we do not recover. It is good that we left, but there is this: that we won't ever be able to go back. Whose fault is this but the human ones? And we breathe the air of their world, somehow, and it is like a gift we never asked for. We want them to take it back. We will take our world again. We would not have traded it for this bad gift. The trade is unequal. We are not sure how or why we breathe, but we believe it is out of a great necessity. We will do whatever it takes to survive. This is both our greatest strength and our worst fault.

DAYLIGHT IS EASY. THEY DON'T come out in daylight. In daylight I walk the beach and the streets and the canals and wish around every corner that I might hear Simon's stupid drunk laugh. He'll tell me he just got too fucked up and forgot who he was for a while. I'll hug him and remember who I am.

This won't happen. It's not really why I search. I search so that I might find proof of the monster killers, the vigilantes who I have seen in black Kevlar gliding through the streets in videos snapped by nosy Internet people. They are like shadows. I want to be one too.

"You already are a shadow," my father said when I first told him this. "You barely speak, barely eat."

My father is right. I have made a decision. I will speak only when it matters to the killing of the red monsters. I will consume only fish you eat with your hands.

I was beginning to believe that the monster killers were nothing more than some fuckers' video editing pranks when I found the first evidence of them, a snag of black fabric on a shard of broken glass ripe for the cutting of night runners. The fabric was silky smooth and smelled like dust and revenge.

I sleep with it under my nose, choking on the smell. I dream of dancing on shadows, gulping jar after jar full of shadows, fucking Simon on a bed of shadows. They curl up around us and hold us together, and I cannot breathe for how tight they wrap us.

My father shakes me awake. "You were gasping," he says. "I worried you were having a seizure or something."

I shake my head. "No," I say. He holds the piece of fabric in his hand. I snatch it back. "That's mine."

He frowns. Purses his lips. Nods, then leaves.

I wish he could stay, read me a bedtime story, like he used to. Make me feel safe again. But shadows have no time for fairy tales.

THE FIRST WE HEAR OF these night ones is the crack of their bombs hitting concrete. The second we hear of them is the boom that tears our shell from skin. The third is the slip of knife in our vulnerable shellless bellies. I have seen nothing solid of them yet, only rumor. I have seen only the shadows their violence leaves behind, buildings burning from the aftermath. They are more our enemy than the metal bird devices above, which drop their own bombs. Those bombs we can run from. They come with the sound of flapping wings. The night ones' do not come with sound. It is more and more dangerous here by the terrible bright of day.

I see the way my old friends watch me. They are hungry. We are all too hungry to go on crushing. It was a pleasure to crush, but it is pleasure no more. We keep on because it has become that which we know, like our home was.

When we doubled back, we were lured by the smell of unruined food fish. Now we follow the smell to a tank packed with more food fish than any five of us could eat, and there are three of us here, in this travel pack. I would not have risked the doubling back if it were not for the sweet smell of a full stomach, the sweet smell of keeping our savage away for a few days more, at least. It is a trap, this we are sure of, but I am not frightened. The bird devices warn us when they are circling overhead.

I did not expect the night ones to be here. I have never seen human ones so black. The regular ones vary in shades, but none of them are so much like shadows as these are. The shadow one weaves between my feet, darting from darkness to darkness but is not as quick as the others. She stands before me, and I look down at her. I see her. In her hands she holds one of their bombs, black as she is and round as a sea globe. What did I expect? The food fish reeked of traps. I thought I was better than they thought me. I thought I was being fished by those who do not know the fishing. I did not realize we would be fished by one who knew the streets as we used to know the dark crevices of our world.

I look down at her. She trembles like one losing its skin. She holds the bomb above her head as though it is a sun to light her way from the dark.

I FOUND THE MONSTER KILLERS, huddled like homeless down near the busted canals. I was drawn to them like a pheromone, like the way Simon's smell used to follow me through our home, even when he was away at work. I stood before them, huddled, their faces too dirty for me to make out in the darkness. I held out their slice of fabric.

"I want to be one of you," I said. "I'm ready to be shadow, too."

They said nothing. I understood this. Instead they stared at me until they heard the crunch of breaking concrete in the distance. They rose from the ground and readied themselves for war. They did not slip masks and suits over their bodies, as I thought they would, but instead rubbed the ash of our breaking city over their skin. Watching them made goosebumps rise along my arms. I tried to follow them, but the shortest and smallest of them pressed her hand against my chest and shook her head. I didn't try again.

As I walked home, I wondered if they might watch me, test me. That was how it was in the stories; you had to pass a test before you joined the club.

The next day five of them were at my door. My parents came and got me.

"Is everything okay, Maria?" my mom asked, eyes wide.

I kissed her on the forehead. I went with them. I took nothing with me.

We walked a reverent silence among streets I had known so well in that other life but which looked new to me now, as though they were a new home. I stopped to smear pieces of Venice across my face. The chalky powder itched on my skin. Some of the monster killers clutched skateboards to their chests. When we were a mile or more away from my old apartment, we stopped. It was then that they talked. The shortest and smallest one talked first. She sounded like a teenager. "We have a plan, right. We put together a tank of fish, right, to, like, lure the red monsters here. Once they're here, you'll, you know, use this, right?" She handed me a handmade bomb wrapped in black tape. It was a misshapen sphere. I thought it would be smooth and slick, like in the cartoons. They told me I would light it when it was close enough to matter. "Then, run, right?" the shortest and smallest one said.

"I will," I said. But I could tell more from what she didn't say; that there may not be time for running, that I would do the thing they could not bring themselves to do. "I'll blow those red fuckers to pieces."

"Cool," she said.

But now, as I stand in front of the red monster, there's this empty feeling in my stomach, like I haven't eaten for months, and I don't think it's anything that death, anyone's death, will cure. I look up at the red monster, at its belly, and it reminds me, with its buggy eyes, of the geckos that used to crawl across my window screen in the summer. We used to have a cat, Simon and I, before the cat snuck out one day and never returned. The cat, I remember, a random-ass memory for this moment, used to stand on the other side of the closed glass window and bat at the gecko's belly. The cat's name was Hero, and she would make this noise like she was crying. I always thought it was because of the gecko, because she couldn't stand not getting what she wanted, the spoiled brat.

But I know now, looking at the red monster, that not being able to catch that gecko was a sick reminder of her lost home. Not that I took her from the outside world where her mom had birthed her, not only that I forced her to stay inside, but also that she had lost the whole way of who she was. Domestication. She'd lost the wild world. She was part of our world now, and her place there was so pointless, that all she had to spend her days with was trying to catch a gecko through the glass.

We don't even register, not usually, to these monsters. What kind of place must the world they came from be? I can't imagine. I don't want to imagine. I just wish, for this moment, that they could have it back.

I hold the bomb in my hand. What happens now? Maybe it explodes, even though I no longer believe that it's worth it, even though I see now that the world has gone to shit and it is everyone's fault and no one's. Maybe this bomb is bunk anyhow, and what really matters is that here two creatures see each other, and I mean really see each other, for the first time. And yeah, there's no way we can understand each other—we can only pretend we know what makes the other watch so forlorn out the window—and it's not like we're going to shake hands or whatever they call those claws of theirs in their giant lobster brains. But does it matter? There is no ending that will bring Simon back.

There is no ending that will save me and the monster both.

FALL OF BABYLON

JAMES MAXEY

And the woman was arrayed in purple and scarlet color, decked with gold and precious stones and pearls, having a golden cup in her hand full of abominations and filthiness of her fornication. Upon her forehead was a name written a mystery: Babylon The Great, the mother of harlots and abominations of the Earth.

Revelations 17:4-5

IT'S RAINING BLOOD.

I'm on my belly atop the Statue of Liberty, jammed against one of the wedges of brass that radiate from the crown, hoping the wind doesn't to blow me from my perch before I take my shot.

The Lamb is marching straight toward me, balanced on the heaving Atlantic like its solid and calm. The Lamb would look at home in a medieval painting of Hell. He's part-sheep, part-human, a cloven-hoofed devil covered in thick wool. Of course, if this were a devil, you'd expect him to be red, or maybe black, not pure white, glowing bright as dawn through the blood rain. Seven ram horns curl atop his head like a crown, with lightning crackling between

Illustration by **ROBERT ELROD**

the tips. The Lamb's been gutted; I'm told he was sacrificed earlier in the day, but that doesn't seem to have slowed him. His purple entrails snake from his chest cavity like tentacles in a hentai movie.

Did I mention he's big? It's hard to pin down his size while he's out on the water, but I can already tell he's a hell of a lot taller than Lady Liberty.

Despite the howl of the wind, I hear Baby and that crazy preacher going at each other in the room below. I think, between the two of us, she's got the tougher job.

All I have to do is shoot a judgmental god in the face. My odds of hitting the Lamb right between eyes are improved by the fact the thing has seven of them. She definitely didn't mention they'd be full of fire.

The thing's almost in range. I wipe blood from my eyes, taking slow, steady breaths as I rest my finger on the trigger of the crossbow.

What a fucked up day.

THE DAY STARTED BAD THE second I crossed onto Long Island and got caught in snarled traffic. I made it to the rehab center three hours late, with the fuel gauge on my Olds Cutlass hovering on E.

People who know I'm related to Baby are surprised I drive such a wreck. My sister's worth millions. It seems like a *little* of that money might have flowed my way. Alas, Baby and I aren't close. It's been three years since we last saw each other. She was supposed to come to Christmas at our stepmother's place last year. She even texted me the day before confirming the plan but never showed up. It wasn't until New Years that she texted again, saying she'd come down with the flu. I knew it wasn't true. I follow her adventures in the tabloids like everyone else. Baby spent Christmas in custody for underage drinking and public nudity, her fifth arrest.

She wiggled out of jail by checking in to a rehab center in the Hamptons. I knew I'd found the right place from the crowd of paparazzi in front of the gates. They were snapping shots of a bearded man waving a placard. The front read, "For all the nations have drunk the maddening wine of her adulteries," which struck me as curiously poetic. Then he turned, and the other side said, "GOD HATES WHORES!"

Poor Baby. I can't imagine a nut like Jude Barnes stalking me 24/7.

The guard at the gate was skeptical of my identity at first, but I had the letter from Baby asking me to pick her up. Why she'd reached out to me was a mystery. Maybe rehab really had changed her.

The Coast Wellness Center looked more like a country club than a hospital. The valet looked mortified when I pulled up, but was saved from getting behind the wheel when Baby burst through the front door and bolted toward the station wagon.

She was dressed in jeans and a neon purple long-sleeved T-shirt, skin tight, but still conservative for her. Her hair was dark brown. I thought she'd let it go back to her natural color, but when she reached the car I realized it was a wig. Large sunglasses hid her eyes.

Her expression was unreadable as she leaned into my open window and said, "You're late, bro."

"Traffic was a bitch."

"You brought the bag I shipped to you?"

"In the back seat," I said, getting out of the car and spreading my arms. "How 'bout a hug? It's been a long time."

She nudged against me, lightly touched my back with her palms, then stepped away before my arms closed around her. "Let's go. I'll scream if I'm here another minute."

"It can't be that bad. This place looks pretty swank."

"It's still a prison. You can't even pee without people watching you." She slid into back seat of the station wagon. "I can't believe you're still driving this heap."

"I can't afford a new car."

"I could have helped out if you'd asked."

I started to say that, if she'd bothered to keep in touch, she might have known I was still driving our grandfather's old car. I held my tongue.

She zipped open her duffel bag. "At least there's room to change in this boat."

I got behind the wheel. "What's wrong with what you have on?"

"Are you kidding?" she asked. "Now that I'm not kissing up to my jailers, I can stop dressing like a nun. I've a reputation to maintain."

I couldn't think of a delicate way to tell her that her reputation wasn't exactly a positive one.

Perhaps to head off what I was about to say, she said, "Just drive."

So I drove. Out of the gate, right into the paparazzi. I was half-blinded by the flashing cameras.

"Awesome," she said. "I was worried the world had forgotten me."

I glanced into the rear view mirror and practically choked. Baby was stripped down to her bra and panties, taking a swig from a huge bottle of Kahlua.

"Where the hell did you get that?"

"From the bag, duh."

"You'll get us both arrested!"

"Don't get your panties in a wad. Nobody gives a—"

Before she could finish her sentence, the rear driver's side window shattered. Baby shrieked as a brick landed in her lap. The Bible-thumper, Jude Barnes, thrust his head through the window and shouted, "Babylon! Mother of whores! Only the blood of the lamb can cleanse the filth of your fornication!"

He thrust a yellow Solo cup through the window. Baby's torso was suddenly coated in foul-smelling, brown-red goop.

"Son of a bitch!" she shouted.

I leapt from the car, not bothering to put it in park, and grabbed the lunatic by the collar. He punched me in the chest. I drove my fist into his nose and felt something pop, then pushed him away. I spun around to find the photographers scrambling out of the way of the driverless car, still rolling. I jumped into the driver's seat just as the rear passenger door opened and Baby jumped out, running down the sidewalk in nothing but her underwear, holding the Kahlua tucked against her like a football. The paparazzi gave chase. I blew the horn, threw the car into neutral, and stomped the accelerator. The growl of the engine caused the vultures to look back toward me. I threw the car into drive as they scattered.

As the car lurched forward, one of them jumped on the hood and pressed his business card up against the window.

"Andrew Carrick, Weekly World Magazine!" he shouted. "We'll pay top dollar for info on Baby. Top dollar!"

"Get off my car!" I shouted, cutting the wheel hard to the right, lurching us up over the curb onto the sidewalk. The sudden jolt knocked him free and he slid from my hood and disappeared from view on the passenger side. There was a sickening jolt a second later. I felt suddenly sick, worried I'd run him over.

Then, I had to jerk the wheel the other direction and get back onto the road since I was now about to run my sister over.

"Get in!" I shouted, as I pulled up next to her.

She dove inside.

"Fucking maniac!" she screamed, grabbing the purple shirt she'd discarded and wiping the blood off her breasts. I fixed my eyes on the road as she tore off her bloody bra. "Drive! Drive! Drive!"

I gunned the engine, tires squealing as we went around the corner at breakneck speed. A motorcycle with two riders pulled up beside us. One guy was driving, while the other a camera in hand, snapping photos of my topless sister.

"Fuck this," I growled, jerking the wheel to the left, cutting them off. The bike veered to avoid me and disappeared into a ditch on the other side of the road.

Baby threw her bloodied shirt out the window, then stretched out on the seat, face down, her body trembling. I thought she was crying, until I realized she was laughing.

"Why on earth is this funny?" I demanded, jerking the wheel to take another corner.

"Oh hell," she gasped. "Why isn't it?"

In the rearview, another motorcycle was now on our tail. I did a double take as I realized it was that Carrick dude, his face all bloodied. I was both relieve I hadn't killed him, and slightly disappointed I hadn't disabled him. I pushed the station wagon to its top speed, a bone-rattling sixty miles an hour. Carrick was able to easily pull alongside and shout, "Top dollar!"

Then, he suddenly slowed, skidding to a stop and craning his neck toward the sky.

I looked up. My jaw dropped. I pulled the car to the curb.

Baby stuck her head out the window and took a long swig from the bottle.

"Shit," she said. "It's the Apocalypse."

I got out of the car. The whole sky was red and glistening, like someone had applied fresh red paint to a previously unseen ceiling above us.

"It's Judgment Day!" came a shout from behind.

I turned and saw Jude, the preacher, running toward us.

The maniac made a bee-line for Baby, screaming, "With violence shall Babylon be thrown down!"

I leapt into his path, putting everything I had into a roundhouse punch. I knocked him flat, but cut my knuckles on his teeth.

Jude writhed on his back, but sounded ecstatic as he babbled, "Fallen, fallen, is Babylon the Great!"

I stared at the sky, listening to sirens from every direction. Were they coming for Baby, or was something bigger going on? Another terrorist attack? Nuclear war? What causes a sky to look like blood? I glanced back at that reporter and was relieve to see he thought the sky was more interesting than my sister, at least for the moment.

"You're hurt," Baby said, looking at my hand.

"Why the hell don't you hire a bodyguard?"

"A bodyguard would have searched my bag before he brought it to me," she said. "The agencies are legally liable if they sit back and watch me drink or shoplift or whatever."

"What the hell happened to you?" I shook my head, no longer able to suppress my feelings. "I try not to believe half the stuff I read, but..."

"Are you ashamed of me? You used to be proud."

Which is true. We had a rough childhood. Our mother was killed in a wreck when we were young. Dad remarried, but when he passed away, we bounced back and forth between our stepmother and our grandfather. Back then, I was the wild child with a chip on my shoulder, always in trouble. Baby was the good girl, the straight-A student and musical prodigy, a bookish nerd whose quiet accomplishments were overshadowed by my dumb antics.

When I was 18 I joined the navy, just as Baby got her first taste of fame. Only 14, she'd recorded a video of her singing "Like a Virgin," doing her own choreography and editing six different music tracks on her PowerBook. The video got a couple of hits on YouTube, until Warner Brothers threatened to sue her for copyright infringement. The story of the giant corporation unleashing its lawyers on a teenage girl made the Drudge Report. Within a week, twenty million people had watched Baby's performance.

Then Baby released her own song, "Not a Virgin Anymore." The lyrics were full of double entendres about a young girl having her innocence stripped away. She'd performed the video with hands ripping off her clothes, leaving her naked by the end of the song, though with carefully placed shadows hiding enough of her to keep the clip from getting yanked from YouTube. A lot of pundits denounced the video, decrying the exploitation of a minor. Only, it was hard to say exactly who was exploiting her, since everything in the video was her creation.

While I was stocking vending machines aboard an aircraft carrier, she hired a lawyer and had herself emancipated, a legal adult at the age of 15. She had her own apartment in LA and a million-dollar record deal. Overnight, the quiet nerd became an out-of-control party girl. The more she misbehaved, the more songs she sold. I'd always hoped her wild girl persona was an act. I figured Baby was cashing in on her fifteen minutes of fame. But…what if it wasn't an act?

"That's a long pause," she said. "Are you pissed at me?"

I crossed my arms. "It hurts that you only reached out because I'm more gullible than a professional bodyguard."

"That's one way of looking at it."

"Is there another way?"

"Probably not," she admitted. She got out of the car. She was now wearing a red halter-top and a short skirt she'd retrieved from her bag. Her wig was gone, revealing her blonde curls. "I'd say I was sorry, but you wouldn't think I was sincere."

"Would you be sincere?"

"Dan, there's stuff you don't know about me. Stuff you can't know. There's a reason I act like I do. A greater purpose. If I could explain, I would, but…" her voice trailed off. "Let me see your hand."

I looked down at my bleeding knuckles. "Note to self: Don't aim at teeth."

"We should take care of that. Human mouths are rife with bacteria."

I looked at the sky. "If there's been another terrorist attack, the emergency rooms are going to be too busy to look at my hand."

"I can disinfect it," she said, placing her bag on the hood and fishing out a steel flask. "Vodka should do the trick."

"You got a whole bar in there?"

"I wish," she said, pulling out a couple of small rectangular strips. "A Bloody Mary would be exactly the right drink for the apocalypse, but didn't pack any tomato juice. Fortunately, I do have a first aid kit." She produced a roll of gauze. "I keep this stuff handy. I fall down a lot."

I offered her my hand. She dabbed my wounds with gauze doused in vodka. It stung like hell.

As she bandaged me, Jude tried to stand, but fell onto his hands and knees, his legs still rubbery.

"Stay down," I growled.

"It's the whore who will fall!" Jude cried, lisping through loose teeth. "Repent! The hour of judgment is at hand!"

"If he were stalking me, I'd drink too," I said.

"Don't give him credit for my being a lush," she said. "I started drinking before I even made that first video. I was just good at hiding it."

"What's his problem with you?"

She shook her head. "He blames me for his daughter's death."

"Murderer!" shouted Jude.

"Apparently, she got knocked up when she was thirteen, and there's not a lot of places to get a legal abortion in Texas. She'd heard the old wives tale that, if you throw yourself down stairs, you lose the baby. She broke her neck."

"Why's that your fault?"

"Apparently, the girl was kind of a fan. When they found her body, *Mystery* was playing on her headphones."

Mystery was Baby's debut album.

As she finished my hand, she asked, "Want to know why I named the album *Mystery*?"

"Not that I don't want to talk about anything you'd like, but right now our priority should be to find someplace safe."

"Safe?" She shook her head. "It's Judgment Day. There's no safe."

"It can't be that bad," I said. "There has to be some rational explanation."

"Even for that?" She pointed over my shoulder.

I turned to find an army of knights on horseback galloping across the sky. Maybe horseback isn't the right word, since the steeds had the heads of lions and tails like scorpions. They raced among the clouds in eerie silence, their flaming hooves finding purchase on thin air. Black armor encased the knights, who carried long lances that crackled with internal lightning.

"Take me!" Jude shouted, rising to his feet, lifting his arms. "Take me!"

One of the riders heard Jude and peeled away from his fellow riders. He landed with a thunderous boom at the far end of the street, throwing up a pillar of smoke as he gouged a crater in the asphalt. The shock wave knocked me from my feet. I tried to get up, but the ground kept shaking as the monstrous steed thundered toward the preacher.

From nowhere, the reporter, Carrick, leapt into the path of the monster, camera in hand, snapping shots like crazy. He looked prepared to jump aside at the last second but the beast was faster than it looked. I blinked, and suddenly Carrick was impaled on the knight's lance. The lion beast paused for a second to shake the corpse free. The, the knight turned its gaze toward Jude.

The preacher's shouts trailed off as the knight lowered his lance, aiming it straight toward Jude's heart. His face went pale as the monster steed galloped forward once more. Jude might have been crazy, but even he could see the thing wasn't coming to save him, but to kill him.

"Run, you moron!" Baby shouted.

That sounded like excellent advice, so I pulled myself back into the car. I turned around to make sure Baby was in the back seat. She wasn't. She was running toward Jude.

"Snap out of it!" she screamed, grabbing the preacher by his arm. From where I sat, it looked like they'd both be trampled. The lion-thing was the size of a rhino.

Cursing my own stupidity, I threw the Cutlass into drive and stomped the accelerator, aiming for a collision course with the onrushing beast. Instead, the thing leapt onto the hood of my station wagon, killing my car. I slammed into the steering wheel.

The beast flew over the roof. Behind me, I heard Baby scream.

Then, I heard her cheer.

I twisted to see what was going on, wincing. The steering wheel hadn't done my ribs any favors. The rhino-sized steed was on its side, its severed head a good ten feet distant from its body. The black rider, at least ten feet tall, had drawn a sword and was hacking at what could only be described as a demon with a pitchfork.

I pushed open the car door and managed to drag myself out. The demon looked female, with long black hair and porn-star breasts, though her feminine traits were matched by an equally impressive length of male genitalia. She was no taller than Baby, but leathery bat wings at least thirty feet long jutted from between her shoulder blades. A black, scaly tail, thick as an anaconda, snaked from her lower back. With a laugh, she used her tail to jerk the knight from his feet, then buried her pitchfork in his torso. The thing disintegrated into a swarm of black flies.

Baby ran up to the demon, lifting her hand to give a high-five. "Way to kick ass!"

"199,999,999 to go," the demon said.

"Why?" Jude said with a sob, dropping to his knees. "Why wasn't I taken?"

"Idiot," the demon said. "You weren't good enough."

I limped forward, not fully convinced of my sanity. "What's going on?"

"Really?" the demon asked. "You don't know?"

"Vile succubus," Jude said, tears streaming down his cheeks. "You're a demon, come to drag our filthy souls to Hell."

"Demon? I'm not one of those saps."

"You're *not* a demon?" I asked.

She rolled her eyes. "I'm an independent angel. My real name is seventeen syllables long and would rupture your eardrums, but my friends call me Halo. You must be Dan."

I wasn't sure what was more disturbing, that I was face to face with a supernatural being, or that she knew my name. I couldn't do anything but stare at her.

"An angel?" asked Jude, who evidently had more of his wits at the moment than I did. "Then…I *am* going to heaven?"

"Yeah, no. I'm not that kind of angel."

"You're a fallen angel?" asked Jude.

"There was no falling involved. I walked out."

"Don't be so insulting, asshole," Baby said to Jude. "She just saved your hide. That thing," she pointed at the swarming flies, "was an angel. One of two-hundred million spreading across the globe, charged with killing a third of mankind."

"What?" I asked.

"The seven seals have been broken," said Halo. "The Lamb has returned to Judah and now walks across the ocean for his final battle with Babylon."

"What?" I asked again.

Halo looked puzzled. "How can you not know what's been going on? God's like the Riddler. He spells out his crimes in advance. The world's had 2000 years to get ready. What the hell do they teach in school these days?"

"They pollute innocent minds with lies of evolution!" said Jude, clenching his fists.

"That's still at thing?" asked Halo.

I looked back at the bloody sky.

"So…that Bible stuff…it's real? Shouldn't we…I dunno, find someplace safe to—"

"The great day of his wrath is come; who shall be able to stand?" Jude said.

"What he said," said Halo. "We need to get someplace a whole lot more dangerous if we want to have a chance. Let's hope your sister's ready."

"I'm getting there," said Baby, tilting back the vodka. She belched and wiped her lips. "Can we loot a liquor store or something?"

"Ready for what?" I asked. "Why are you being so cryptic?"

"Reality is cryptic," said Halo.

"This isn't the first time Halo and I have met," said Baby. "She's been giving me career advice for a while now."

I'M NO BIBLE SCHOLAR, AND Halo and Baby took all of two minutes to explain the entire Book of Revelations to me, so if some of this gets muddled, I'm sorry. The takeaway is that Judgment Day begins when a lamb with seven horns and seven eyes is sacrificed and found worthy of judging the world. The sacrificed Lamb then opens a book that's held shut by seven seals. With each seal that opens, he unleashes various horrors upon the earth. The Four Horsemen of the Apocalypse aren't just something heavy metal bands put on album covers. Instead, they're set loose to punish a wicked world, along with an army of two hundred million angels charged with killing a third of mankind.

"That's what's happening now," said Baby.

"You're telling me two billion people are being slaughtered while we're standing here?" I asked, incredulous.

"That's more or less accurate," said Halo.

"Why is there wiggle room?"

"You noticed the sky's changed to blood?"

"Kinda caught my attention, yeah."

"We're not in the material world any more. The Lamb has shifted the globe into the spiritual realm. Here, the physical laws are subservient to symbolism and faith. It's a world of waking dreams. People believe they're being killed, so they're dead, at least until they wake."

"This is just a dream?" I asked. "Then what's the problem?"

"As long as we're here, there's no waking. The Lamb will keep us here for all eternity if we let him."

"Let him? We have a say in the matter?"

"With this, yes," said Halo, holding out a small wooden chest, just big enough to hold an egg. "Open it."

I took the box. It wasn't very heavy. The wood was fine grained, etched with stars and swirls, which were coated with dust. The clasp was simple, made of brass. I flipped it open and looked inside.

"A golf ball?" I asked, rolling the contents into my hand. It was a smooth white stone, maybe marble. It was warm to the touch. There was a single thin braid of black hair wound around it.

"That's the stone that killed Goliath," said Halo.

"Whoa," said Baby, leaning in for a closer look. "You've got the best toys."

"You know how the Old Testament God was a bully?" asked Halo. "A sadist who slaughtered the firstborn children of Egypt? Who blasted Sodom and Gomorrah to the gravel because he disapproved of how the residents used of their genitals? The maniac who drowned the whole fucking world in a fit of spite?"

"A God of righteous vengeance," Jude murmured.

"Then, you notice that around the time David became king, God mellowed out? No more smite-fests?"

"I'll take your word for it."

"The mellowing out wasn't voluntary," said Halo. "When David fought Goliath, God placed the spirit of his wrath into this tiny stone. The pebble punched a nice, clean hole through Goliath, but some buddies and I were waiting on the other side. We grabbed the stone before it hit the ground and encircled the rock with a braid woven from the hair of a fetus, trapping this aspect of God inside."

"And that works why?"

"Because God can't hurt you if you're sinless, and original sin doesn't pass into a person until they're born. The hair holds him as securely as a chain. But, even if the wrath can't escape, this is still one bad-ass pebble. It might be the only thing in the world that can kill the Lamb."

"If God's wrath is trapped inside, why is the Lamb dangerous?"

"The Lamb is the manifestation of God's judgment, not his anger. It's a fine distinction, but the end result is still destruction."

"So…we're going to put the stone into a slingshot and throw it at the Lamb?"

"I'm thinking crossbow," said Halo. "I've got a modified bolt with a little cage to hold the stone."

"Wouldn't a rifle be better?"

"We debated using a musket, but worry that might destroy the hair. Fortunately, Baby assures me you're good with a crossbow."

"I am?"

"You're not?" asked Baby. "Didn't Pop-Pop used to take you hunting with one?"

I shook my head. "He used to hunt during bow season, but the only thing I ever shot was a straw target out behind the barn."

"How was your aim?" asked Halo.

"I mean, not terrible, but…look, why can't you take the shot?"

"Even with the hair around it, we free angels are sensitive to the power radiating from the stone. It's only safe for me to touch the gopherwood case. If I tried to use it as a weapon, I'd be dead before I had time to pull the trigger."

"So…you want me to kill…"

"The Lamb of God," said Baby.

"Is that…is that even…remotely ethical?"

"It's always ethical to protect yourself from a bully," said Halo.

"But…isn't this bully…God?"

"An aspect of God, yes."

"Don't let that intimidate you," said Baby.

"I'm intimidated as hell."

"If you don't help, he's going to kill me," said Baby. "And I don't mean as one of the faceless billions the angels are going to slaughter. I mean he's going to rip me limb from limb and personally toss me into the fiery pits of hell."

"Why?"

"Because I'm the current manifestation of Babylon."

Seeing the confusion in my face, Halo jumped in. "The Lamb's judgment ends in a final battle with a woman known as Babylon the Great. She's the last embodiment of the goddess Ashera, once worshiped throughout the Middle East. She was a goddess of female sexuality, of life and fertility, the embodiment of sexual freedom. Then a band of zealots with a commitment to patriarchy and strong opinions about who should sleep with whom came out of the desert carrying an ark filled with an angry God and wiped out all the tribes that worshipped Ashera."

"But," said Baby, "as long as men worship female sexuality, the worship of Ashera continues, even if almost no one knows her name."

"A lot of men lust after your sister," said Halo. "Basically, anytime a man downloads nude pictures of Baby, he's worshipping her, imbuing her with spiritual energy, making a rival god of her."

"And God is jealous," said Baby.

"That's why the Lamb's heading for New York," said Halo.

"To find Baby?"

"Because New York harbor is where the most famous idol of Ashera is located."

"It can't be that famous. I've never heard of it," I said.

"To the Roman's, Ashera was worshipped as Libertas," said Halo.

I was still confused, so Baby spelled things out. "The Statue of Liberty. He's coming to tear down the Statue of Liberty. And when he gets there, I'm going to be inside." She tilted back the flask, frowning to find it empty. "And, I'd like to be a lot drunker."

WHICH BRINGS ME BACK TO my perch atop the Statue of Liberty. Did I mention it's raining blood? And that I'm having to listen to my sister engaging in loud sex in the room below, losing her virginity to a creep like Jude Barnes? News that Baby was a still a virgin took me by surprise. Apparently, by maintaining her virginity, she's been able to store all the accumulated sexual energy of the mobs who pay tribute to her. It seems that Halo explained all this stuff to her when Baby was still fourteen, when Halo discovered my sister the same way the rest of the world did, via YouTube. Record producers saw a future superstar. Halo saw a goddess waiting to blossom. As to why Jude is her partner, I'm a little fuzzy. Maybe the preacher was the nearest warm male body she wasn't related to. As to why Jude agreed, I suspect he's been lusting after Baby all along. Once he learned he hadn't been raptured, he didn't have any reason not to give in to his baser instincts.

The Lamb strides closer and keeps getting bigger. I thought I'd be shooting more or less on the level of his eyes, but I'll be shooting almost straight up. I'm holding out to the last second. I've only got one shot.

He's close enough I can smell those prehensile entrails he's waving. I pull the trigger.

The bolt is instantly caught by the wind. It's not only going to miss the eyes, it's not going to hit at all. Suddenly, Halo's dark wings unfold from below and she launches herself at the falling bolt. The second her fingers wrap around the shaft she screams. Flames wreath her as she falls from the sky, the bolt clasped against her breasts. The Lamb kicks out with one his cloven hooves, catching Lady Liberty dead center of her chest. There's a rending sound as the statue twists on its pedestal. I'm flying through the air, buffeted by the storm, dropping toward the raging waves.

Then Liberty drops the tablet she carries and stretches her arm toward me. Giant green fingers gingerly pluck me from the air as the statue lands feet first in water that, for her, is only knee deep. The statue's features shift from a stoic stare to a sly grin.

The torch in her other hand flickers, then flares into a blinding light. She rises from her crouch, thrusting the white blaze into the Lamb's dangling entrails. There's a horrible sizzling sound and the smell of burnt meat as she stands on tiptoe to twist the torch in the Lamb's guts. The big guy roars. He grabs her by the crown and lifts her as easily as I could lift a toddler. As she rises, the hand that holds me passes near the now vacant base of the statue and she drops me. I land without breaking my legs, but the whole base is slick with the oily blood. I lose my footing and slide toward the edge before my fingernails find purchase.

Above me, the Lamb holds Liberty above his head with both hands. He roars again and throws her toward the city. She spins head over heels for half a mile before crashing into a skyscraper. Every window in the building shatters as she slides down the face, landing with her limbs limp, the torch guttering in her lap. Her face twists. At first, I think it's a look of pain, but then she raises her fist and shouts, with a voice like a thousand megaphones, "That all you got?"

The Lamb stomps across the waves in pursuit. She aims her torch and blasts him with a beam of light. By the time he reaches her, his wooly coat has caught fire, but it doesn't slow him. He grabs her by the throat and slams her into a nearby building. When she keeps fighting, he slams her again, and the whole skyscraper twists and topples.

The Lamb tilts back his head and unleashes a bleat that sounds like sadistic laughter, as if he's pleased by the falling building. They're stomping through the financial district. Maybe the Lamb hates Wall Street as much as the next guy. As evidence of that theory, he uses Liberty's flailing form like a club to batter another building into rubble.

I can't just stand here and watch this. I don't know where Halo fell, but I have to try to find her. There's a big shaft just ahead of me, what's left of the staircase that used to go up into Liberty's body. I slip and slide across the bloody rubble, then make a jump for the nearest intact step, a good six feet down. I land less than gracefully but pull myself up and start racing down the steps three at a time.

I find Halo near the bottom, midway to the first landing, crawling. Carrying the bolt hasn't been good for her health. The voluptuous succubus I met earlier is now little more than a skeleton. Her skin, once creamy and translucent, is now charred and crispy, falling off in big flakes, revealing a good chunk of her skull.

"You...missed..." she gasps, as she lifts the bolt.

I grab the missile. "Won't happen again. For one thing, I've lost the crossbow."

"Great," she says.

"It's not important," I say as I get my shoulder under her arm and help her limp out of the building so we can get a view of what's going on. "With this wind, I'd never make the shot. We need a helicopter or something, some way for me to get above this thing. I'll jump down and stab him."

"How...heroic," she pants.

"Just desperate. Baby's getting her ass kicked."

Halo nods. "Prophecy's hard...to shake. At least we know...she won't be fighting alone."

"For all the help we've been, she might as well be alone."

"No." Halo shakes her head. *"There I saw a woman...sitting on a scarlet beast that was covered with blasphemous names...and had seven heads and ten horns."*

"Um," I say.

"Revelations 17:3."

Just then, there's a howl from the other side of the statue's base. I turn the corner to see the Lamb staggering backward. He's on fire again. Jets of what look like lava splash against his torso. I strain to find Baby amid the destruction. Their battle has left half of Manhattan flattened. I wonder where she is.

Finally, I spot her. She's in the sky, riding a dragon with a wingspan so wide the tips disappear among the clouds of smoke. The scaly thing has seven long necks, like a hydra, with its dragon mouths spitting geysers of molten brimstone at the Lamb.

"Is that—"

"The great dragon," says Halo. "He has the most to lose if the Lamb wins. If he loses this battle, he'll be cast in to the pits of hell for all eternity."

"I don't think he's going to lose," I say. As big as the Lamb is, the dragon is bigger. The creature lands amid the ruins of Manhattan, bracing himself on legs the size of sequoias as he sinks his teeth into the Lamb's charred flesh. Baby is blasting the Lamb with dazzling beams of light, blinding him. In his agony, the Lamb stumbles, howling. The dragon presses his attack, destroying buildings with each sweep of his massive tail.

The Lamb drops to one knee. He raises both fists, then pounds them against the earth. The ground cracks open, revealing a massive pit of smoke and flame that grows beneath the dragon's feet. The dragon flaps his wing to fly away, but the Lamb grabs the nearest neck and breaks it, then uses it as a line to reel the beast in, snapping its necks one by one.

Baby's still on the dragon's back, holding on for dear life. When this thing goes down, she's going with it.

"We have to save her," I shout. "Can you fly us—"

"I can barely stand," says Halo. "Though…there's a way to regain some strength."

"How?"

"Jude wasn't completely wrong when he called me a succubus."

"What does—"

"I'm a bit like a vampire," she explains. "Only instead of sucking your blood, I drink your soul."

I furrow my brow.

"I won't drink it all. There's no time to fully drain you anyway. But a kiss will restore some small portion of what I've lost."

"Take what you need," I say, closing my eyes.

Her dry, thin lips crackle as they press against mine. She smells like a steak that's been burnt to a crisp. Her nails dig into my back.

Without warning, her tongue snakes between my teeth, forcing itself down my throat. I gag, but she doesn't let go. I can't breath. The world spins. It feels like she's licking my heart.

She lets go and I drop to my knees. The backs of my hands are wrinkled, aged. My arms look thinner than they did a moment ago.

I look up. She's not as voluptuous as she was when I first saw her, but she looks filled out, full of life. My life.

"Don't drop that bolt!" she says, grabbing me by the collar. "Definitely don't let it touch me!" Her long wings flap and we lift into the air.

Five of the dragon's heads hang limp.

We lurch across the sky, tossed about by the tempest. My heart rises in my throat as we plummet in a downdraft, but Halo just laughs and folds her wings, diving even faster, until she spreads them wide and we zoom upward.

"I've been flying since the dawn of creation," she boasts, clutching me tighter as we rise above the struggling monsters. "Nothing can touch me in the—"

Her voice cuts short as her arms go limp. As I tumble, I see one of the mounted angels looming above us, his lance jutting from her left breast, wet with gore. I spin and see I'm falling right toward the Lamb. There's still a tuft of wool relatively intact amid his crown of horns. It's like landing on a mattress, jarring, but nothing is broken. Was it luck that I've fell here, or did Halo aim me?

It doesn't matter. I scramble on my belly until I'm between the closest eyes. I gaze out at the destruction, the city blocks flattened, the flames stretching for miles. Any doubt I had about whether fighting this thing was right or wrong vanishes. I rise to my knees, lifting the bolt overhead with both hands and plunge it into the Lamb's brow with all my strength.

The bolt bounces off. I don't even scratch him. I nearly lose my balance from the recoil. Why didn't this work? If this thing is some all powerful weapon…

I eye the braided hair that wraps the tip. Removing it will free the wrath of God. It might make our situation infinitely worse. Or maybe…

The dragon only has one head left. Baby's still hanging on, unable to do a thing while the Lamb is thrashing the dragon so badly. I've no choice.

I tear the hair away with my teeth and strike again.

This time, the bolt plunges into the skin and through the bone as if they were mashed potatoes. I keep pushing until my arm is shoulder deep in the Lamb's boiling gray matter. The Lamb howls, jerking his head, throwing me into the open air. As I fall, I see the Lamb's grip on the dragon's last head weaken. The beast latches on to the Lamb's throat with a thunderous growl. Lava splashes through his teeth as he blasts brimstone directly into the Lamb's jugular. But I can't focus on whether on not this attack is working since I'm plummeting directly toward Hell.

Liberty's hand juts out and snatches me from the air. She places me atop her crown, then takes her torch in both hands. The Lamb is writhing in agony, his skin bubbling and boiling. There's a huge smoking crater in his brow, right at the point I pierced him with the bolt. Baby leaps from the dragon's back and plunges her torch into the crater.

Light explodes from every orifice of the Lamb. He stops howling in agony. He stops everything and simply falls. His ropy entrails entangle the dragon and they both tumble toward the hellfire. Baby makes a jump for the edge of the pit and hooks a single arm across the lip. The ground shakes violently as the Hell pit starts to close.

"Run!" she gasps.

I run, sliding down her face to land on her shoulder, scrambling toward freedom. I make a leap for a steel beam near the edge of the pit and stick the landing. I turn, shouting, "Get out of there!"

But she loses her grip and vanishes into the ever-narrowing gap. Before I can even call out her name, the crack closes, and she's gone.

I throw myself onto the broken earth, vainly, foolishly clawing at the rubble, as if I might somehow free her. My tears blot away by vision. I rub my fingers raw for a while, then wipe my eyes. I study the ground, searching for any sign of an opening.

It's then I discover that the sidewalk I'm sitting on is completely intact.

I look up and find myself surrounded by towering skyscrapers. Through the haze of light cast by the city, I see a single star in the night sky, Venus I think. I rise, and see a dozen people on the street staring at me. I look at my ruined hands and suddenly it all makes sense.

Halo was right! It was only a nightmare, and now we're awake. I race down the sidewalk, heading for the waterfront, laughing like a maniac. I feel like Scrooge on Christmas morning. All a dream. A dream.

Then I reach the harbor and my laughter dies. I stare across the waters, toward a distant island, where a hundred floodlights illuminate the base of a vanished statue.

Not everyone woke, it seems.

Fallen, fallen, is Babylon the Great.

But she went down fighting.

And she didn't go down alone.

BIG DOG

TIMOTHY W. LONG

IT WAS A DIFFERENT WORLD inside the box.

The pod rattled loud enough to make her ears ring for days. It smelled like exhaust and raw fuel. Her eyes stung from spent shells and multi-stage accelerants. Vertigo ate at her gut every time she looked outside, and just when she thought she was used to all of these sensations she would be picked up and tossed back into her chair hard enough to knock the breath right out of her chest.

The world rocked back and forth as Commander Katie Cord attempted to keep up with the viewports. Each three inch thick glass window provided a limited view of the world ahead, and what she saw was not pleasant. The act of actually turning to view her 'six' was worse thanks to a creaking chair that more often than not, smacked her head against the side of the padded portcullis.

What she saw of the hills of Saipan were beautiful but there were also patches of scorched earth among the trees and grass.

But for all that she wouldn't give this up for the world.

"Six degrees lift. Hit 'em with the fifty-fives again." She bellowed into the radio. It hung a foot from her head and she had to reach for it because holding on, she'd learned early on, could practically

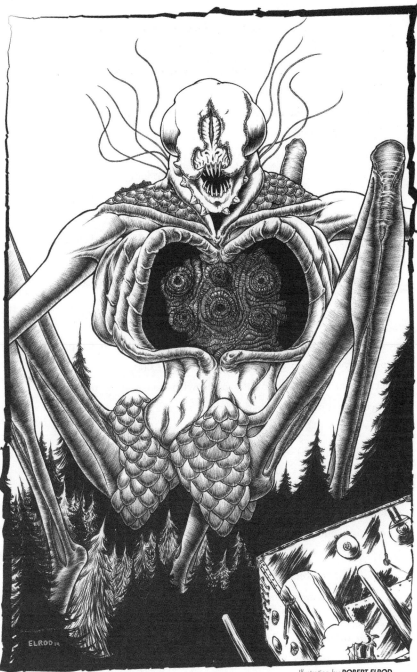

Illustration by **ROBERT ELROD**

dislocate her shoulder.

The machinery screamed around her as the beast fought to move sixty-seven hundred tons of metal, gears, grease, fuel, and ammo. Not to mention five souls all of whom were under her command. A staggering step, and then she was in the air again. Exhale, wait for it and then just like that, smashed into her padded chair.

Katie lowered her headgear exactly eight seconds later as her commands were relayed to waiting gunner, Mack. She knew her seat was uncomfortable but the gunner had to hang on for dear life every time the big guns fired.

"Hit six!" the gunner rattled back.

"We got a oil leak in seven primary," Kilmer called from the reactor room. "I need two or three minutes to get it under control."

"Sorry, Kilmer. We don't have time to stop and shut down a boiler."

"I'll do what I can but these are not the ideal working conditions."

"Noted," she said and clicked off.

"Movement right, I make it forty five degrees," her topside spotter yelled into the nearest porthole. O'Hare's position was perilous at best. His mount swayed with each step of the beast. During trial runs, Katie had sat there for a few hours, and if there was a scarier place on Earth, she'd never heard of it.

At least in the hole she was protected by a couple inches of American steel. A direct hit was nothing. Big Dog could take it. It was the Kaiju she had to worry about. The minute one of them got close enough to engage in actual combat she was going to be sent home in a bunch of little boxes."

Commander, I see movement," the man next to her said in a thick German accent.

I wish the movement was a bullet seeking your head, she didn't say out loud.

Heinrich Glaus, former commander of the famed Panzer Corp was smug. He wore his adopted American uniform with the same aplomb he'd worn his Nazi clothing. His shoes were spit-shined so that they gleamed in the dank pod and his rank insignia shined like gold.

Another shuddering couple of steps and she saw it, too.

"It's a Mark one?"

"Mark two, begging the commander's pardon. We are headed for some fun time, *ja*?"

"You think this is fun? I'd hate to see what you do in your down time."

"Mainly listen to music. I must confess that sitting in a metal box for years has damaged my hearing some but when I hear Grieg's music I can, for a time, forget all of this."

"Do you forget the screams of men? Asshole." The last word was under her breath. The man probably didn't hear it, but she really needed to learn to hold of her tongue.

Dammit. What would her very proper and very Kentucky father say if he heard his daughter using such language? Since Germany had surrendered six years ago, her feelings of hatred for her nation's former foe had not lessened. They'd killed her Teddy, and she would never forgive them. Any of them.

"It was a bad time for us. You know? It was a bad time for all of us. I did not like what I did just as I do not like this."

He didn't like this? What did he like, the screams of millions of Jews as they were fed to the fires? So many questions remained after the surrender, and with the truce in effect many of them remained unanswered. Germany had agreed to reparations but when the threat of Kaiju, as the Japanese had named their new allies, had spread, so had the need to present a united front with the assistance of the European nations.

When Katie's career in the Air Force had nearly come to an end, thanks to a test flight gone wrong, she'd thought that a peaceful life lay ahead for a year, or so. At least until the beasts picked up their attacks and spread their seed and rage across the rest of the world.

"We need delta wing and we need them now. Let command know." She squinted at the shape ahead. She used to wear eye glasses but had given them up in recent months to appear more able. She was not about give up command of the largest machine of war the US had ever created.

"On the way."

"How did they know? How did they know we were coming here?"

"Did you think they would leave a nest unprotected, Commander?"

"But ground pictures didn't pick up anything this size."

"We can take it. Think of the glory from this mission when we take down a class two and bring home a sample of the beast."

"I don't know. This feels wrong."

Big Dog continued it's lumbering steps. Glaus yanked the radio transmitter to his mouth and shouted directions, and then made adjustments as they drew nearer to the enemy. The Kaiju might be huge and they might be nearly unstoppable but they were still as dumb as rocks. Rocks that could swat fighters from the air and crush tanks with hands the size of busses, but still, tactics needed to be adhered to.

"*Ach!* It's a class three. No, I make two of the creatures."

Katie grabbed the command receiver and triggered it.

"Lightning one, lightning one. This is Big Dog. Where is that wing?" she yelled. Katie triggered the transmitter several times, and then asked again.

"Big Dog, we are sending you some love. Stand by." The man had a Southern Drawl heavier than her own.

"Can you hurry it up before we engage?"

"We hear you, Big Dog. General Patton sends his regards, ma'am," the man replied.

"The general is here?"

"Ah. Patton is a great strategist. Perhaps there is hope," Glaus replied.

"If you didn't believe in this mission, then why the hell are you here, Glaus?"

"I am here, Commander, because I believe in the mission, and I also believe in you. Now lead us forward," he said and lowered his viewfinder.

Big Dog had not been her idea. She was brought in late and that was only thanks to a favor that General Monroe and his admiration for her work on the latest destroyers. Many of them lay at the bottom of the ocean, thanks to the Japanese alien allies, but many of them still patrolled near home, and that was enough for her. When she'd proved herself to have a good eye for tactics against the beasts she'd been moved up to the project.

Big Dog was the first of it's kind. A machine large enough to contend with the Kaiju. Work had begun after the third disastrous battle of Fukujima when all was had been going in the Americans' favor. Then the wave of advanced and larger beasts had descended on their forces and decimated them. The war had been all but at an end when the alien's craft, damaged and lost near Earth, had sensed the detonation over Hiroshima and come to investigate. It was sheer bad luck that the ship had crashed near Fukishima, making a new island in the Japanese sea.

"Target ahead. It's firing. Shift fifteen degrees. No, make it twenty five," Glaus bellowed.

"Shit!" Katie yelled as commands were translated to drivers.

Below them the boilers screamed as they poured power into four squat legs. Big Dog swayed to one side, and then took a couple of shuddering steps. Something whistled overhead and created an explosion she felt in her gut a few seconds later.

"That was too damn close, Glaus!"

"If you'd care to switch positions?"

She frowned. He was quicker than her but not by much. She turned her attention to the map of the terrain that hung a few feet away and just over the portholes. Just another mile and a half and they would arrive to deliver their payload.

If they arrived.

"Shift starboard fifteen," Glaus shouted.

Katie braced herself again but was slammed into her hard seat? Why didn't she design this part better? Something with more padding and webbing to keep her from getting tossed around. The hard canvas like straps that made up her seatbelt bit into her chest and shoulders.

Something screamed overhead, and she looked up instinctively but saw only the dull metal. Bombs exploded in the distance. She clicked over her backup radio to hear the chatter.

"Delta, I have two targets. Engaging," one of the pilots squawked.

The man's voice sounded frightened but there was also the hint of exhilaration she'd always felt behind the stick of an aircraft. It wasn't for women just ten years ago. They worked in factories and prepared food and supplies for men in the field. After a decade of war and learning (though Eisenhower would never admit this) from the Soviets that a female was more than cheap labor. They could fly, drive armored vehicles, and fight as well as men.

Katie bellowed orders at engineering to keep the beast righted. Ballast shifted as Glaus called out command after command to avoid being hit by one of the Kaiju rounds. The strangest part of the creatures, apart form their massive size, glowing green skin, and scales the size of Tucker luxury automobiles, was their weaponry. Entirely organic they could fire projectiles that were heavy and struck with great force. They could also unleash acidic bombs that obliterated everything in their splash path.

The creature rose seventy feet into the air. Its abdomen opened and extruded a pair of the rounds. It took a step toward them and then the bombs were on the way. They accelerated with a propellant that no one in intelligence had been able to fathom. It seemed to react to oxygen and then convert it's outer coating into an accelerant. The balls didn't move like standard projectiles, but they picked up speed as they flew, often arcing into the air before striking a target. She'd seen three such balls eliminate a platoon and fifteen tanks before an out of control and ancient P-51 Mustang had smashed into the attacking Kaiju's head causing the beast to lose an eye. Portable artillery had been brought up to finish the howling beast and it's squad of Japanese Kaiju controllers. They'd rode on a bamboo platform, three of them lying on their stomach, hands touching the creature to create the strange telepathic link.

At one time she'd had dreams of capturing a small one and seeing the results of Army intelligence, but by the time they'd brought one home, sedated with enough cattle tranquillizer to kill an entire herd of cows, it has been close to death. The only connection they'd manage had put the creature in a panic and it had self-immolated leading to the loss of six building at Area 51, and at least fifty-seven deaths.

She'd been leading the research on Big Dog when the base had been destroyed and barely managed to make it out alive. Since then she'd embarked on this quest to bring back a sample rather than an entire beast. If her reasoning was correct the sample would be viable since it was separated from the Kaiju.

"Bring the forty-eights online, Gunny Mack," she called and then got slammed into her seat as Glaus shifted their stride once again.

"Aye," called back the gunner.

Big Dog shuddered as the guns extended from portholes. She stared at her console until all six barrels showed they were ready. Red lights clicked off and green lights underneath glowed.

"Glaus, let's take it down."

"One moment, Commander," he said, and then shouted commands.

Big Dog shifted to the right and then came to a shuddering fifteen-degree adjustment so quickly she almost broke her damn neck. She slammed into the padded chair for the hundredth time and cursed once again.

"Easy!" she yelled.

"Just testing. I apologize, Commander. I have to know our maneuverability. When I drove a Panzer it took a few days to get the handle on it."

"Hang of it," she corrected him. "And I don't want to hear any more tank stories. Just do your job."

"Yes, *mein heir*," he replied stiffly.

She swallowed and took out the eclipse lender, as she'd called it after getting the first one back from the engineers. She'd designed it but they'd given it a truly hideous name. Katie lowered a bar and lined it up. With the shuddering and rhythmic steps of the Kaiju, it was still nearly impossible to determine their path. She could strap on the device with the support of the metal extension rod and as long as her head wasn't ripped off by another wild maneuver she might actually get lined up.

The visors had a phosphorous layer that allowed her to pick out the footprints left behind. It was all rhythm, something she learned in one of her countless piano lessons as a kid. She could follow the beat and determine it's next step.

This one's steps told her it would veer to the right after three more steps. She focused on the warriors strapped on the beast's shoulders. They were indistinct at this distance. They'd tried sniping the soldiers but the Kaiju had seemed to feel their deaths and go into a rage that led to it losing control and in the process losing its ability to extrude its weapons. The first time that happened the explosion had been like a nuclear detonation.

"I wish we could just tiny nuke the bomb on these bastards." Katie gritted her teeth.

This battle might be a test but it would also lead to a loss of life and one of those lives might very well be her own.

"That would be unwise. I was an observer on the first attempt to remove the alien craft from the waters of Okinawa."

"I heard what happened," she tried to cut him off.

"The beasts were furious, Commander. It was a massacre. The island, as we call it, opened up and out poured such a menagerie of beasts it was like leaving Dante's Inferno with Hell on our heels. Flying beasts with four and six wings intercepted the craft and drug them to the ocean. Our assault force on the water was sent to the bottom. We suffered over six thousand losses and this was all, as the theory goes, due to the material. The nuclear material. Even Einstein was baffled."

"I don't need a goddamn history lesson," Katie shot back.

Big Dog shifted around her as guns were readied, shifting the weight to the front of the metal beast. She moved the eclipse lender aside and tried to concentrate on the task at hand.

"We always need a history lesson. My country would have done well to pay attention to 1914 but we were blind."

"Shut your mouth. Just shut your goddamn mouth, right now. As your commander, I order you to."

"You do not wish me to speak of the past or you do not wish me to speak at all?" he asked.

His blue eyes were as piercing as ever, but she could tell she'd hurt him.

You know what I mean. You know. You're the reason my husband is dead! She wanted to scream, then drop out of the stupid webbing, pick up a wrench, and beat this man to death. Her husband had died inside a tank.

"There's a second one!" Glaus gasped and pointed.

Gunny Mack came over the intercom a half second behind with the news.

"Got a Mark three on his six. Ah shit-biscuits."

"We're going to die in this stupid metal box."

"We are not going to die, Commander," Heinrich said with

such finality she wanted to believe him.

"I want the one of sixes readied," she called to Gunner Mack.

"Readying the rounds." His Jersey accent came back strong.

Katie considered the path of both beasts. The Mark three towered over the Mark Two by at least forty feet, and with that height came so much mass that even their largest shells might do nothing more than clean its teeth. On three legs, this was a newer Kaiju, something they'd never faced before. Mark Threes had been seen but never in combat. During the battle of Saipan in 1949 a Mark Three had threatened but hadn't been required because the American forces were so soundly trounced the Three had slunk back into the depths.

"Commander, I don't think we stand a chance."

"Two degrees high," she yelled. The size of the guns meant that the slightest shift resulted in a greater arc and it took a careful touch to get the angles just right. In test after test she'd beaten the mighty Heinrich Glaus at every version of artillery and tank shelling they threw her way.

What she hadn't been prepared for was actual combat with the exception of flying the X-187 Marauder, the plane that had been set to upgrade the US Air Force before the war became one almost entirely on the ground.

"Mark, two degrees high."

"Watch for the soldiers. It appears they have spotters on both shoulders," Glaus said.

"I know." She slid her binoculars down and spotted them as well.

Jets roared overhead as the first of the fighters arrived. They stayed high but, as they closed in, the planes dipped low to deliver their payloads.

Dozens of missiles fell toward earth. Propelled but unguided they relied on inertia and the pilots. It also didn't take into account the stuttering steps of the giant beasts, and that's why most of the first wave missed.

Explosions rocked the ground and tore up terrain. Smoke rose into the air and billowed. A second flight screamed in and delivered another blast. Most of the ordinance struck but it was like hitting an elephant with a BB gun.

"Fire two and four!" Katie yelled, and then wrapped her hands around her head.

The pounding as the smaller guns bellowed was like sitting near a gong. The pulse struck her hard enough to rattle her teeth.

"One and Three ready," Gunner Mack called over the comms.

"Fire one and Three." She took her hands off her ears long enough to hear her own voice, and then slapped them back around her head.

The firing went on and shells arced into the sky.

They were still a kilometer away but closing fast. The shells arrived in a few heartbeats.

The monster tried to shift to the side but it was too late. Several of the shells struck and blew the beast back. Detonations rocked up and down the coast as shells continued to fall.

"One of the eights at the ready," Gunner Mack called.

"We have to line up. Keep them warm, gunner," Katie said.

Heinrich dropped down from his perch and appraised Katie's condition.

"None the worse for wear, I see."

"Just do your job. I can take care of myself." She glared.

The man nodded once and resumed his watch. She slapped the Eclipse Lender to her eye to inspect the damage.

The shells had done damage, and a lot of it. On top of the Kaiju's shoulder men clung to the remains of their wooden platform. Many had fallen but the three who appeared to be meditating were still strapped next to the monster's neck, hands extended as they continued their silent vigil. Why did it make the monsters crazy when the men were killed? Why? What sort of symbiotic connection existed that was so deep it transmitted each other's pain.

Or was that it? Did the men feel pain just as the Kaiju did when the Japanese warriors were struck?

"Damage?" she asked Heinrich.

"The new magnesium shells worked marvelously. I can see that chunks are missing. The Class Two is hurting and has slowed."

"What about the drivers. Can you see them? Can you make out their faces?"

Heinrich was silent or a few seconds. He shifted to a longer lens then looked back down into the cockpit.

"They are in great pain. Did we hit them?"

"If we'd hit them this entire area would have gone up."

"The Two is moving," Heinrich said.

She didn't need the reminder. If they stayed here much longer they were dead.

"We need to get closer."

"No, we need to run. I see its chest cavity undulating. Is that the word?"

"Yeah." Katie rolled her eyes. "Gunner, get those plates in place. Brace for impact, and I want crews standing by with soda," she yelled and hit a button on her console.

Men moved into action rerouting boiler steam to the six-inch plates. Her console reported the shields were moving into position.

"Slow to one quarter flank and squat," she called out and punched more buttons.

Big Dog came to a near stop, and then shifted its weight to back legs. Front legs pistoned down, lifting her big puppy's front end into the air. Her view of the world disappeared. She stared for as long as she could even raising herself against the webbing until all she saw was sky and a pair of Kaiju intent on tearing Big Dog to scrap.

The plating came into place completely covering their view. She tried to think of the men topside that were diving into cavities in the ship or cowering behind the plating.

The shells hammered at Big Dog. He shuddered and shook but, to her surprise, they bounced away just as Heinrich had said. The angled plating had been the German's idea based on his days commanding Panzers.

Katie slid her own periscope down and stared at the Kaiju, cursing her new and limited view of the action. The glass was hard to see through thanks to damage from the last salvo. Something had struck the glass and made it dirty on the port side. She strained her eyes but only made out vague shapes.

The fighters came screaming overhead to buy them time. Missiles leapt away and flew at the Kaiju. The class three howled at the planes and fired on them. A shotgun blast of heavy balls took four planes but at least a dozen escaped.

"Acid!" someone called from topside. Might have been Peter but his voice was high and scratchy and hard to make out.

"How much?" Katie yelled into the intercom. The shifting and rocking of Big Dog made it almost impossible to hear her own thoughts.

Gunny must have been feeling lucky because he fired a fresh salvo of rounds. They screamed over the distance and hit the class two low. The explosions ripped it off the ground and sent the beast crashing forward.

"It's not too bad. Deploying counter measures."

Katie grimaced. Counter measures were simply bags of baking soda, but at least the stuff would stop the plating from being eaten away.

"Angle the one O sixe milimeter down ten degrees and fire," she called.

A few seconds later her commands became action and Big Dog shuddered as it's largest guns fired.

"Plate down six feet," she ordered. It was too hard to make out the action.

"Plate down," Gunny Mack confirmed.

Her view shifted long enough to make out the Class Three coming into view.

"Engineering. Kilmer, we need to be fast. Can you give me full power and take us to port at speed."

"On it."

"The leak?"

"Still there but we got most of it contained."

"Are we moving to flank?"

"I'm trying."

"It better be your best because that Class Three is about to pound us."

"Damage!" Glaus said, and she nearly leapt out of her seat.

The shells arrived and took the Kaiju right in the back of the head. The explosion was immense as the beast died. There was some soft material back there but the chance of making such a strike was hard to pull off.

The ground shook as the Kaiju went up. The rolling terrain and accompanying tropical trees shuddered, then were blown over by typhoon forced wind. Fire spread, and then came a small mushroom cloud.

"Son of a bitch, that was a big explosion."

"*Ja*, and the class three is moving now. Fast. It doesn't seem to have been affected by the blast," Glaus said.

Big Dog lurched to the side just as it fired. The shotgun blast of hundreds of pellets the size of boulders arced toward them. Big Dog kept moving as it shifted from 'ass down' to 'ass on the run', but there was a problem. Even if they managed to turn around, a feat that would take minutes instead of seconds, even if they went to flank speed, there was no way they were outrunning the class three.

"How soon?"

"Not long now. It's running."

She ordered the plate lowered. If she kept it up it would only delay the inevitable and she preferred to see their doom approaching.

"What's it doing?" Glaus asked.

She had no answer.

The guns thundered relentlessly as they were loaded and fired in tandem. Forty-eights and one o sixes with their own unique sounds. But the pattern was so fast it was staccato and music to her ears.

Then a fresh wing of fighters spread across the battlefield and unleashed hell. Missiles raced across the sky to impact with the building sized beast. Explosions danced across it's mid section, arms, and legs. The Kaiju howled in fury and extended whip like armatures to bat at the gnats swarming past.

Something else whistled overhead and stuck the creature, giving it pause.

"What the hell?"

"Battleships are firing."

"But that's a death warrant," she said.

"It will also buy us time."

"It's not worth the loss of life."

"I do not agree. If we locate a weakness in the beasts then a million deaths may someday be averted."

"You would say that." She muttered under her breath, "Fucking Nazi."

"As I have explained, your anger toward me is misplaced.

"Not now, just shut up about you and how your country followed orders to kill millions. Is that why you're on this mission? Redemption."

"As a matter of fact it is, *fräulein*."

Katie wanted to shoot back an angry retort, but she never got the chance. The class three Kaiju did something unexpected, something she'd never seen or heard of before.

It leapt into the air.

"Oh no," she said, but her words were not enough. Despair

crashed down just as the beast did. She wavered in her seat as sudden fear ate at her gut. She needed more time. Time to think and plan.

The Kaiju landed hard enough to shake the earth. It was so massive that Katie had to wonder how the rest of the world didn't feel it coming. As it rose up on all three legs, its mouth opened, head tilted back, and it bellowed at the sky. The sound was like a typhoon had arrived.

The Kaiju Soldiers hung on for dear life as their ride came to a stop. Its chest opened in hundreds of locations as it extruded weaponry to demolish Big Dog.

"How do we stop that?"

Katie thought of her husband stuck in a metal can while being shelled by men like Heinrich Glaus. She was terrified of what it would feel like when the beast crushed them to scrap. Would she die screaming?

"Commander! What'd we do?" Gunny Mack yelled into the intercom.

What do we do? We die, she wanted to shout back.

"Commander Cord, listen to me. We have to move. We must do something or we will all die."

"We're all going to die," she repeated the words.

The engineer must have had enough silence because he triggered the shielding. It started to slide into place.

Heinrich Glaus let himself free from his webbed seat and dropped to the ground. He moved to her command chair and leaned over the console to look her in the eye.

"There are times when warriors are scared. They must swallow that. They must use it. I spent years stuck in a tank while I did the bidding of a madman, and this is my only hope for redemption. Do you see?"

She stared at the man before her and something slid into place. He had been scared? The mighty Heinrich Glaus?

"Get away from me, you monster!" she cried.

"No, *fräulein*, that is the monster," he said and pointed at the porthole.

She shook her head and stared at her console.

The beast was coming, and they were going to be crushed. If they just had a way to put the creature down.

She snapped her eyes front.

"Back in your seat, Commander," she said, and then lifted her transmitter.

"Engineering, extend the support. Do it now!"

The shield reacted and slid into place as hundreds of pellets struck them like thunder.

"We can't stand this assault," Gunner Mack cried into the transmitter.

"Stand, that's what I want. Bring us upright, and I mean now; fully upright. Divert every bit of steam we have. Buy us some time by aiming below the Japanese. Don't hit one but make the Kaiju think we will. If it has any sense of preservation it should try to shield them."

The engineers didn't bother to argue. They must have just conveyed her orders because Big Dog slid back, and then, with boilers howling, her viewpoint rose into the air.

"Faster! I don't care if you have to kill all the other systems. We need to be upright now and get the brace in place!"

The mode was not fully tested. It worked, that was for sure, but standing Big Dog up was a mechanical feat the experts had sworn would never work properly. The support was mainly used for bracing during heavy work like lifting but now it would act as the third leg of a tripod.

She was thrown back into her seat and Heinrich, for all his nimbleness, barely made it to his station. He dragged himself up the webbing and almost reached his seat when the Kaiju struck.

Hands the size of trucks and bearing seven willowy fingers hit hard enough to nearly knock Big Dog over.

"Fire everything we have!" she yelled into the transmitter.

"We'll have to drop most of the shielding for that," came back Gunny Mack.

"Just do it. I have a plan."

"Plan better involve kissing my..." he trailed off as the transmitter clicked.

The plating moved out of the way, and she was face to face with the monster's chest. Holes were undulating as rounds appeared. If her plan didn't work the beast would hold them in place and blow them to pieces. Skin the color of aquamarine, like a bunch of glowing algae, flowed over flesh the color of liver. The beast bellowed again, and it was all she could do to get her hands over her ears.

The guns roared and punched into the beasts shoulder directly under the Japanese soldiers. The Kaiju reacted by moving a hand to protect them.

"We don't have time to make this pretty. I want that tester ready to fire. Can you do that?"

"But it's still alive, why would we need a sample now?" Then Heinrich smiled. "Ah, I see. I'll need help."

"Fine." She unsnapped her seatbelts and slid out of the chair and was immediately tossed to the floor.

The guns opened up and bought them some time. At this range they couldn't miss but they also couldn't come up to velocity.

The Kaiju fell back and dragged them after. She clung to her seat and lifted herself to the fallen transmitter.

"I want the front arms up. All the way up. I want to hug this son of a bitch!"

If they heard her she was unaware because the rocking beast tossed her across the enclosure. Hienrich managed to reach out and grab her arm before she could slam into the wall. He hauled her to his side and got his hands around her waist to pull her to her feet. Katie resisted the urge to bat his hand aside.

"Is it ready?"

"Very nearly. I think the firing mechanism may be jammed. You get ready to hit the release, I'll get it back into position."

"Be careful or you'll lose a hand."

"I'll lose more than that if we fail."

Brought to Big Dog's full height, she stared into the face of the Kaiju. Its mouth was filled with razor sharp teeth the size of cars. It had nostrils of a sort but they were composed of willowy membranes that fluttered as it sucked in breath.

Heinrich slithered into a workspace and started banging things around.

Big Dog came to it's full height and Katie grimaced a the visage before her. The beast's eyes didn't glow with malevolence as she had thought. They were thoughtful and bespoke some intelligence. But that alien intelligence, new to this world, was using its might and might of its brethren for one purpose: the destruction of her and her allies.

"Try it!" Heinrich yelled.

She moved to the console but the beast struck, batting at Big Dog. The metal around her groaned and parts shrieked. Gunny fired again this time blowing holes in the creature but it was tough and thick and, while it hurt the Kaiju, it could not kill it. There was simply too much of the monster to kill.

"Are you going to try it?"

"I'm trying!" she yelled back.

The beast struck again and this time she was tossed across the pod. She hit the wall and saw stars. Another one of those and she was done for.

The console was only a few feet away. All she had to do was get to her feet. Move. One foot after another. She'd been good at that since she was two years old. Now it seemed impossible as the world reeled around her.

She fought vertigo as Big Dog nearly tipped over but Engineering worked some magic and, with boilers pushed to the edge, Big Dog righted itself on legs strained to the edge.

"Now, I can see it. We must strike now!" Heinrich bellowed.

She crawled across the floor on hands and knees and reached the console. She hauled herself up the seat and stared blankly at the buttons as stars swirled in front of her face. She found it by touch and triggered the switch that would arm the needle.

"It's online," she yelled back. "I think."

"Do it."

"Get out of there."

"I can't. I am holding the firing pin. There was damage from the beast, and if I let go it won't line up to fire."

"You'll be killed."

"No, *fräulein*. I won't. Please, do it."

Big Dog rocked one more time as Gunny Mack yelled into the intercom. "This is it. He's going to strike at the pod."

The pod; her. She took a deep breath and wondered if this was the last thing she would do before being crushed like a tin bucket.

Katie triggered the device.

The explosion blew the back out of Big Dog. The needle was a piece of reinforced metal shaped like an actual hypodermic. At three feet in diameter and over a hundred feet in length after the telescoping inner tubes fully deployed, it was designed to pierce a Kaiju and retrieve a sample.

The Kaiju howled in fury as its chest was punched through. It stumbled back and stared in shock at the giant metal robot before it. Blood, blue and frothing leaked from its mouth.

Katie almost felt sorry for it.

The needle retracted and the Kaiju stumbled to the side so she hit it again.

The second strike didn't have as much power but it still sank into the beast's chest.

The Kaiju turned away, took a few stumbling steps, and then collapsed. It's third leg swept around and struck Big Dog. Even on three legs it couldn't withstand the force of the blow and toppled.

Katie managed to drag herself into her seat and snap shoulder pads into place.

The rending crash of machinery was horrific and went on forever. She screamed and, after a few moments, realized she was still breathing. Her consoles were a mess. Sparks flew and smoke filled the cavity. One of the port windows had come lose and slid open and fell to the ground.

From her vantage point, she watched a leg kick like a dying dog.

"Fräulein?" a pitiful voice asked.

She unsnapped herself and braced for the four-foot drop to the floor, which a few minutes ago had been a wall. She struck it and pulled herself to the hatch that Commander Heinrich Glaus had descended to save their lives.

She peered over the side and saw him clutching a metal canister in both hand. It was huge and heavy and he heaved it at her. She caught it and pulled it up with both hands. The container was heavy and blue blood had leaked on the side.

"Go. Take the X and go. We are done. The boilers will blow soon. Just go."

"I'll pull you up then we can get the others free."

"Go. My legs are crushed, and I can't feel anything below my chest. I am dead. You must take the sample, you must. If you stay and die then all of this sacrifice would be for naught." He took a deep breath and met her eyes. "For what it is worth, *fräulein*, you are a brave commander, and it was my honor to serve under you."

Heinrich Glaus tried to salute but failed and fell silent. His eyes remained on hers as life faded.

Katie moved.

She hauled herself and her precious package along the wall and then triggered the entryway into X. She had to angle her body to slide into the cockpit. There was barely room behind the seat for the canister but she jammed it in and hit power. The entry slammed shut at the same time as the canopy overhead.

She hit the radio and called for Gunny Mack or Kilmer in engineering but neither answered.

She sobbed as she called in the *Mayday*, and then launched, hoping the craft wasn't about to be slammed into a blocked hatch.

Even on it's side, the X-227 Marauder was a beast in its own right with powerful engines, a squat fuselage, and stubby wings. As the called over and over for any survivors the plane's engines kicked in.

She closed her eyes and the plane's turbines roared.

Katie was pressed back in her seat so hard that she nearly passed out. She dragged the stick to the side and managed to right the tiny jet. As she cleared the battle site, she looked in the rearview mirror mounted over her HUD and watched as Big Dog exploded.

"Craft X-227, identify yourself."

Katie spoke codes into the radio and waited.

"Big Dog, it's good to hear you. The general's waiting to hear your results. Make your way to these coordinates, and we'll be waiting with a warm deck and dinner. How is Big Dog?"

"Big Dog is a loss but the mission was a success. I'm the only survivor. I'll be recommending Heinrich Glaus for the Medal of Honor. He saved all of us."

"Giving a medal to a stinking Nazi? What gives?"

"He paid for his sins many times over. I'll just leave it at that. X-227 signing off. See you in a few minutes."

Katie sat back in the seat and hit the afterburners. She got one last look at the smoldering remains of the Kaiju and the dog that had killed it, then they disappeared as she rocketed into the sky.

THE GREAT SEA BEAST

LARRY CORREIA

THE GREAT SEA BEAST REVEALED itself.

First, spines of bone, each one as big around as a tree, broke the ocean's surface. Next came the great bulbous head, its skin a deep red except for where it was covered in barnacles and black growths from the depths. Then the eyes appeared, two great white oozing blobs, and beneath those was a mass of writhing tentacles, longer than anything found on even the largest of the giant squid. There were still freshly drowned corpses of Minamoto clan sailors trapped in those tentacles.

As Munetaka watched, the tentacles moved the bodies into the vast wet hole that served as the creature's mouth, to be ground into a red paste between teeth like mill stones. The head alone was larger than his ship, and when the shoulders broke the surface, it was larger than a castle. It was so large, so inconceivably vast, that it was like watching the sea birth a new island, only this island was heading straight for them at a seemingly impossible rate of speed.

It was incredible. It was a god made flesh.

The ocean crashed around the creature as if it were a rock cliff. Waves created by the monster lifted the *Friendly Traveler* and sent it hurtling back down. His tiny wooden ship was nothing before the

Illustration by **ROBERT ELROD**

Great Sea Beast. Several other Minamoto clan vessels had already been smashed into splinters by the thing's wrath. Their lord's warship was broken and sinking. They were on their own.

He spied the jagged cliffs. "Hold this course!" Nasu Munetaka bellowed at his panicking crew. He looked toward the opposite horizon. The sun was just beginning to rise. "Hold this exact course."

It would close with them in a matter of minutes. They would all die, crushed, drowned, or devoured. The brave sailors adjusted their sails and kept them on the wind. Lesser men leapt overboard or cowered in fear. The other samurai were struggling in vain to figure out the magical horn they'd taken from the *gaijin*, while their priest begged the water dragon to rise from his coral palace beneath the sea to protect them.

But Captain Nasu Munetaka did not ask the heavens for aid nor did he resort to foreign magic. He simply stood at the stern of the *Friendly Traveler*, calmly stringing his bow, watching the demon that had haunted his dreams come for them.

He had been waiting half his life for this moment.

His hands did not tremble.

TWELVE YEARS BEFORE, HE HAD woken up screaming.

Someone was carrying him, cradled in their arms like he was a baby. They were trying to be gentle, but every touch was made of agony. The half of his body which had been out of the water had been burned crispy by the sun, and the half that had been submerged had been eaten away by salt water. His skin was peeling off in black or blue strips.

Munetaka was the son and grandson of warriors, so he tried not to scream. His throat was so dry it was more of a soundless hiss anyway, and his body was so wrung out that there was no indignity of tears. Then he remembered through the haze of sun drenched pain how he'd come to be here. The village had to be warned. Frantic,

Munetaka clutched at his rescuer's shirt and tried to tell him of the crimson demon rising from the sea, but he couldn't form the words.

"Bozu! Help us. The fishermen found this boy washed up on a reef."

With eyelids dried partially open, he could barely see, but Munetaka knew they were inside. He could feel absence of the angry sun. The rescuer laid him on a mat. Thousands of hot needles stabbed through Munetaka's back. He'd never before realized that his skin served the same purpose as his father's armor.

Someone knelt next to the mat. Cold hands touched the sides of his face and tilted his head for examination. "A shipwreck?"

"Yes. They said he still had a death grip on a broken board."

"He must have been in the water for several days... Ama! Get my medicine pouch. I'll need some water boiled. These wounds must be cleaned."

"We forced some drink down his throat when we found him. He didn't vomit most of it back up."

"Good, then he may still live... Can you hear me, boy?"

The crimson demon comes from the sea. Run. You have to run. You have to get away.

The memories came back, breaking through the walls of his mind. He was too young for a voyage up the coast, but he had tagged along on his father's patrol, sneaking in to hide amongst the piles of rope. By the time he was discovered they would be too far from home to turn back. His father was a stern man, as was required of a Minamoto clan ship captain, but Munetaka knew that he secretly enjoyed having his son onboard his ship. Someday Munetaka would be a captain too, and he'd be the one to keep the seas around Kamakura free of pirates and Tairu clan scum, just like his father, and his father before him. Once found, he'd not even received too much of a beating. He suspected his father had been more than a little proud of his daring. The captain had even told his men that Munetaka was their good luck charm. It was the happiest day of young Munetaka's life, until the luck ran out and he had watched helplessly as the ocean turned red and the Great Sea Beast slaughtered everyone.

He snapped back to the world of sunburned pain. His flesh was so softened by days spent soaking in saltwater that even the tatami mat was cutting through him and the monk was fretting as Munetaka bled all over the polished wooden floor of the monastery. The monk was asking him another question.

"What happened?"

Death had happened, only somehow it had forgotten to take him.

TEN YEARS BEFORE, HIS LORD had condemned him.

"You waste my time with this?" Lord Minamoto Yorimasa raised his voice. "I should have you killed for your impudence, boy."

Munetaka kept his eyes on the floor. He could feel the angry gaze of the court on him.

"Your request is denied. There will be no expedition. The Great Sea Beast is a lie. You are the only witness. A child who drank too much saltwater and cooked his brains in the sun imagined a demon to blame for his father's carelessness. Your father died in a storm like a fool. Knowing your family he was probably drunk and drove *my* ship onto the rocks. A stupid man, always wasteful and drunk."

The shame was unbearable. His father had been the best captain in the clan, but the truth was whatever the lord commanded it to be.

"My advisor said you display a constant tremor in your hands. You are too young to already be a drunk like your father. You are an embarrassment, and yet you dare to come before your lord and ask that I grant you an expedition to hunt for an imaginary monster? Especially now while the Tairu clan encroaches on our lands. What do you have to say for yourself, Munetaka?"

It was said that the exposure had stunted his growth. His voice was as small as his body. "Should it come again, we are all in danger. If we cannot hunt it down and kill it, we must be ready for when it returns."

The lord laughed. "Now you are telling jokes for my amusement. You must wish to be the new court fool. Even if such a thing was real, then it must be a spirit of the ocean. It could not be defeated with arrows or spears."

"No, my lord, I saw it clearly. It was no ghost or spirit. It was shaped like a man and walked upon the seabed. Its skin was like a whale and its face was like many squid, but it was still a creature of flesh and bone."

"And you alone are the only one who has ever seen such a magnificent sight."

"There are other witnesses," Munetaka said softly. "Only last year, three fishermen near the lighthouse at—"

"Peasants!" the lord snapped. "Their word means nothing. Their minds are soft, and your drunken tales have filled their hearts with fear. My fisherman are scared now because of you. Production suffers as they imagine a big red shadow beneath them, piss themselves, and flee back to shore. Even some of my samurai have been dumb enough to listen and believe your fanciful tales." He turned to glare at one of his retainers.

The young scribe Saburo lowered his head and backed out of the line, shamed by the attention.

"My lord. forgive me, but I remember clearly what I saw. The crimson demon was far bigger than your castle." He dared to raise his voice. The retainers began to mutter at his bold words. "It lifted my father's ship in one hand as it licked the sailors from the deck, and then dropped us when it was done."

"Silence!" The whispering stopped. The lord would have no scandal his court. "Listen to me very carefully, young Munetaka. Go back to your village. There will be no more mention of this sea monster. You will not speak of it again. It never happened. I have declared that it does not exist. Your father, despite his weakness, served me well, and that is the only reason I am being so lenient with you now. Return to your studies. I've been told that you show no talent with the sword and you are a disaster upon a horse, but the clan will find some use for your life eventually. Dismissed."

EIGHT YEARS BEFORE, HE HAD discovered his purpose.

"Nasu Munetaka, if rumor is to be believed, you are possibly the worst student who has ever been sent to me. You are small. You are weak. You shake like a leaf. Hold out your hands."

"Yes, sensei." Munetaka did as he was told and stuck his hands out, palm down.

"They expect me to teach the art of the bow to such as this?" The old man watched Munetaka's hands tremble. "Pathetic. They told me it is because you swallowed too much seawater, but I suspect that you are simply a wretched pig dog who lacks character. You have already demonstrated that you are a liar."

The other students snickered. Even though he'd been forbidden to speak of the Great Sea Beast for years now, their daimyo's condemnation had followed him everywhere. Nasu Munetaka was considered a liar for telling the truth. "Yes, sensei."

"Lower your hands. Your last sensei told me you have been squandering your inheritance on gambling and pleasure women, and that you often come to training reeking of alcohol. You're a disgusting mess, but if there is to be a war against the Tairu, we will need bodies. If you are late again to class again I will use you as a target."

The sensei continued down the line. "You will draw until the second thumb joint nestles upon your jaw." The other students had already prepared their bows and they stood eager at the edge of the grass of the practice field. Munetaka hurried to catch up. His father had been a superb archer and Munetaka would not fail him. "Each of you will release two hundred arrows today. First your arms will ache, then your fingers will bleed, and then you will experience pain like nothing you have ever imagined. You will pray for death long before that, but you will not stop until I tell you to. Ready! Draw!"

The targets were men made of straw. They seemed very far away. Munetaka raised the yumi. It was longer than he was tall, but because it was designed to be gripped on the lower third, he could still use it. His hands were shaking so badly that he had a hard time nocking the arrow.

"Release."

A dozen arrows flew down range. Most of them fell short and stuck into the grass. Not a single target was struck. Munetaka's hands were shaking so badly that he wasn't ready in time.

"Hurry, idiot. You will draw back fully and then release the arrow in the same motion." A few of the other students laughed. "Shut up. Did I give you permission to find that amusing? Now, Munetaka."

It was incredibly difficult to pull it back and the yumi creaked as it bent.

"Imagine it is your sea monster," one of the other boys shouted.

And for just a moment, he did, and they were on a sea of red. His fingers slipped. The string slapped into his left wrist with a *snap*. The arrow flew wild to the side, burying itself deep into the ground.

The sensei casually backhanded the loudmouth. "Multiple idiots. Wonderful. But if it really was bigger than our lord's castle, that would probably still have struck your monster. Try it again, fool, and no distractions this time. The rest of you wait."

His father had often told him that the arrow knew the way, so it had to be true. He could only trust that his father would guide the arrow's flight. Muscles strained as he struggled to pull back the string as he glared at the target, imagining that the straw man was his sensei, and as his fingers reached his cheek, he let go.

Red fletching appeared in the center of the dummy's chest.

The sensei nodded at Munetaka. "It is rare that a liar can shoot true. Again."

His wrist stung from the string. He took another arrow from the bundle, and since the yumi seemed to fight him less this time, had it nocked far more quickly than the first.

The second shot hit within a few inches of the first arrow.

"Again!"

The third was just above those.

"Hmmm…" The sensei stroked his long mustache thoughtfully. "Maybe the rest of you should arrive stinking of cheap booze, too… Now imagine it is this sea monster of yours, Munetaka. Show us what you would do to it now."

He was a screaming child on a sea of red, holding onto a fragment of a boat, struggling to stay above the waves, as tentacles fed men into a wet hole filled with giant teeth.

Only he was no longer a little boy. *Father guide my arrow.*

His hands did not tremble this time.

The fourth arrow streaked directly through the center of the straw man's face.

FOUR YEARS BEFORE, THE HUNT had begun.

Munetaka was woken by the grunting of pigs. A wet, pink snout was biting at his face to see if he was edible so the young samurai slugged the pig in the eye. It squealed indignantly and retreated. He found himself lying in a pile of straw, his back against a peasant's shack, and a sake jug in his lap. It sloshed when he moved it, so he choked down the remainder. It was the cheapest swill in Kamakura, but it got him drunk enough to sleep, and that's what counted.

"I figured you'd wake up if that pig started eating you." There was a man leaning on the fence. His kimono bore the mon of the Minamoto clan. "If not, then that was some strong drink."

"Who're you?" Munetaka asked as he scratched himself.

"The better question is who are you, Nasu Munetaka?"

"Who's that? I'm just some drunk ronin," he lied.

"No. I recognize you. You do not look so different now, like a shorter version of your father. They say you would have been a handsome one if the sea hadn't poisoned you so, that's why you are still nothing but skin and bones." The man gave him a sad smile. "They say you're the best archer in all the land. They say you killed a hundred Tairu soldiers at the battle of Uji."

"*They* say lots of stuff." He had no idea how many he'd killed, but he'd shot at least twenty. It was hard to keep track. Lord Yorimasa had still lost though, and after his suicide they'd tossed his head in the river.

"Yet now you've been reduced to a life of crime, smuggling, and drinking. That's rather sad. It's to be expected though. You can't tell someone their entire life that they're a liar without honor, and not expect them to make it the truth."

"You're lucky I'm too hung over to string my bow to shoot you, friend." The man seemed kind of familiar, but Munetaka couldn't place him. "Do I know you?"

"I'm Saburo," he answered as he climbed over the fence.

"The scribe?"

"Scholar, diplomat, things like that, in fact I've just returned from a mission to the Song court all the way across the sea, but I still remember your tragic story."

"Yeah… Just a story…" Munetaka rubbed his bleary eyes. "Our dead lord saw to that."

"Most of all I'm a collector of stories. The *gaijin* have stories too." Saburo removed a piece of paper from his kimono and handed it over. "Like this one, about a war between witches and a king, where foul sorcery was used to turn a leviathan of the deep into a giant monster to wreck the king's fleets. It comes all the way from a land called India."

Munetaka could not read the strange foreign writing, nor could he recognize the coastline shown on the map, but at the bottom was a drawing and it was… "No." The eyes, the tentacles, the spine, the blood red hide, It was *perfect*. His mouth was suddenly very dry. His hands began to shake so badly that it threatened to crumple the ancient paper. "It can't be."

"So it is the same then?"

Even though Saburo was of higher station, Munetaka leapt up and grabbed the scribe by the shoulders. "Can you take me to its lair?"

"It is very far away."

"I know a good ship."

"It is in a strange, *gaijin* land. We'll need warriors."

"Then we will find them!"

Saburo grinned. "I've always wanted to be part of a story."

SIX MONTHS AGO, HE HAD found the source.

The samurai had fought their way through the jungle temple, leaving a trail of dead and dying in their wake. One of the foreigners charged them with an oddly curved dagger. Munetaka drew an arrow and launched it in one smooth motion, piercing the throat and sending the *gaijin* to the stone. Two more cultists followed, screaming, but Munetaka released two more arrows in rapid succession and dropped them both. He stepped over the dying and observed his crew. They were hacking the last of the cultists to bits. Worshippers of foreign devils were no match for Munetaka's experienced warriors.

In honor of their god of the depths, the cultists painted their skin red. Munetaka had painted their temple red with blood to defy it.

"That's all of them, Captain. We took no casualties."

"Good work." Munetaka gave the ronin an appreciative nod. "Spread out and search."

This land was always hot. The air was constantly moist. It made their equipment rust and their armor chafe. For years they had followed clues and consulted with wily foreigners. They had been caught up in battles and plagues. They'd crossed an ocean, a dozen kingdoms, and marched hundreds of miles, and every inch of it had been filled with discomfort and misery. It stood to reason that such an awful creature had been spawned in this cursed land. Despite all of those tribulations, the warriors he had gathered still followed him. He didn't really understand. Munetaka had no real station. There was no honor to be gained in following someone considered to be a delusional madman, yet they followed his orders and trusted him with their lives.

Perhaps, if the Great Sea Beast hadn't ruined his life, turned him into a drunk, and gotten him disgraced with his clan, Munetaka might have made a good captain after all…

They entered a great stone room, lit by flickering torches, covered in gaudy carvings and murals. In the center of a great basin was another statue of the Great Sea Beast, dyed red from the accumulated sludge of thousands of human sacrifices. Munetaka snarled, "Damned foreign devils."

"Remarkable. This is the home of the cult of the Great Sea Beast." Saburo was examining the murals. He alone could read their gibberish. "This is the repository of all their knowledge." The scribe seemed giddy with excitement.

"All I need to know is where to find it and how to kill it."

Saburo traced his finger down the wall. They had struck enough of these temples that Munetaka recognized the story shown in the pictures. Witches dragging a leviathan from the depths, cutting it apart, and torturing it with their *gaijin* sorcery until it had been twisted into the savage creature that had ruined his life. However, this series of pictures was different than the others.

"Interesting. They cut a bone from the leviathan. A horn… When the witches blew on the horn it made sounds that could awaken and summon the Great Sea Beast." Saburo reached for a thick wooden lever on the wall and pulled it down.

There was a sudden grinding inside the wall. Munetaka had an arrow nocked within an instant. Rusty chains rattled through channels in the floor. The stone wall split, then slowly ground open. "What manner of *gaijin* trickery is this?" He pointed his yumi into the room, but there were only shadows. "Fetch a lantern."

Flickering light filled the newly revealed chamber. There was something odd hanging from chains attached to the ceiling. The mysterious device's surface was grey and porous of texture. It was an oddly curled bone, only it was as big as an ox, and standing next to it was one of the red painted priests wearing only a tiger pelt. He began gibbering furiously in their strange language when he saw the samurai approaching.

"You'd best shoot him quickly. He says that if we come any closer he will unleash the monster and send it against our home island," Saburo whispered.

"Good." Munetaka made an exaggerated show of gradually drawing back his bow. "Let him."

The priest rushed and pressed his mouth to the bone. Air resonated through a maze of chambers. A deep, eerie rumble filled the temple. The sound seemed to grow and grow. The hair stood up on his neck. It was a long alien wail that shook all the warriors to their bones.

Munetaka could have killed the priest immediately, but let the monster come. That took care of finding it. The priest looked up, triumphant, but seemed a bit surprised when Munetaka showed absolutely no fear. Realization dawned that the samurai wanted the beast exposed. Only then did Munetaka drill him through the heart.

The assembled ronin stared at the body for a moment, unsure what their captain had just allowed to happen.

Munetaka took a flask from his pocket and took a long drink.

There was no turning back now. "Take the horn back to the ship. Have the priest cleanse this *gaijin* filth from us." He began walking away. "It's time to go home."

TEN DAYS AGO, HIS CLAN had learned the truth.

The crew of the *Friendly Traveler* had seen the smoke rising over the horizon hours before they'd seen land. There were bloated corpses floating on the surface as they approached the harbor. After such a long journey it had not been the joyous homecoming most of them had been hoping for.

There had been a town here once. Now it was nothing but a ruin. Buildings had been crushed. Fires had caught and spread out of control, consuming everything. There had only been a small castle, but it had been smashed to pieces and spread across the rocky shore. There were bodies everywhere. Peasants were trying to pull survivors from the rubble.

Two men stood at the rail, watching the dead float by

"Is this what you wanted, Captain?" Saburo asked.

"No…" There were children crying in the streets.

But now they understand.

His crew was shocked by the carnage. They were hard men, but it was hard to comprehend destruction on this scale. He'd warned them… "Take us in. I want to find out what direction it went."

The docks were gone. Several masts sticking out of the water explained the fate of most of the ships stationed here. One warship had been picked up and hurled three hundred paces inland, and half of it was sticking out the side of an inn. There were other warships still in one piece, but they had most likely arrived after the Great Sea Beast had left. They had been gone so long, and there had been a clan war going on when they'd left, so Munetaka wasn't sure who would be in charge when they got back, and he was too pragmatic to risk flying his clan's flag. When he saw that the other warships were Minamoto he ordered their own flag raised.

The crew of the Minamoto warships were so stunned that they barely noticed the arrival of the *Friendly Traveler*. Munetaka hailed them, answered several angry challenges, and was then allowed to come alongside a much larger, newer warship. Ropes were hurled back and forth, and the *Friendly Traveler* was hauled in close, partially so they could communicate more easily, but more likely because they looked like pirates and the clan was not about to let them escape.

There were shouts as they drew closer, warnings that the harbor was treacherous with sunken ships that could damage their hull and questions about if they too had seen the giant crimson demon, which was half the size of a mountain.

Munetaka was surprised to see the personal mon of the Minamoto daimyo on the guard's armor. Lord Minamoto Yoritomo himself—the successor of the man who shamed him—approached the rail. The entire crew bowed… Except for Munetaka.

"What're you doing?" Saburo hissed. "Are you drunk?"

"Only a little," Munetaka answered.

The Lord's eyes narrowed dangerously at this sleight. Dozens of Minamoto soldiers nocked arrows, waiting the order to execute the impudent captain. "Who are you?"

"I am Captain Nasu Munetaka, son of Captain Nasu Tadamichi. Twelve years ago the Great Sea Beast killed my father and sank his ship. I alone survived. I saw this monster, and I told the truth. I intended to hunt it down and send it back to Jigoku. Your predecessor called me a liar and a fool. He mocked me and dishonored my father. He declared this monster a myth." Munetaka pointed toward land. All eyes followed.

There was a giant footprint, shaped like that of a lizard, only as wide as the Lord's warship and pressed deep enough into the sand to fit a house.

"Do you believe me now?"

HIS ENTIRE LIFE HAD COME down to this moment.

The sea outside Kamakura was red with blood and lit by burning wreckage. The air was choked with smoke and the screams of the injured. The Great Sea Beast's arms were humanoid, only its hands ended in three webbed fingers, and it was swatting boats from the ocean like a child in a bath tub. Hundreds of arrows were lodged in its hide. It had been struck by balls of flaming pitch from the warships and the whaling harpoons of desperate sailors, yet it showed no sign of slowing.

A Minamoto warship rammed straight into the monster's stomach. The flesh dimpled as the bow gave, but it did not pierce the ancient flesh. The Great Sea Beast let out an ear splitting roar, scooped the warship up and hurled it inland. The tiny dots spinning off of it were sailors and samurai. The ship landed on the rocks and exploded into a million pieces.

"Saburo!"

The scribe ran to him. "Yes, Captain?"

"Sound the horn."

"But we don't understand how the *gaijin* magic works! It could just enrage it further."

"Excellent... Do it now."

The scribe knew not to question. "Yes, Captain!" He ran to do as he was told.

Munetaka picked one particular arrow from his quiver. Though the shaft had belonged to his father, he'd replaced the arrowhead with one he'd fashioned himself. It was slightly different in shape from his regular armor piercing points, but the balance was perfect. He'd carved a piece of bone from the gaijin horn. If it had really come from the body of the leviathan the Great Sea Beast had been fashioned from, he would send it home. He'd had the arrow blessed by priests of every faith he'd come across in his travels. Surely some god would be listening.

Saburo blew the horn. It was nothing like the strong, resounding bellow created by the tiger priest, rather it was a harsh note that trailed off into a painful warble.

Yet, it worked. The Great Sea Beast turned and roared a furious challenge. It started toward them. The waters were shallow, so it seemed to grow taller as it walked across the seabed, exposing even more of its corpulent self to the air. The waves became increasingly violent.

Taking out his flask, Munetaka enjoyed one last drink. It was the finest sake in Nippon, and he'd saved it for a very special occasion. Only the best would do for today. Putting the flask back in his kimono, Munetaka took another look at the horizon, then back at the creature, carefully estimating its speed. "Hold this course no matter what."

"There's rocks straight ahead, Captain!"

"No matter what!" he shouted.

Closer.

He readied the special arrow. There would be only one shot.

The other ships were forgotten. A warship clipped the beast's side and was sent spinning away. A single, crazed samurai leapt from that ship onto the beast's flesh, stabbing at it while trying to climb up its body as if it were a mountain. The monster did not seem to notice. It was entirely focused on the *Friendly Traveler*. The warrior lost his grip on the slick hide and disappeared into the churning waters.

Closer.

Munetaka took a deep breath then slowly exhaled. His body moved in time with the violent rolling of the deck beneath his bare feet.

"We're almost on the rocks!"

"Steady…"

The Great Sea Beast loomed over them. The air stunk of rotting fish. A black rain began to fall upon them, and he realized it was demon blood weeping from a thousand shallow cuts.

His hands did not tremble.

The golden edge of the sun broke over them. Vast white eyes, accustomed to the darkness of the deep ocean twitched and mighty lids slammed shut with an audible *slap*. He'd looked directly into those giant merciless eyes so long ago, and he'd wondered afterwards why it had spared him. At the time he'd thought it was because he was insignificant. He was a bug to the Great Sea Beast, not even worth crushing.

Now he understood he had lived because it was his destiny to end this abomination.

While staring into those white orbs before he'd seen that there was a tiny circle in the center, an off white pupil, only visible when you were close enough to choke on its stench and its tentacles could taste your blood on the water. He intended to put an arrow through that pupil and straight into the creature's brain. Two hundred paces away, at an extreme angle, from a rocking ship against a rapidly moving creature the size of a castle, and his target was as big around as the bottom of a sake cup.

Only Munetaka had spent many long hours studying the bottoms of empty sake cups.

The arrow knows the way.

Munetaka drew back the bow in one perfect motion.

Father, guide my hand.

He let fly.

The entire crew held their breath as they watched the arrow streak through the blood rain.

The huge lid blinked open the instant before the arrow struck.

The arrow disappeared, sinking right through the clear jelly of the pupil.

It twitched.

The crew gasped.

There was an incredibly long pause. Then the creature's eye began to spasm wildly, like it was about to leap from its head. It leaned back, head jerking, tentacles thrashing. Webbed fingers clutched at its face. The horrific noise it let out threatened to split the world. The noise trailed off into a moan.

"Turn hard to port! Hard to port!" Munetaka ordered. "Now!"

The crew did as they were told. Seconds later their hull made a sickening sound as it ground against the rocks. Salt spray came up over the side from an impact, but they kept moving. To stop was to perish.

Lumbering forward, the Great Sea Beast continued to clutch madly at its misshapen head, but it was too late. The blessed arrow had worked its way deep into vulnerable tissue, and no living thing could survive for long bleeding from inside its brain. It stumbled then began to fall. It was like watching a great tree being felled by an ax, only they were beneath the tree.

Munetaka's crew knew what to do. They understood what would happen if they didn't get out of the way in time. There was no need to give instructions because they were already working hard. So Munetaka simply stood there, watching, as the Great Sea Beast fell. Live or die, it no longer mattered. His duty was complete.

The Great Sea Beast collapsed. The gradual impact of its bulk threw up a huge wall of water before it. They were lifted and pushed on the wave as sailors held on with all their might. The *Friendly Traveler* was hurled through the maze of rocks. They hit open water, violently spinning, and a few men were flung over the side. Yet, they were through the rocks. Normally that would have raised a cheer amongst the crew but the monster was still collapsing on top of them, and all they could do was watch and hope.

It struck. The world was consumed with thunder. For a moment all of them were blinded by spray.

The Great Sea Beast's head smashed into the rocks right next to them, tons of flesh and bone compacting and rupturing against the unyielding earth. A spine came crashing down, shearing effortlessly through the *Friendly Traveler's* mast and rigging. Captain Munetaka stepped calmly aside as the razor tip of the spine cleaved through the deck where he'd been standing.

And then they were away.

The Great Sea Beast lay still. Ooze pouring from its head in such great quantities that the *Friendly Traveler* was floating on a sea of black.

It was silent except for the creaking of wood and rope.

"It is finished."

THEY WERE HEROES.

The crew of the *Friendly Traveler* were welcomed in Kamekura and showered with gifts. Lord Minamoto Yoritomo granted every member of his crew lands and titles. Songs were sung about their long journey along the shores of foreign lands, and their battle against the Great Sea Beast grew larger with each telling of the story.

Captain Nasu Munetaka sat alone beneath the shade of a tree, watching the tide come in. It was good to escape the noise of the adoring crowds, but the silence made him realize a few things. His father was avenged. His family's honor restored. Yet, what good was a samurai without a purpose? He took out his flask and raised it to his lips. He was a great captain and probably the best archer in the world, but he did not know what came next…

Are there other monsters in the world?

Then perhaps I shall find them.

He poured the rest of his sake into the grass.

His hands did not tremble.

ANIMIKII VS. MISHIPESHU

C.L. WERNER

MARCEL CLERVAL STOOD ATOP THE gantry and stared across the scarred landscape of Michipicoten Island. Before his mining company had arrived, the place had been almost pristine wilderness, devoid of any mark of man's construction beyond the old lighthouse at its eastern extremity. The Canadian government had been loath to relinquish the island, to allow it to slip away from the protection of the Ministry of Natural Resources. It had been a long and tedious legal battle fought in both Canadian and French courts of law to get them to accept the legitimacy of his company's claim to the island.

Centuries past, Michipicoten Island had been known as Isle Maurepas, named after the Count of Maurepas, then serving as France's Minister of the Marine. Jean-Frederic Phelypeaux had been a powerful man in his time, responsible for the funding and maintenance of France's naval forces. Many awards and honors had been bestowed upon him. Among these had been the Isle Maurepas in France's New World colonies. The documents proving the land had been awarded to the Count of Maurepas hadn't come to light until after the Second World War, discovered in the bombed-out cellar of a family named Phillipe outside Rouen. Ownership of the

Illustration by **CHUCK LUKACS**

island was in the form of allodial title, granting the count and his descendents complete control over the land without any restrictions or duties owed to any higher authority, even the French Crown.

Devastated by the war, the Phillipes had sold the title to an American serviceman for a few hundred dollars. From the soldier, the deed had passed through a string of American and Canadian speculators before finally coming into the hands of Munsaint Limited. The first surveyors dispatched by the corporation had done so under the pretence of studying forest caribou, the true nature of their job concealed by the front company they ostensibly worked for. It had all been cleverly arranged, investigating the mineral composition of the island had been simply another part of their research into the caribou population and its conservation. The samples they brought back told far more about the natural resources within the island. It was rich in copper and a second expedition determined the mineral wealth to be extracted was almost unbelievable in magnitude. When global copper prices began to rise, Munsaint set their lawyers to enforcing their claim on Michipicoten Island.

Now the operation was in full swing. The wild island had been transformed in the space of a few weeks into a thriving enterprise. A modern dock had been erected on the west side of the island, bunk houses for miners, warehouses for equipment and storehouses for ore had been built all along the shoreline. The copper veins were so close to the surface that it had proven efficient to cut the timber away and strip mine several acres at a time. Two enormous bucket-wheel excavators had been brought in to clear away the masses of dirt to expose the ore. The waste deposits extracted from the growing pit were discarded in the little lakes dotting the island. Marcel thought it immensely convenient that some retreating glacier had left those natural depressions behind. It made the operation faster and more convenient.

The executive looked past the scarred terrain to gaze in pride at the titanic excavators. They were mounted on gigantic crawlers, each supporting a boom sixty meters long. When operating at peak efficiency, each of the machines could clear 180,000 cubic meters of overburden in a workday. They represented a considerable expense for Munsaint, imported from Germany and with expensive compliments of operators and mechanics to maintain them. Marcel felt, however, that the excavators would quickly prove their value.

Value? For all the trouble clearing their ownership of the island, Munsaint was expecting a considerable profit. Marcel knew if Michipicoten Island didn't pay significant dividends, he'd soon find himself out of a job. Beyond the expense of the legal battle, beyond financing the men and materials to extract the copper, there was the public relations cost to consider. Conservation groups were howling for blood, calling Munsaint everything from barbarians to Nazis for the despoiling of the island. Munsaint had been compelled to endow a few scientific studies to prove that their operations on the island wouldn't harm the indigenous wildlife, and it had taken extra effort to find credible naturalists who would endorse the results Munsaint expected their research to reveal. More capital had been expended to smooth over politicians in France, Canada, and the United States to ensure no environmental agencies disrupted their work. Indeed, Munsaint had been compelled to process the extracted ore in America so several senators could justify their support of the operation by claiming the mine was creating jobs for their constituents.

Most vexing of all, at least for Marcel, had been the protests of the Ojibwa tribe. They held that the island was a sacred place and must not be defiled by the greed of men. Their legends claimed a great monster slumbered beneath the island, and the copper Munsaint was taking had been put there to ensure the beast's sleep. Their ancestors had suffered terribly from the monster until their medicine men discovered it could be placated with copper. Using the metal, they'd lured it to the island. It had soaked up the energies of the ore like a snake sunning itself on a rock. Eventually, the monster wearied and crawled into one of the lakes.

While it slept, tribes from across the region brought all their copper to the island and buried it in the ground so that the monster could never again stir from its lair.

Marcel smiled at the absurdity of the legend. The monster, a thing they called Mishipeshu, was said to be a great scaly beast, the greatest of the creatures they called water panthers. So mighty was Mishipeshu that even the natural foes of the water panthers, the mighty thunderbirds, had been unable to oppose him. Only by placating the brute with copper had the Ojibwa finally been able to end his depredations.

Well, if Mishipeshu had ever existed, Marcel had entombed it far more thoroughly than the Ojibwa. Tons of overburden had been dumped into the lakes, reducing them to nothing but muddy puddles. There was a lesson there, for all backwards, superstitious people who insisted on standing in the path of progress, if only they had the wit to see it.

Marcel turned away from the strip mine and looked out towards the waters of Lake Superior. An empty ore barge was just pulling up at the dock to take on another load. At present capacity, the mine was able to send a load of ore to be processed once every two weeks. Marcel thought they could double that capacity once enough land had been cleared. He still fumed at the decision to process the ore in Chicago rather than someplace closer, but he was realistic enough to understand the concessions demanded by political graft.

The executive had been leaning against the metal rail of the gantry. Now he recoiled from it, staring first at his hands and then back at the railing. Perplexed, he reached out and gripped the rail again. There was no mistaking it; he hadn't imagined the weird pulsation, the shiver that was vibrating through the metal. Marcel shook his head, unable to account for the weird phenomenon. Shouts from mine workers around the camp told him he wasn't the only one to notice the occurrence.

A moment later, however, the miners and their boss had bigger things to occupy their attention. A stand of half-dead trees near the camp began to sway. Chains suspended from the winches at the dock began to shudder. It was a matter of seconds before every bird left on the island flew into the air, squawking and shrieking as they hurriedly made their way inland. Then the tremor struck in earnest.

Marcel was sent reeling as the whole gantry began to creak and groan, threatening to tear itself free from its moorings and pitch him into the strip mine hundreds of meters below. The executive clung to the railing, unable to believe what he was experiencing. An earthquake? Here? It was impossible?

Away to the north, Marcel could see the earth heaving, undulating like a turbulent sea. The great spoil heaps came crumbling down, splashing across the landscape in an avalanche of waste. Near one of the lakes, a great plume of dust and debris shot into the air, propelled hundreds of meters skyward with a force almost volcanic in its violence.

Marcel's mouth dropped open in horror, all color draining from his face as he considered that prospect. Volcanic activity? Was it possible Michipicoten Island was simply the caldera of a sleeping volcano? Had their digging and drilling disrupted some tectonic pressure beneath the island? Was the whole place going to erupt in a firestorm of magma?

Even that apocalyptic explanation would have appealed to Marcel a moment later, for at least it would have been something his secular, materialistic mentality could have accepted and understood. When the earth heaped about the lake suddenly lurched upwards, when it came cascading away from the titanic body of an unbelievably huge creature, everything he had ever believed in, every concept of reality he'd held, was shattered.

The thing was as big as one of the bucket-wheel excavators Munsaint had brought to the island. One hundred and fifty meters long from the tip of its ophidian snout to the end of its long bifurcated tail, sixty meters high at its scaly shoulder. As it shook the loose earth from its body, Marcel could see that the monster was some sort of immense reptile, its scales possessing a dull cobalt hue along its sides and back but fading to a dingy yellow along the belly. Its build was lean, somehow conjuring the impression of a serpent despite the four clawed legs protruding from its bony shoulders. A bony ridge ran along its back, each of the triangular backplates showing black against its cobalt scales. At the ends of the bifurcated tail were two slender barbs of bone, conjuring to Marcel's mind the incongruous image of an earwig's abdomen. The head was an ugly wedge at the end of a long, snaky neck. At once both flat and elongated, the wide jaws supported an array of serrated teeth with a set of long, cobra-like fangs protruding from the upper jaw. The eyes of the creature were narrow, slit like the lenses of some great hunting cat. Those red eyes had an eerie awareness and malignance about them, betraying intelligence far more calculating than that of a mere animal. At the rear of the flattened, rattler-like head, two spikes of bone projected rearwards partially shielding the thing's neck.

Marcel didn't need an Ojibwa medicine man to tell him he was looking upon the great water panther, Mishipeshu. He didn't need to be told the monster was a beast of evil. He could sense that in his bones, in his very soul. When the reptile reared back, when it opened its jaws in a primordial ululation that hissed across the island like a symphony of vipers, terror at last overwhelmed the shock and awe that had gripped Marcel and his miners. Almost to a man, the miners fled towards the docks, screaming and waving their hands at the ore barge.

Marcel scrambled down from the gantry. He didn't shout a warning to his men, didn't tell them that, as he leapt down from the gantry, he could see the barge pulling away from the island, retreating out into Lake Superior. He was too pragmatic to risk the advantage circumstance had gifted him. The Ojibwa said that Mishipeshu was a man-eater. Well then, the monster could glut itself on the workers. While it was busy gorging, Marcel would retreat across the island to the safety of the old lighthouse.

As he ran across the perimeter of the mine pit, Marcel could feel the earth shuddering beneath his feet. His ears rang with the ghastly hisses and growls of Mishipeshu as the enormous reptile lumbered across the island. Once, he risked a look towards the camp, watched as terrified miners began to throw themselves into the icy waters of the lake and try to swim to the quickly retreating barge. He could see Mishipeshu crawling towards them, its forked tongue flickering from between its jaws as it tasted their scent in the air.

A grinding roar, the blast of a steam whistle sounded from nearby. Marcel spun around, horrified to see one of the gigantic excavators crawling towards Mishipeshu, its cutting boom raised in the absurd parody of a knight's lance. What were the idiot Germans doing? Why hadn't they fled with the rest? Did the fools think they were Siegfried sallying forth to vanquish Fafnir? This wasn't some Wagnerian farce! This was a living, breathing monstrosity!

Mishipeshu turned away from the camp as it heard the challenging blast of the excavator's whistle. Hissing its own defiance, the reptile scurried across the piles of overburden, its mammoth claws punching into the walls of the pit as it crawled down to confront the excavator. For an instant, the monster hesitated, glaring balefully at the second excavator at the far end of the mine. That machine's crew had been off duty when the water panther awoke. There was no one available to spur it into action.

The Germans drove their machine at full speed towards Mishipeshu. The monster whipped its tail at them, the bony spikes slashing across the side of the boom. Mishipeshu reeled back in confusion, surprised by an enemy that wasn't a thing of flesh and blood.

As the water panther reeled back, the cutting boom came screaming downwards, crashing against the reptile's flank and grinding against its scaly flesh. Mishipeshu writhed out from beneath the sawing blade. Sludge, which was too thick to ever be called blood, welled up from its horrendous wound. It roared angrily at the excavator and from each of its cobra-like fangs a stream of caustic bile was projected onto the excavator.

Steel bubbled and plastic vaporized as the poisonous slime splashed across the excavator. The crew screamed in despair as the boom's weight was compromised. The front twenty meters of it sagged leftwards on what integrity remained in its frame. Unbalanced, the entire machine crashed onto its side.

Mishipeshu hissed again, but this time there was a suggestion of victory and satisfaction in the ophidian sound. The reptile lunged forward, pouncing upon the toppled excavator like some titanic catamount. The German crew's shrieks became ever more intense as the water panther probed the control booth and maintenance cabins with its claws, digging the men out from their machine like a bear clawing termites from an old log.

Marcel fled, clapping his hands over his ears so he couldn't hear the ghastly cries of the Germans as they were devoured by Mishipeshu. He knew the beast wouldn't be long, and he also knew that it would take far more meat to ease the appetite of something so enormous. Still thinking of the lighthouse, of the security it could offer, he ran about the periphery of the pit. Desperately, he tried to ignore the quaking ground, tried to convince himself the gargantuan footfalls of Mishipeshu weren't coming closer.

Ahead, Marcel could see the lighthouse rising above a stand of trees the miners hadn't yet cleared away. He cried out in delight, fired his exhausted body for the final effort that would carry him to his refuge.

Then, overhead, he saw the flashing flicker of Mishipeshu's tongue. Marcel spun around, throwing his arms across his face to blot out the awful sight, the vision of Mishipeshu crawling up from the bottom of the mining pit, its red eyes glowering hungrily at him.

It was the last thing Marcel Clerval would ever see. The next instant, the water panther's immense jaws closed about him and the screaming executive was gone. Only the scarred landscape of Michipicoten Island remained as his legacy to the world.

The scarred terrain of the island, and the rampaging monster his greed had unleashed.

ALARM KLAXONS SCREECHED ACROSS THE concrete canyons of Chicago, civil defense sirens blaring from the rooftops of skyscrapers and radio towers. Beyond these, the crump of artillery lobbing shells into the cold waters of Lake Michigan rumbled throughout the city. Helicopter gunships circled above the brooding inland sea, their crews dumping depth charges into the lake. Jet fighters screeched across the skies, napalm bombs loaded on their wings. Columns of tanks roared along Lake Shore Drive, trundling past expensive high-rises, their armored advance cracking windows in luxurious condominiums. Mobile missile batteries followed the tanks, the box-like carriages for their weaponry trained upon the grim expanse of water eastward.

A terror inconceivable to the citizens of Chicago had descended upon them. Hordes of refugees choked Michigan Avenue and the other streets still open to civilian traffic. Ferries, tugs, motor launches—anything that could float—was drawn up in the Chicago River, assisting in the Herculean task of evacuating the city.

Destruction loomed over Chicago, annihilation both strange and inconceivable to the sensibilities of the scientific age. A monster from the mists of legend had suddenly erupted onto the modern world. Mishipeshu, the great water panther of the Ojibwa, a reptilian horror of gargantuan size and titanic strength. The beast had ravened down the length of Lake Superior, annihilating communities great and small. The militaries of both Canada and the United States had been helpless to stop the creature. Shipping in the Great Lakes had ground to a halt. Hundreds of thousands had fled their homes, retreating inland in an effort to escape the monster's approach.

It was only recently, with satellite photos and orbital tracking of the monster, that the grim conclusion that its path would bring it to Chicago had been appreciated. Indeed, there were some who claimed that, from the curious diversions Mishipeshu's trail had taken, the water panther was deliberately making for the city.

Bombs, missiles, artillery of every caliber and description had been loosed against Mishipeshu. Whatever substance composed the creature's structure, however, was impervious to the ordnance deployed against it. Injuries inflicted upon the beast healed at an astounding rate, regenerating with a speed directly proportionate with the severity of its wounds. The military was placed in the curious position of trying to inflict the minimal damage to the beast, hoping to weaken it by degrees and slow its advance without activating whatever biological system would throw its restorative properties into overdrive.

Briefly atomic and chemical weaponry had been considered, but the prospect of contaminating the whole of the Great Lakes and their tributary rivers was too hideous to contemplate. Similarly, germ agents had been dismissed. As long as Mishipeshu kept close to the waterways, only conventional ordnance could be deployed against it.

For all the artillery and depth charges, the bombs and missiles, Mishipeshu emerged from the frigid waters of Lake Michigan. The gigantic reptile, resembling nothing so much as some dragon of the Dark Ages, strode up the beach, wading through the desperate fire of the tanks arrayed along Lake Shore Drive. The brute's tongue flickered from between its jaws, tasting the air, savoring the scent of the terrified masses trying to flee the city.

The artillery barrage, the direct fire from the tanks intensified as the water panther crawled over the greenery of Grant Park, its claws gouging great furrows in the earth as it propelled its reptilian mass towards the towers of the Loop, the commercial heart of the city. Again, the hideous tongue flickered from between its jaws, tasting the smell of panicked humanity in the air.

Hissing with the violence of a raging cataract, Mishipeshu charged towards one of the towering apartment complexes. The reptile's claws gouged great furrows in the building, its tail lashing and stabbing at the structure to tear away great chunks of concrete and steel. The building, a weathered veteran from the Roaring 20s, was unable to endure the assault. Shuddering and groaning, it crashed against its neighbor, bringing both structures crumbling down in a cascade of dust and debris.

Vengefully, one of the circling fighters dove down upon Mishipeshu as the monster began to claw bodies from the rubble. Napalm cylinders flashed through the air, their silvery casings gleaming in the sunlight as they hurtled towards the water panther. Oblivious to the weaponry loosed against it, the monster continued to gorge itself on the inhabitants of the buildings it had demolished.

Mishipeshu vanished in a great ball of flame. The reptile's anguished shriek rang through the urban canyons. The fighter swung back around to confirm the kill.

As the plane swept down towards the fire and smoke, caustic slime came shooting out from the destruction. The pilot had time to shriek once as Mishipeshu's venom melted through the canopy of his fighter, and then proceeded to corrode his flesh. Unguided, the fighter careened onwards, smacking into the side of the hulking Trump Tower, shattering its mirrored façade.

Mishipeshu came crawling from the flames, fingers of napalm still clinging to its scales, charred bones standing naked and exposed where the reptile's regeneration had yet to repair its injuries. Maddened by pain, the water panther aimed its fangs skyward, projecting venom at the circling helicopters and fighters. It hissed in frustration as its poison failed to strike down any of the swift-moving craft. Lashing its tail, the monster leapt upon the side of a skyscraper, scrambling up its height in an effort to close with the circling planes.

As it neared the summit of the tower, however, Mishipeshu's eyes narrowed, its entire body shivering in agitation. It leaned its head back, gazing away from the planes and helicopters, looking up into the sky itself. A sky that had been clear minutes before but which was now rapidly darkening with thick clots of cloud.

Mishipeshu hissed angrily, its tongue again flickering as it picked the scent of its ancient enemy from the air.

Animikii, the mighty thunderbird, was coming.

THE VIBRATIONS OF THE WATER panther's essence attracted Animikii's attention, resonating even in that higher plane of existence to which the thunderbirds had ascended ages past. Mishipeshu's presence could be perceived as a shadow, a blot shifting across the harmonics of that alien dimension. Only the interference of water could shield the monster from the notice of the thunderbirds, but in seeking prey Mishipeshu had cast aside such protection.

It took Animikii some time to restructure its substance and awareness into a state that could penetrate into the purely physical constraints of three-dimensional aspect. The breech between existences was preceded by the rapid cloud formations. When Animikii actually penetrated the dimensions, the violation was announced with a deafening peal of thunder, a sound that *boomed* across half a continent.

The thunderbird soared high above the urban sprawl of Chicago, its sharp eyes piercing through the veil of clouds that swirled about it. Slowly, gradually, its body took on tangible shape, diminishing into the confines of physical matter. Half-forgotten sensations like temperature, smell, and sound impacted upon Animikii's mind, forcing its mentality to reduce and adjust to the demands of this new existence.

Far below, Animikii could see the blotchy shadow of the water panther. Mishipeshu was far greater in size than any of its breed had ever been before. Of all the thunderbirds, only Animikii had the strength and power to challenge such a monster.

Challenge it Animikii did. Hurtling down from the sky, soaring through the circling aircraft, the mighty thunderbird cackled its threat to Mishipeshu. The slipstream caused by the giant's flight sent helicopters hurtling earthward, sent fighters spiraling out of control. Cars were buffeted across the streets, trees and lampposts were uprooted. Before the hurricane force of Animikii's wings, Mishipeshu was forced against the ground, digging its claws into the asphalt and cement to stabilize itself.

Animikii swept past the crouching water panther, climbing skywards and ascending to the vantage presented by the megalithic Willis Tower. Radio and television antennas snapped beneath the thunderbird's weight as it settled upon the tower. The glass sides of the skyscraper reflected Animikii's terrifying shape as it flew past. The thunderbird was a featherless creature covered in dark red leathery skin that faded to a dirty brown at the wings. Its legs were short and coated in a scaly texture such as might grace the tail of a rat. Massive talons tipped each foot, each individual claw ten meters across and a third again as wide. Animikii's leathery wings stretched to encompass a span of several hundred meters, and each pinion was ribbed after the fashion of a bat. A short stump of neck rose from above the creature's torso and atop this rested a small head with an elongated beak. Horns curled away from either side of Animikii's skull, framing its stormy eyes while its beak was rendered grotesque with a profusion of jagged fangs.

Flapping its wings, Animikii sent a thunderous clamor rolling across the city. The monster turned its head from side to side, cackling menacingly at the water panther down in the streets below.

Mishipeshu responded to the thunderbird's goading. Lunging

to its feet, the water panther charged along the street, its lashing tail battering the shops and offices arrayed along the boulevard and swatting the vehicles that had been abandoned everywhere. The primordial hate between its kind and the thunderbirds sent a bestial fury surging through its cold reptilian heart.

Animikii cackled again and came hurtling downwards. The thunderbird's stormy eyes blazed, bolts of lightning flashing from each orb to sear down into Mishipeshu's body. The reptile hissed in pain as the electricity scorched its scales, yet still it charged onward in a bounding lope that combined the scurry of a lizard with the pounce of a cat.

The thunderbird's lightning flashed again, blackening Mishipeshu's back. As Animikii went soaring past, however, Mishipeshu's bifurcated tail whipped upward, the great bony prongs stabbing into the leathery flesh. The water panther's tail lodged in Animikii's body and, as the thunderbird's momentum carried it onwards, Mishipeshu was dragged after it, pulled back down the street.

Impaled by Mishipeshu's tail and overcome by the beast's dead weight, Animikii's flight ended in a devastating crash against the side of an office building. Glass and concrete rained down upon the thunderbird and its adversary as the structure collapsed beneath their weight. A cloud of dust billowed away from the destruction, for a moment obscuring the two monsters from those men still able to witness their conflict.

As the dust cleared, the mammoth shapes of the monsters could be seen. Animikii, injured and bleeding, swatted at Mishipeshu with its wings, using its pinions to pound the water panther against the ground. Mishipeshu responded by raking its claws across the thunderbird's breast and spitting its caustic venom across Animikii's body. The water panther's tail, the bony spikes ripped away by the calamitous impact, swatted at Animikii, trying to bludgeon the flying monster.

Lightning again flashed from Animikii's eyes, searing into the face of Mishipeshu. The water panther yowled, hurling itself back in an agonized sprawl, sludge streaming from the scorched ruin of its eyes. Allowed a respite, the thunderbird lifted itself back into the air. It circled the prostrate water panther once, then dove down and sank its talons into Mishipeshu's flank.

The blinded water panther flailed and thrashed at the end of Animikii's talons, spitting venom from its fangs in every direction in a futile effort to strike its foe. The weakened thunderbird carried its prey across the city, crashing to earth in Daly Plaza. Mishipeshu struggled even more fiercely as it slammed into the ground, cracking the cement and rupturing water mains. Its claws raked across Animikii's hide, tearing great furrows in its enemy.

Those gunships yet airborne streaked towards the plaza, loosing a steady barrage of missiles into both of the weakened monsters. Animikii reared back, shrieking angrily as it sent lightning from its eyes crackling towards the helicopters. Three of the aircraft were burned from the sky before the others escaped into the man-made canyons of Chicago's Loop.

The brief respite afford to it allowed Mishipeshu to writhe out from beneath Animikii's grip. The water panther struck at Animikii, sinking its fangs into the mighty thunderbird. Corrosive poison pumping through its body, Animikii tried to rise once more into the sky, but the weight of Mishipeshu brought it slamming back to earth.

A slap of Animikii's wing broke Mishipeshu's hold, sending the water panther slamming into the base of Daly Center and obliterating the fountain set before it. With its beak, the thunderbird pried loose the cobra-like fang Mishipeshu had left embedded in its body.

The water panther crashed through the lower floors of the skyscraper, but instead of working itself free it clawed its way higher, crawling through the inner structure until it was above its foe. Blinking its partially regenerated eyes, the reptile glared down at the thunderbird. Erupting from the face of Daly Center, Mishipeshu pounced upon Animikii.

The thunderbird lifted into the air in that brief instant before the water panther could strike. Mishipeshu hurtled past it, slamming face-first into the street. Before it could wriggle away, Animikii dropped down upon the stunned reptile. The fanged beak ripped at Mishipeshu's wounds, tearing slimy goblets of flesh from the beast. Throwing its head back, Animikii forced each morsel of flesh down its gullet.

Again, the defenders of the city tried to assault the wounded monsters. A tank platoon rumbled out from behind the corner of Clark Street, opening fire on the two beasts. Animikii rose from its dying prey. The thunderbird's eyes flashed lightning, its wings swept forwards in a titanic gale, catching the electrical discharge and transforming it into a crackling skein of death. The tank crews were cooked inside their armored machines by the electric hurricane.

Animikii soared upwards, the wounds dealt to it already mending as the regenerative properties of Mishipeshu's flesh was absorbed into the thunderbird's metabolism. Once again, Animikii flew across the city, landing upon the spire of Willis Tower. The thunderbird settled upon its perch and cackled in triumph. Then it swept its gaze across the concrete canyons, over the artificial constructions of centuries of industrialization and mechanization, of ruthless consumption and exploitation.

Mishipeshu had been freed from its ancient slumber by such things, these corrupt essences that inflicted such disharmony upon the world. As Animikiii tried to render its own essence into that phase which should allow it passage into its own plane of existence, the thunderbird found conditions too hostile to the effort. The imbalance inflicted by the men who had so greatly profaned the land was too immense for Animikii to overcome.

The thunderbird's cackle became malignant, its stormy eyes glaring down at the fleeing crowds. The few who remembered the old Ojibwa legends might have appreciated how insignificant the destruction of Mishipeshu was beside the advent of Animikii. The water panther was a monster that would prey upon men, devour them like any beast of prey. The thunderbird was different. It didn't prey on men, it judged them and destroyed all who didn't please it.

In this modern world of steel and smoke, of greed and hedonism, how few would be spared the wrath of Animikii?

ABOUT THE AUTHORS/ARTISTS

JAMES LOVEGROVE was born on Christmas Eve 1965 and is the author of more than 40 books. His novels include *The Hope, Days, Untied Kingdom, Provender Gleed,* the *New York Times* bestselling Pantheon series—so far *The Age of Ra, The Age of Zeus, The Age of Odin, Age of Aztec, Age of Voodoo,* and *Age of Shiva,* plus a collection of three novellas, *Age of Godpunk*—and *Redlaw* and *Redlaw: Red Eye,* the first two volumes in a trilogy about a policeman charged with protecting humans from vampires and vice versa. He has produced two Sherlock Holmes novels, *The Stuff of Nightmares* and *Gods of War.*

James has sold well over 40 short stories, the majority of them gathered in two collections, *Imagined Slights* and *Diversifications.* He has written a four-volume fantasy saga for teenagers, *The Clouded World* (under the pseudonym Jay Amory), and has produced a dozen short books for readers with reading difficulties, including *Wings, Kill Swap, Free Runner, Dead Brigade,* and the *5 Lords Of Pain* series.

James has been shortlisted for numerous awards, including the Arthur C. Clarke Award, the John W. Campbell Memorial Award, the Bram Stoker Award, the British Fantasy Society Award and the Manchester Book Award. His short story "Carry The Moon In My

Pocket" won the 2011 Seiun Award in Japan for Best Translated Short Story.

James's work has been translated into twelve languages. His journalism has appeared in periodicals as diverse as *Literary Review, Interzone,* and *BBC MindGames,* and he is a regular reviewer of fiction for the *Financial Times* and contributes features and reviews about comic books to the magazine *Comic Heroes.*

He lives with his wife, two sons and cat in Eastbourne, a town famously genteel and favoured by the elderly, but in spite of that he isn't planning to retire just yet.

By night, **DAVID ANNANDALE** brings doom to untold billions as a writer of Warhammer 40,000 fiction for the Black Library, most recently in the novels *The Death of Antagonis* and *Yarrick: Imperial Creed.* As the author of the horror novel *Gethsemane Hall,* he hopes to end sleep for you forever. And in his Jen Blaylock thrillers, he does his best to blow up everything in sight.

During the day, he poisons minds as he teaches film, video games and English literature at the University of Manitoba. If you have any fragments of hope still left, you can have them crushed at his website (www.davidannandale.com) or by following his Twitter account (@David_Annandale).

KANE GILMOUR is the bestselling author of *Ragnarok* and *Resurrect.* He is a frequent co-author with Jeremy Robinson in the Jack Sigler/ Chess Team series, and he also writes his own thriller novels.

In 2014, he hopes to release the first in a trilogy of Kaiju novels, called *Monster Kingdom.*

In addition to his work in novels, Kane is the writer of the sci-fi noir webcomic, *Warbirds of Mars.* He lives with his family in Vermont. When he feels tremors in the ground, he wonders if Kashikoi has awakened.

Follow him at kanegilmour.com and on Facebook at facebook. com/kane.gilmour.author.

NATANIA BARRON is a word tinkerer with a lifelong love of the fantastic. She has a penchant for the speculative, and has written tales of invisible soul-eating birds, giant cephalopod goddesses, gunslinger girls, and killer kudzu, just to name a few. Her work has appeared in *Weird Tales, EscapePod, Steampunk Tales, Crossed Genres, Bull Spec,* and various anthologies.

Natania's debut novel, a steampunk/mythpunk fantasy, *Pilgrim of the Sky,* released in December 2011 from Candlemark & Gleam. She is also the co-editor of *BullSpec.*

In addition, Natania's also a founding editor at GeekMom and a co-author of *Geek Mom: Projects, Tips, and Adventures for Moms and Their 21st-Century Families,* released October 2012 from Potter Craft. When not venturing in imagined worlds, she can be found in North Carolina, where she lives with her family. Her website is www.nataniabarron.com and you can follow her babblings on Twitter (@nataniabarron).

HOWARD ANDREW JONES' swashbuckling fantasies of Dabir and Asim have appeared in a variety of publications over the last decade, and their first novel, *The Desert of Souls,* was released in February 2011 from St. Martin's Thomas Dunne Books imprint to critical acclaim. The second, *The Bones of the Old Ones,* was released in December of 2013. Both novels made the Barnes & Noble 'Year's Best Fantasy' list, and *The Bones of the Old Ones* received a starred review from *Publisher's Weekly.*

Jones has written two novels for the Paizo Pathfinder Tales adventure line, *Plague of Shadows and Stalking the Beast,* and assembled and edited eight collections of neglected historical fiction writer Harold Lamb's work for the University of Nebraska Press.

When not helping run his small family farm or spending time with his wife and children, Howard can be found hunched over his laptop or notebook, mumbling about flashing swords and doomhaunted towers. He has worked variously as a TV cameraman, a book editor, a recycling consultant, and a college writing instructor. He blogs regularly at the Black Gate web site (www.blackgate.com) and maintains a web outpost of his own at www.howardandrewjones. com. He can be found on Facebook as Howard Andrew Jones and on Twitter (@ howardandrewjon).

JONATHAN WOOD is an Englishman in New York. There's a story in there involving falling in love and flunking out of med school, but in the end it all worked out all right, and, quite frankly, the medical community is far better off without him, so we won't go into it here. His debut novel, *No Hero* was described by *Publisher's Weekly* as "a funny, dark, rip-roaring adventure with a lot of heart, highly recommended for urban fantasy and light science fiction readers alike." Barnesandnoble. com listed it has one of the 20 best paranormal fantasies of the past decade, and Charlaine Harris, author of the Sookie Stackhouse novels described it as, "so funny I laughed out loud."

His short fiction is in *Weird Tales, Chizine,* and *Beneath Ceaseless Skies,* as well as anthologies such as *The Book of Cthulhu 2* and *The Best of Beneath Ceaseless Skies, Year One.* Visit jonathanwoodauthor.com.

JAYM GATES admits "I probably shouldn't start a professional bio by admitting that my first real writing consisted of grade-school adventures to haunted, monster-infested islands. I suppose it's less odd than admitting that I wrote *Ivanhoe* fan fiction. I would claim that my tastes are better now, but an anthology of zombie erotica might negate that argument. Instead, I'll say my tastes have matured.

"My themes tend toward the dark and sleek, both in reading and in writing. I love historical flavorings, New Weird worlds, mythical monsters, cyberpunk rebellion, sword and sorcery grit and high-tech imaginings. A bit of everything, blended into something cool and new.

"After a couple of years away from editorial work, I'm ready to jump back in. There's nothing like seeing authors and artists I first published signing contracts for novels and selling short stories to some of the most exciting new markets. Some of the fiction I've acquired for various projects has gone on to be featured in year's best collections and reprinted in other venues.

"I'm back to writing a little, too, mostly in development projects and gaming. A few new short stories are floating around, on the lookout for a new home."

Educated in the tenets of Wuxia and giant monsters by the esteemed Son of Svengoolie and a regular dose of Chicagoland's Samurai Sunday, **EDWARD M. ERDELAC** is the author of the acclaimed weird western series *Merkabah Rider* and *The Van Helsing Papers,* as well as *Coyote's Trail* and *Buff Tea.* His fiction's appeared in over a dozen anthologies including most recently, *Sword And Mythos, Atomic Age Cthulhu,* and *Monster Earth.* He is also a sometime Star Wars contributor, having contributed tales of ion powered prizefighters and ancient dark lords to the annals of *A Galaxy Far, Far Away.*

He lives in the Los Angeles area with his wife and a bona fide slew of kids and cats, and can be found online at emerdelac.wordpress.com, or at emerdelac@gmail.com.

BONNIE JO STUFFLEBEAM lives in Texas with her husband and two literarily-named cats: Gimli and Don Quixote. Her fiction and poetry has appeared in magazines such as *Clarkesworld, Strange Horizons, Goblin Fruit,* and *Daily Science Fiction.* She holds an MFA in Creative Writing from the University of Southern Maine's Stonecoast program and reviews short fiction at her blog, Short Story Review. You can visit her on Twitter (@BonnieJoStuffle) or through her website www.bonniejostufflebeam.com.

JAMES MAXEY: "I've been an avid reader since I first picked up a book. Luckily, I was within biking distance of three different libraries growing up. I was a skinny kid. If only I had maintained that link between biking and reading, I might be a skinny adult.

"I'm also a writer. I wrote my first book as a kid, an adventure about pirates and ghosts. When I was a teenager, I used to write superhero adventures. Then I went to college and was steered toward writing "literature." It took me several years to shake that off, and today I write the sort of books I devoured by the shelf when I was sixteen, fast-paced fantasy, SF, and superhero adventures, which I use to explore deeper questions about life. My goal is to always be thought-provoking and always be fun.

"I've had short stories in about a dozen anthologies and magazines. My novels to date are: *Nobody Gets the Girl, The Dragon Age trilogy, Bitterwood, Dragonforge, Dragonseed, Burn Baby Burn, The Dragon Apocalypse, Greatshadow, Hush,* and *Witchbreaker.*"

TIMOTHY W. LONG has seen the world courtesy of the United States Navy. He has also been writing tales and stories since he could hold a crayon and read enough books to choke a landfill. He has a fascination with all things zombie, a predilection for weird literature, and a deep-seated need to jot words on paper and thrust them at people in the hopes they will nod, smile, and maybe pat him on the back and buy him a cold one.

Tim writes for Permuted Press, the largest publisher of post apocalyptic fiction in the world. He is the author of the horror novels *Beyond the Barriers, Among the Living,* and the sequel, *Among the Dead.*

His other works include the deserted island "zombedy", *The Zombie Wilson Diaries.* He also co-wrote the post-apocalyptic novel *The Apocalypse and Satan's Glory Hole* with Sir Jonathan Moon. This book was recently named the preferred version of the end of the world by a consortium of rapture survivors.

True story.

Tim's latest book is the serialized *Z-Risen: Outbreak* and he is also hard at work on the final Among the Living book titled *Among the Ashes*.

LARRY CORREIA is a *New York Times* bestselling fantasy novelist. His first novel, *Monster Hunter International,* despite being self-published reached the *Entertainment Weekly* bestseller list in April 2008, after which he received a publishing contract with Baen Books. *Monster Hunter International* was re-released in 2009 and was on the *Locus* Best Seller list in November 2009. The sequel, *Monster Hunter Vendetta,* was a *New York Times* bestseller. The third book in the series, *Monster Hunter Alpha,* was released in July 2011 and was also a *New York Times* bestseller.

Correia was a finalist for the John W. Campbell award for best new science fiction/fantasy writer of 2011. The Dead Six series started as an online action fiction collaboration with Mike Kupari (Nightcrawler) at the online gun forum "The High Road" as the "Welcome Back Mr Nightcrawler" series of posts. These works predated the publishing of Monster Hunter.

CL WERNER has crafted numerous tales for Red Leaf Comics, the Black Library, and other cutting edge publishers. He recently stopped by CBI studios to talk with publisher John Michael Helmer about his career writing comics, novels, and war games.

ROBERT ELROD is a self-taught artist who works with a variety of mediums including pencil, color pencil, ink, watercolor, gouache, acrylic and digital. His artwork has appeared on the covers of several novels and anthologies from small-press horror authors and publishers, including Permuted Press.

Tickling A Dead Man: Stories about George is his self-published comic book in which he relentlessly tortures his misanthropic title character by forcing him to face his deepest fears and anxieties. His comics have also appeared within the pages of the "Best New Zombie Tales" series from Books of the Dead Press.

Robert has contributed pinup art to publications by Bluewater Comics, Creephouse Comics, Creator's Edge Press, Abandoned Comics, Angry Dog Press, British Fantasy Society, Lovecraft eZine, The Big Adios, This Is Horror, and Ragnarok Publications. To see more of his work, visit www.robertelrodllc.com.

CHUCK LUKACS [loo-cuss] has been illustrating for science fiction and fantasy gaming markets for over 17 years, occasionally teaches illustration in Portland, OR, and has spent a number of years studying ceramics, bookarts, wood engraving, alternative energy, traditional archery, and homebrewing. Lukacs's paintings and prints have won awards and appeared in conventions, galleries and museums internationally. He was featured in *Spectrum 7, ImagineFX June/2010* (UK), *FantasyArt Magazine* (Peking University), and has authored two fantasy art tutorial books: *Wreaking Havoc,* 2007 and *Fantasy Genesis,* 2010.

Clients include: NBC/Universal, Wizards of the Coast's Magic the Gathering, Impact Books, Pyr/Prometheus Books, Paizo, SuperGenius, Upper Deck, Games Workshop, Road Runner, and Atlantic Records.

Visit him at ChuckLukacs.com, FantasyGenesis.blogspot.com, and PortlandStinkeye.blogspot.com.

MATT FRANK is based in the Golden Land of Texas and loves to draw monsters and anything else that happens to be very, very cool.

His works include: *Ray Harryhausen Presents: Back To Mysterious Island and Ray Harryhausen Presents: Wrath Of The Titans: Cyclops*

(BlueWater Productions), *Beast Wars Sourcebook* (IDW Publishing), *Marvel Handbooks* (Marvel Comics), *Black Paw: Return Of The Dragon* (Gleaming Scythe Productions), *Godzilla: Kingdom Of Monsters, Godzilla: Gangsters And Goliaths , and Godzilla: Legends* (IDW Publishing), *Transformers: Flash Forward* (Fun Publications), and *Mars Attacks The Transformers* (IDW Publishing).

BOB EGGLETON is a science fiction, fantasy, and horror artist, and has been honored with the Hugo Award for Best Professional Artist eight times, first winning in 1994. He also won the Hugo Award for Best Related Book in 2001, won the Chesley Award for Artistic Achievement in 1999, and was the Guest of Honor at Chicon 2000.

Eggleton's drawing and paintings cover a range of science fiction, fantasy, and horror topics, depicting space ships, alien worlds and inhabitants, dragons, vampires, and other fantasy creatures. His view on spaceships even from childhood was that they should look organic, hence he was disappointed with the space shuttles and rockets NASA eventually produced, as they were nothing like fantasy artists of the '20s and '30s had promised.

His fascination with dragons originated with his childhood interest of dinosaurs, which can be seen in the book *Greetings from Earth,* and he has illustrated cards for the *Magic: The Gathering* collectible card game. Eggleton received encouragement from his father, in the form of books, supplies, visits to museums of space and aeronautics and support during the career choices he made, and dropped out of art college because he felt it was not for him. Eggleton is a fan of Godzilla and worked as a creative consultant on the American remake. While in Japan he appeared as an extra in one of the more recent films.

TIM MARQUITZ is an author and editor, having recently compiled and edited the Angelic Knight Press anthologies, *Fading Light: An*

Anthology of the Monstrous and *Manifesto: UF.* His writing credits include the "Demon Squad" series, the "Blood War Trilogy," co-writer of the "Dead West" supernatural horror series along with Kenny Soward and J.M. Martin, several standalone books, and numerous anthology appearances including *Triumph Over Tragedy, Corrupts Absolutely?, Demonic Dolls,* and *No Place Like Home.*

In mid-2013 Tim partnered with Joe Martin to launch Ragnarok Publications, and acts as the independent publishing house's Editor-In-Chief. *Kaiju Rising: Age of Monsters* is Ragnarok's first anthology, but by no means its last.

NICKOLAS SHARPS is an advertising/public relations Major at Point Park University in Pittsburgh, PA. He maintains Ragnarok's various social media pages on Facebook and Twitter, and also assists with acquisitions and project development. He has also contributed as a book reviewer to the Hugo Award-winning SF Signal and Elitist Book Reviews.

His first published work, "Toejam & Shrapnel" appears in *Manifesto: UF* from Angelic Knight Press, and he aspires to be a novelist. *Kaiju Rising: Age of Monsters* is the first anthology project Nick brought to Ragnarok's Creative Director, Joe Martin, and they have already brainstormed on several more.